THE MONK'S
SON

THE MONK'S SON

W. R. WILKERSON III

BOOKS

BELLINGHAM, WASHINGTON

4152 Meridian Street, #6
Bellingham, WA 98226
888-88-CIROS

www.cirosbooks.com

PUBLISHER'S NOTE: This novel is a work of fiction. Names, characters, places, and incidents either are the product of the author's imagination or are used fictitiously, and any resemblance to actual persons, living or dead, events, or locales is entirely coincidental.

ORDERING INFORMATION
Quantity sales. Special discounts are available on quantity purchases by corporations, associations, and others. For details, contact the "Special Sales Department" at the address above.

Orders by U.S. trade bookstores and wholesalers. Please contact Biblio Distribution: Tel: (800) 462-6420; Fax: (800) 338-4550.

Printed in the United States of America

Cataloging-in-Publication Data
Wilkerson, W R.
  The Monk's Son / W. R. Wilkerson III.
  p. cm.
  ISBN 978-0-9676643-1-6
1. Monks—Fiction. 2. World War, 1939-1945. 3. Orphans—Fiction.
4. Drug abuse—Fiction. 5. Friendship—Fiction. 6. Homosexuality—Fiction.
7. Psychological fiction.
I. Title.
PS3573.I4368.P3   2007
813.54—dc22   2006938328

Cover design: Catherine Lau Hunt
Interior design: Beverly Butterfield, Girl of the West Productions

FIRST EDITION
11 10 09 08 07   10 9 8 7 6 5 4 3 2 1

For Michael Earle
who saved my life in 1971

From great hell comes paradise

1

BEFORE DAWN, BEFORE THE kitchen staff arose, Brother Dominic was awake. He clambered out of bed and shuffled over the cold stone floor to a plain wooden cabinet. Taking a white porcelain pitcher from a bowl on top of the cabinet, he carefully poured water into the bowl. Drowsily he splashed cold water onto his face. It was not meant to be warm but merely part of his ritual of rousing himself first thing in the morning.

Dominic toweled his face dry and brushed his teeth. Then he replaced the pitcher on top of the cabinet. The water he would dispose of later.

He opened a drawer in another part of the cabinet and extracted a clean robe. Slowly and meticulously he dressed, putting on his underwear, then his socks, and finally the brown habit that had been like a second skin for virtually most of his adult life. It was belted by a white rope studded with knots—twelve in all—signifying the Stations of the Cross. He lowered himself onto the pine kneeler at the foot of his bed and softly mumbled his prayers. Eyes closed in reverence, Dominic slid his rosary through practiced fingers. After more than two decades of repetition, the prayers had become more of a drone than a recitation. He made the sign of the cross neatly across his chest, then scooped up the wicker basket from the floor next to his bed and left the room.

Brother Dominic was of medium height, and his stone-chiseled features highlighted deep-set green eyes that gazed out softly upon the world. He had a long, protruding jaw and a high forehead that gave way to baldness on top, though the sides of his head were carpeted in thick, black hair. Tufts of hair protruded from his ears, and he had long, slender fingers that delicately handled his medicines and plants.

He padded quietly down the corridor, past rows of private cells where the nineteen other monks still slumbered in quarters exactly like his. When he reached the dormitory's back door, he opened it as quietly as he could, yet the hinges still squealed in protest. Several times he had asked Brother Christopher to oil them. Christopher, who was always so busy, never got around to it.

Dominic slipped outside. Just a few yards beyond was the back gate of the massive cloister wall, one of two points of access to the monastery grounds. Except for a stain of orange in the sky, it was still dark. Dominic knew by heart where to find the overgrown footpath next to the meandering stream. This footpath cut across open fields and ended where the woods began. Centuries earlier, the monks of his order had built the cloister close to this stream to harness the power of the water.

Pushing through the waist-high wild grasses that extended over the countryside in summer, he tramped down the path, singing to himself the plainchant sung in chapel with the other friars. Although not terribly gifted, Dominic did enjoy singing. It kept him company when he worked alone while the rest of the world was asleep. Save for the distant sporadic lowing of cows and the talkative stream, there was hardly a sound.

As the sky brightened, he stopped for a moment to admire his surroundings. Not a cloud drifted in the sky. He was in the middle of a large field that was part of the cloister's acreage. The gray sandstone buildings of the monastery began to turn a pinkish hue. He could see the chapter house, infirmary, dormitories, mill, and chapel. In the distance a plume of smoke from a farmhouse chimney drifted into the air. There was the smell of the grass after last night's rains. He took a deep breath, letting the fresh air fill his lungs.

A lone seagull sailed into view. Its sharp, intermittent cries reverberated over the landscape. Dominic followed the bird with his eyes as it circled high in wide arcs, carving up the dawn. "You're a long way from the sea, my friend, aren't you?" he said.

Not until he was a considerable distance from the monastery did Dominic realize he had forgotten his list. *Must have left it on my desk*, he thought. As the monastery doctor and apothecary, it was his practice to make a list of the herbs he needed to make medicine. This was the last thing he did before retiring at night. After double-checking it, he would put it in the pocket of his habit, ready for the morning.

Forgetfulness has been catching-up with me recently.

Rather than going all the way back to retrieve the slip of paper, he decided to search from memory. "Let me see, let me see," he said, thinking out loud. "What was on the list?"

Before he had a chance to recall a single item, he stumbled upon a valuable find. "Ah, *Rosa canina!*" he said, bending over a plant and touching it. "Where have you been? I've been looking for you all week!"

Eagerly he fished inside his wicker basket for a trowel. Tool in hand, Dominic dug down into the soil close to the plant. Then he tugged on the plant with his free hand and began digging a circle around it. Angling under with the trowel, he grasped the plant firmly and tugged harder. The roots gave way, sending him flying backward into the grass. Chuckling, he got back on his feet and stowed his prize in the wicker basket.

He was brushing the clots of dirt from his habit when suddenly an unusual sound caught his ear. It was a brief, shrill whine that echoed off the stone walls of the cloister buildings in the distance.

At first he thought it was the seagull, but when he looked up, the sky was empty. He stood still for a moment. A mild breeze wafted over the fields, bending the tall grasses backward and forward. In the background the stream murmured softly. After thirty years Dominic had come to know this babbling brook intimately and was able to identify every sound it made. Like a mockingbird, it could mimic and imitate, deceive and hoodwink the listener into thinking it was something it was not. But the sound he was hearing—it was like one that was seared into his very soul, evoking distant but painful memories he carried with him always.

He didn't want to believe his ears. *The stream's talking quietly to itself. Yes, that's it. Nothing more. You're hearing things. Shame on you. Age is creeping up on you.*

Dominic studied his surroundings once more, looking all around. He sighed heavily and returned his attention to collecting plants.

The sound suddenly repeated itself, this time more distinctly. It rang out as if from every corner of the field, cutting the air and shattering the silence. Then, as quickly as it came, it stopped. It sounded like an animal of some kind. A cry of distress—of that Dominic was absolutely certain.

The strange sound came again. He froze. Then he knew. It was not that of an animal at all.

It was the cry of a baby.

Suddenly the whine was drowned out by a single bell ringing out across the fields. Dominic's heart sank. It was St. Martin's bell. From the colonnaded gallery it called the monastic community to prayer, office, meals, and sleep. In answer, monks would drop whatever they were doing and make their way to the cloister chapel, to the refectory, or to bed. In this case it was the bell for the Holy Office of Matins, the morning prayer service. Dominic was overcome by a feeling of both helplessness and panic, torn between rescuing the child and returning at once to the cloister to fulfill his monastic office.

The sun began clearing the rooftops. He looked back over his shoulder at the monastery. The buildings loomed large in the distance. He tried telling himself that the child would be found by its parents or guardians shortly. But this did little to quell his mounting frustration. As he scanned the empty countryside, his hopes faded.

Dear God, please show me where. I beg of you.

The bell stopped, and with it the cries. He was desperate to hear them once more, just long enough to locate the child. But all he heard was the wind moving across the fields. There would be consequences if he remained longer, and he knew he had to return to the abbey. As it was, he would probably be late. Like the others, he could not miss a Holy Office. Those who did, without an acceptable excuse, were assigned extra duties by the abbot for a week. On top of their normal workload, this proved to be trying.

Just then he heard a long, piercing wail coming from the direction of the stream. The baby was behind him, he guessed, no more than fifty feet away. He made no further attempt to fight his feelings. Frantically he rushed from one spot to another, pushing back the blades of grass. Next to the stream, hidden deep within the tall, thick grasses and wrapped in a tattered brown blanket, was an infant, not more than a few days old.

"Benedictus!"

Dominic dropped the wicker basket. Gently he picked up the crying infant and carefully wrapped it in the folds of his habit. Unnoticed, he spirited the infant into the cloister, muffling its cries under his garments. No one saw him. It seemed everyone except Brother Thomas was in chapel.

Safe in his cell, Dominic examined the child on his bed. It had been stung on its thigh by a bee. The area was swollen. Dominic removed the stinger and applied an ointment to reduce the swelling. He kept the ointment on hand as during the summer one brother or another was always getting stung by something out in the garden. Using an eyedropper, he orally administered an herbal chamomile compound he gave to the brothers as a tranquilizer to calm them. He hoped it would have the same effect on the infant.

BROTHER ANDREW hurried toward the chapel. He was late. On the way he thought he heard the cry of a baby coming from Dominic's cell. He pressed an ear against the door and stood motionless, listening.

THE INFANT had calmed down. Dominic wrapped it in a clean blanket, placed it in the middle of his bed, then hurried off to the kitchen. Brother Thomas, the monastery cook, was drying the dishes.

"Can you spare some warm milk?" said Dominic.

Thomas peered closely at him, then dried a teacup and put it away in the cupboard. "Not feeling well?"

Dominic nodded. "Upset stomach."

Thomas washed his hands in the basin, then wiped them on his apron. He began heating some milk.

"I need two mugs," said Dominic, waiting for the milk to warm.

When the milk was ready, Thomas poured two mugs. "Feel better," he said.

Among the hundreds of glass bottles in the laboratory, Dominic found one with a rubber nipple. He waited until the milk had cooled, then transferred it to the bottle and carefully inserted the nipple into the baby's tiny mouth. To his relief, the infant took the milk immediately. After drinking half the bottle, he fell into a sound, peaceful sleep.

Dominic knew his empty stall at Matins would arouse suspicion. He was often late, but rarely did he miss an office. Generally only extreme illness prevented a monk from participating. As the abbey's physician, he felt his primary duty was to nurse and tend to the infant, just as he would a sick brother.

INSIDE THE chapel, the monks knelt with their heads bowed in a silent examination of conscience. So far, Dominic's absence was unremarkable. Known as a gentle man of medicine whose ongoing love affair with nature rivaled his devotion to his religion and his vows, Dominic spent hours studying nature, entranced by its beauty and wonder. He was often so lost in his work that he was late for prayers and meals.

Abbot Immaculus, who was an imposing six feet two inches tall when standing, knelt at the head of the group. Brother Andrew hurried into the chapel, approached the abbot, and whispered into his ear.

"A *child*?" the abbot said, completely forgetting where he was.

A few of the other monks looked up. Andrew continued whispering.

"In the abbey?" the abbot said, even louder.

Andrew nodded. The abbot looked over at Dominic's empty stall. He rose from his seat and quickly left the chapel. When he arrived at Dominic's door, he threw it open. His piercing blue eyes seemed to burn right through Dominic, who was seated on his bed next to a bundle in a blanket.

"What is the meaning of this?" the abbot bellowed. Coupled with his resonant voice, his looming presence was intimidating.

The infant awoke and immediately began crying.

"The child was abandoned," said Dominic. He took the bundled child in his arms and began rocking it, but the infant would not stop crying.

"Abandoned?" said the abbot. "Abandoned where?"

"Out in the fields."

The infant's wails grew louder, drowning out their conversation.

"I can't have this conversation here," said the abbot. "Have someone look after the child. Come with me."

By now a small group of curious onlookers had gathered at Dominic's door. Dominic saw Thomas and motioned for him to come in.

"Thomas, would you mind?" he said, gingerly placing the infant into his arms. "I shan't be a moment."

IMMACULUS STOOD with his back to Dominic, gazing inattentively out the window, hands clasped behind his back. Only the loud ticking of the clock on the mantel invaded the silence of the abbot's wood-paneled study. Dominic stood in front of the abbot's desk. With each passing second, the silence grew more deafening.

"Do you know what you've done?" the abbot said finally. "You've admitted one who is unordained into these consecrated walls!"

"We're talking about a child," said Dominic. "A mere infant, abandoned, powerless to survive on its own. Surely you cannot be implying that a Holy Office takes precedence over human life?"

Immaculus said nothing.

"Correct me if I am wrong, Abbot, but in Our Lord's eyes, all infants are considered sacred—"

The abbot calmly raised a hand, stopping him short. "Dominic, I'm not interested in your biblical interpretations. How can you be so sure the child was abandoned?"

"There was no one else around. The child was completely alone, in the middle of the fields."

"Dominic, two serious offenses have been committed here. One, a child has ostensibly been kidnapped. Two, one of our most sacred rules has been violated. Perhaps you're familiar with it? Unless ordained, laypersons, irrespective of sex, social standing, or circumstance, are not admitted into many areas of this monastery. By bringing this child into the abbey, you have violated that sacred rule."

Rocking uneasily on the balls of his feet, Dominic nervously fidgeted with the rosary in his pocket. "I needn't remind you that this is all cloister property. If someone wanted to abandon their baby, what more ideal place than an abbey full of monks with nothing better to do but pray and eat all day?"

"I resent that," Immaculus grumbled.

"I apologize. But it is a common misconception, and because our doors are closed to the outside world, that misperception is allowed to persist."

The abbot shook his head. "Dominic, you are here to observe and obey rules, not to take it upon yourself to interpret them. Being the cloister physician, your first duty is to obey the wishes of your abbot and your order."

Dominic removed his hand from his pocket and clenched it into a fist. He was angry. "But I also took another oath, Abbot—an oath to save life, not to turn my back on it in times of trouble!"

"You also took a vow of obedience. Or have you forgotten?" The abbot looked back over his shoulder at Dominic to see what kind of reaction he had elicited, then turned his gaze toward the window again.

"Did you honestly expect me to leave him there?"

Immaculus scratched the top of his bald head. "Why didn't you tell me about this before Matins?"

"I considered this an emergency. I thought I would explain after the office."

"What gender is the baby?"

"It's a boy."

"Thank heaven for that. I could see the penance I would be doing if the child were female."

"I'M AFRAID to ask," Brother Thomas whispered when Dominic returned to his cell. He was sitting in a chair next to the bed, an open Bible on his lap.

Dominic closed the door quietly behind him. "How's he doing?"

"He's sleeping peacefully now. What did Immaculus have to say?"

Dominic looked up. On the wall above the bed, a painting of St. Francis of Assisi caught patches of colored sunlight from a stained glass window set high up on the wall. "He said we can't keep the child."

"And the reason?"

Sitting down on the bed, Dominic looked at the baby sadly. "In the eyes of our abbot, bringing a child into the abbey constitutes the grossest breach of monastic discipline." He ran a hand over the sleeping infant. "He demands blind obedience. In his mind the vows we have taken declare that we give our unconditional loyalty and obedience to God, our order, and, of course, to him. And though I understand that failing to attend an office is a punishable offense, I am a doctor. It's my duty to heal the sick, no matter who they are or where I find them."

Thomas closed the Bible. "So what did he do?"

"He just listened impatiently. You know how he gets when he's angry." Dominic removed his shoes. "I did my best. I described the deceiving sounds of the fields and the stream, the baby's cries I had mistaken for bird calls. But I couldn't stand there and tell him that one of my vows had won out over the other; how I had struggled out in those empty fields to come to a decision; vacillating between the two worlds I love, between my vows as a monk and my duties as a physician. That I'll save for the confessional."

Thomas shook his head. "Immaculus is suspicious about the amount of time you devote to your outdoor activities when you have a perfectly adequate greenhouse at your disposal for growing what you need."

Dominic sighed. "He hides behind his vows when something emotionally uncomfortable arises and expects us to do the same."

Thomas returned the Bible to Dominic's crowded bookshelf, struggling to make room for it amid the other books. "Crabby old Immaculus. Always hated children. God forgive him."

SERGEANT OLIVER leaned over the infant, pretending to examine it while scratching notes in pencil in a small black notebook.

"Where exactly was the infant found?" he said.

"Out in the fields," said Dominic. "Behind the monastery."

PC Harmon stood next to his duty sergeant. He tried to concentrate on keeping his back ramrod straight in order to look commanding. He had never been on a call like this before.

Sergeant Oliver pensively stroked one end of his handlebar mustache. "What time was this?"

"Early," Dominic said. "Before six, I would say."

Raising his index finger, Oliver tugged on his collar, which was too tight. The portly officer then ran the same hand down his coat, smoothing out the imaginary creases in his dark blue uniform that struggled to contain his bulging shape. Dominic thought the officer's buttons would pop off and the white chevrons on his coat sleeves would come undone.

"Mind taking us there?" Oliver said.

"Of course not," said Dominic.

He escorted both men out the same back door he had passed through earlier that morning and into the summer fields. It was noon now, and the sun was uncomfortably hot.

After retracing his steps, Dominic stopped. "Right here," he said, pointing to the place near the stream where he had made his discovery.

The two police officers studied the area. PC Harmon pulled back the tall grasses for a closer look. Oliver stood in silence, making notes, then turned to survey the surrounding country-side. The fields still swayed under the weight of the midmorn-ing breezes, and the chattering stream glinted in the sunlight.

As Oliver continued making notes, he asked, "You say there was no one else around?"

"Yes," said Dominic. "That's correct."

"Any theories?"

Dominic folded his hands in front of him. "Whoever put the child here knew exactly what they were doing. They were at least wise enough to know that the grasses would shield the infant from the sun. I'm forced to conclude that this was no mistake."

"To your mind, then," said Oliver, "this abandonment, or whatever we might call it, was planned?"

"That is my opinion, yes."

"I see," said the sergeant. He brought the pencil to his lips as he walked around the site in circles, studying it intently. He stopped and made another notation. "Right. We're finished here," he said, folding up the small notebook and storing it in his breast pocket.

They returned to the monastery, where Immaculus offered them tea and refreshments in his study.

"In my experience," Oliver said, pausing to take a sip from his cup, "it is not uncommon for young Gypsy mothers to abandon their unwanted after birth. In some instances the newborns are even drowned and their corpses buried." He picked up a shortbread and dunked it in his tea. "Abandonment is a way of life with these people." He took a bite out of the shortbread. "In the meantime, if you wouldn't mind looking after the infant, he would receive better care in your hands than ours—just until the parents are located."

IMMACULUS PACED round the study after the officers had left. "I'm not counting on those imbeciles for results!" he said to Dominic. "We shall mount a search ourselves. We shall go to the village, door to door if necessary, until we find the parents or the rightful claimants to this baby. Do you understand me?"

Dominic said nothing. He calmly slipped his hand into his pocket and fingered the rosary.

"The sooner we get rid of this child, the better," said the abbot, his eyes dark.

"And if the parents cannot be found, may we keep the child?"

Immaculus looked at Dominic in horror. "Have you lost your mind?"

"But—"

"Out of the question!" The abbot walked in a wider circle this time, stopping at one window. Peering out, he continued, "We have committed ourselves to a life of solitude here. Relinquishing all that is worldly allows us to fully embrace the benefits monastic life offers—a world rich in spirituality and scholasticism. But in this life we have chosen to lead, we are also given some great tests. The first is chastity. It is, above all else, the most difficult vow we make, especially for a young monk. Youth is a time when lust still courses through a man's veins and he hungers for carnal pleasures. But thankfully, as youth fades, so do these urges of the flesh."

He turned from the window and faced Dominic. "Another test," said the abbot, "is parenthood. Parental feelings usually crop up in middle age, sometimes when we least expect it. And when it does, we are overwhelmed by a void. It's a feeling that something is missing from our lives. Fortunately, like lust, it too dissipates with time."

Dominic looked straight-faced at Immaculus, trying not to betray too much emotion. To him, finding the boy had been no accident.

"I can see now that you are faced with this particular challenge," said the abbot. "I remember well your coming to us shortly after losing your wife and child. You have been with us many years. You must now take my advice. The Lord determines life and death. Not even the most gifted healers—yourself among them, Dominic—can change that."

"I pray every day to strengthen that belief. I must admit it is always a struggle. I do believe, however," said Dominic, "that keeping the child would renew my monastic commitment."

Immaculus shook his head. "Dominic, distance yourself from these thoughts and notions once and for all. If you don't, I promise that they will succeed in destroying your calling to be a monk, and possibly even your faith."

Dominic stared at the floor. He was silent for several moments. Looking up at the abbot, he said, "May I keep the baby in my cell?"

"What? And wake the others with its crying? Certainly not. The child will stay in my quarters."

That night, however, the infant kept the abbot awake for hours on end. Immaculus tried everything he knew to stop its crying. Crudely he rocked the makeshift crib Brother Christopher had erected in his room, cooing and singing in a squeaky falsetto while mechanically tickling the infant under the chin. He tried feeding it with Dominic's improvised baby bottle, but the infant refused to take it.

At his wit's end, Immaculus dropped to his knees next to the crib and clasped his hands in prayer. He rolled his eyes toward heaven. "Sweet angel of Mercy, give me a sign, an answer to this matter. I've spent my entire life without children. Why must you test me thus? Why?"

Nerves racked, his body aching with fatigue, he paced the stone floor, desperate for ideas. Secretly he wished the infant would disappear. He stared down into the crib. "If I told you we were keeping you, would you stop crying and go to sleep now?"

Miraculously, the infant stopped crying. Breathing a sigh of relief, Immaculus once again folded his hands in prayer and shook them in affirmation. "Praise God. Now to sleep."

Exhausted, he crawled into bed and blew out the candle. "Gypsies," he grumbled, pulling the bed clothing over himself. "I might have known."

He settled his head against the pillow and closed his eyes. *Sleep is such a divine state*, he thought. But just as he was about to drift off, the baby burst out crying again.

"Jesus and all the saints!"

The abbot leaped out of bed. Without relighting the candle, he stormed into the next cell, where his assistant Brother Vincent was sleeping, and threw open the door. "Send for Dominic!" he yelled. "Send for Dominic! I can't take this any longer!"

Vincent woke with a start and ran to fetch Dominic, throwing on his habit as he went. Seconds later he returned with Dominic, who wordlessly picked up the infant. Immediately the baby stopped crying.

The abbot closed his eyes and sighed in relief. "Well, I can certainly see you have the magic touch."

In the middle of the night, the crib was quietly transferred to Dominic's cell.

"HE WILL probably sleep for two or three hours," Dominic said the next morning as he stood in the doorway of his cell, both eyes trained on the crib. Brother Thomas nodded.

"When he does start to cry, he needs either a clean diaper or a new bottle, or both. I've gone over with you how to put on the diaper. Do you remember, or would you like me to talk you through it again?"

Thomas gave him a strained smile. "We'll muddle along until your return. Now off with you."

"Thank you, my friend," Dominic whispered, and disappeared down the corridor.

IMMACULUS AND Dominic walked the three miles to the village. Their first stop was the church to see the clergyman, the Reverend White. He knew of no missing infants and sent them to inquire at a few households nearby, where they were told the same thing. They did learn that the village had its own midwife in residence, who certainly would be aware of any recent births.

A middle-aged woman with a cheerful, intelligent face opened the door. "Good morning to you, sirs. My name is Ann," she said after the friars introduced themselves. She invited them in, stepping aside to allow them entrance into her tidy foyer.

"I was just about to have a spot of lunch. Would you care to join me?"

Nodding graciously, the abbot and Brother Dominic followed Ann into her dining room. Over a simple meal of tea and sandwiches, the abbot explained the purpose of their visit. Ann listened, then asked several questions about the appearance and condition of the baby.

"There were a few women in this area who were pregnant recently," she told them. "I expect to be called, but they don't always ask for help, you know. Especially the ones with children already at home. A family with too many mouths to feed might not want any more. It's a tragedy."

She fell silent, then rose from her seat to clear the table. When she returned—after what seemed to the monks like an eternity—she said, "Thank God the child was left in the fields where someone would find it."

"We'll go back to the Reverend White," Immaculus said. "Perhaps there is a family in town who would take in the baby."

He stood up, as did Dominic, and they headed toward the door. "Thank you for a most delicious meal," Immaculus added.

Ann smiled and looked at Dominic before saying to the abbot, "You will probably be in need of a wet nurse to take care of the child until someone is located, or at the very least some bottles and a bit of instruction on what to do, yes?"

"We would be most grateful for some instruction," Dominic blurted out.

Clearly taken aback, Immaculus looked at him sternly but said nothing. The midwife nodded. "I'll get my things ready and be at the abbey midmorning tomorrow, if that's alright."

The abbot barely managed a murmur of agreement, his lips a thin line across his face. Ann smiled and closed the door after them.

"IF ONLY you had ignored the child's cries," Immaculus said as they approached the abbey. "If only you had heeded the bell for office instead, all this could have been avoided."

Dominic did not reply.

Anticipating his return, the abbot's other assistant, Brother Daniel, had prepared a large bowl of hot water. Immaculus found the cloth-draped bowl on the floor in front of his chair when he entered his study. Dominic added some mineral powders and salts to the water. The abbot flopped down wearily in a chair. He rolled his habit up to his knees and with great effort removed his socks and shoes. Rapturously he soaked his feet in the water. Not since a pilgrimage to Palestine's holy sites in 1921 had he walked so far. Every part of his legs and feet ached.

"Perhaps the child and his family had gone on a picnic?" the abbot mused.

"I doubt it," Dominic said. "It was quite early, close to five thirty. An unlikely hour for picnicking."

Immaculus rubbed his legs. "Perhaps the parents misplaced the child? They put it down in the grasses and forgot where it was. And since the child was asleep, they couldn't hear it. That wouldn't be hard to do. The tall grasses could easily conceal an adult lying down, much less a child."

Dominic watched the steam rise from the bowl of hot water. "Whoever put the child there made preparations for it to be there for a while. The child was lying on a small blanket it had presumably been wrapped in. Genuinely concerned parents would have searched frantically for their child. They may even have knocked on our door. We would have heard from them much sooner."

The abbot kept rubbing his legs. "We shall pray the child's parents or another family comes to claim him. For now, you are to look after him. I shall excuse you from all other obligations save your pharmaceutical and medical ones. Taking care of this lost soul is to become your full-time duty until we know more."

EVERY NIGHT, by the flickering light of his candle, Dominic prayed to the painting of St. Francis on his wall. He prayed not on his padded kneeler, but on the hard, cold stone floor of his cell until he could barely rise from the stiffness in his legs. He prayed in his laboratory while he made medicines and when he was alone out in the fields. And he prayed over the baby's crib at night before he retired.

He prayed that the family in question would not be found.

2

BARE TREES AND CHILLY WINDS served as potent harbingers of the coming winter. The same thick stone walls that had kept out the marauding invaders of the Middle Ages, the thieves and highwaymen of the eighteenth and nineteenth centuries, and for the most part modern-day burglars were no match for the cold. There was no central heating in any part of the monastery. The only source of warmth for most of the monks consisted of a single blanket folded in two and a hot water bottle at bedtime.

All the friars were fast asleep when a low rumble in the middle of the night shook the countryside. One old monk, thinking the apocalypse was at hand, threw himself out of bed and fell onto his knees in prayer. In Dominic's cell the infant began wailing in his crib. Dominic sat up in the dark and stared up at the ceiling until the roar of what he thought were planes had passed and everything was silent once more. Then he got up and nursed the child until he was quiet again.

"I'LL MAKE a thorough inspection of the water pipes before winter sets in," Brother Christopher told Immaculus. They stood in the abbot's study, warming themselves in front of one of the building's few fireplaces.

"Thank you, Christopher. Was anything broken last night? I believe I heard every window in this building rattle during that unearthly shaking."

Christopher was about to respond when Brother Andrew barged into the room, waving a newspaper.

"Abbot! The Germans have bombed Coventry," he said. "That rumbling we heard last night was the sound of German bombers flying overhead."

Immaculus picked up his spectacles from his desk. Still folded, he brought them up to the end of his nose and calmly studied the headline.

"Where did you get this?" he said.

"One of the brothers found it this morning at the top of the drive outside the main gate."

Newspapers, the abbot thought. He had forbidden them ever since he had first taken office some two decades before. All outside literature not preapproved by him was not allowed within their walls. He had restricted a monk's reading to the contents of their library. To him, newspapers were a secular concern, not an ecclesiastical one. They did not reflect monastery life. Rather, they were the extensions of a world he had left behind so long ago. The cloister, he felt, was built for the sole purpose of creating a lifestyle dedicated to retreat and spiritual contemplation. And although some in their order favored greater involvement with the outside world, Immaculus preferred to thoroughly exclude it. That was the vision of their order's founders centuries ago.

The abbot's face flushed red in anger. He shook the newspaper in the air. "This is a cloister, not Whitehall! Our interests here are purely spiritual, not temporal. Anyone found with a newspaper will receive the severest punishment I can impose. Do I make myself clear?"

Andrew looked at the floor.

Still holding the newspaper, Immaculus turned toward the fireplace and said to no one in particular, "Today at Prime we will pray for those who have lost their lives and for those who now find themselves in crisis."

Then he tossed the newspaper into the fire.

SERGEANT OLIVER called on Immaculus that afternoon. "Night blackouts are mandatory now until further notice," he said.

"What about fuel lamps?" said the abbot.

"The same, I'm afraid. Candles will have to do. All windows must be curtained after six in the evening."

Immaculus nodded grimly. He paused, then asked anxiously, "Any news of the child's parents or guardians?"

The sergeant played with one of the buttons on his coat. "We've scoured our records. We've contacted every station in the surrounding area. There have been no reports of any missing babies. Of course we'll continue making inquiries. But these latest developments in the war hamper our investigation. I need you to keep the child for a while longer, until we're past these current events."

"What if we decide to keep the child ourselves?"

Oliver looked at the abbot in surprise. "You want to have a go, then?" he said.

The abbot nodded.

"Generally there is much paperwork to be done in such cases. Given the current state of affairs, however, I think we can make an exception. We'll deal with the formalities later—that is, if the parents or rightful guardians turn up."

THAT EVENING Dominic was praying on the floor of his cell when the abbot paid him a visit.

"How is the child doing?" said Immaculus after he opened the door and peered into the room.

Dominic rose to his feet unsteadily and pressed an index finger to his lips. Silently he motioned the abbot toward the crib. Immaculus looked down at the sleeping infant and smiled. In what he thought was a whisper but actually was loud enough to echo off the small room's four walls, the abbot said to Dominic, "I need to speak with you. Let's go next door."

In an empty cell, furnished like the others with a wooden crucifix on the wall over the bed and a few pieces of furniture, Dominic lit a candle. Shadows began dancing on the walls. The abbot paced for a moment, then turned to Dominic.

"Sergeant Oliver came to my office this afternoon," he said.

Dominic braced himself for the bad news. Ever since he had brought the child into the abbey, he had mentally prepared himself for this moment. He glanced at the shadows on the wall and held his breath.

"He has indicated to me that the search to find the parents of the child has yielded no positive results," said the abbot. He paused. Dominic felt himself grow weak. He began to breathe again, albeit uneasily. His heart raced.

"We will keep the child," said the abbot. "Recent events currently plaguing the world and the fruitless efforts of the police have changed my mind. Apart from teaching, illumination, and the preservation of knowledge, part of our history has been to provide shelter to those in need in times of siege. We would be most remiss in our responsibilities if we did not extend that same protection to one totally incapable of defending himself in these uncertain times. When the parents or another suitable family is found, we will deal with the situation then."

The words stunned Dominic. It was impossible for him to discern whether he had truly heard them or not. A lump formed in his throat. He dropped to his knees and buried his face in the abbot's hands.

"Oh, thank you, thank you, thank you," he wept.

Balancing precariously on a chair, Dominic was attempting to string a heavy cord from one wall of his laboratory to the other, attaching it at each end to a metal loop. Momentarily discouraged, he stepped off the chair. He ran a finger across a small scar above his left eye, a souvenir he had gotten thirty-five years ago in a game of tag with his eldest sister.

Katharine. What would she do in this situation? He still looked up to his good-hearted and resourceful sister even though they hadn't seen each other often in the last few years. She was still his guiding light whenever he truly needed one.

Dominic considered the tasks before him: setting up a nursery for the infant in his cell, clearing away medicines to make room for things the infant needed.

He heard the clinking of glass outside his door and went to open it. Brother Thomas stood in the hall with a large cardboard box in his arms, shifting his weight from one foot to the other.

"Done?" Dominic said. "So fast?"

Thomas settled his cargo against the doorjamb. "Where shall I put these?"

"Over there," Dominic said, pointing to the table.

Out of breath, Thomas carefully put the box down. Its contents jingled as he did so. "I had the other two help me," he said. "Instead of making afternoon tea, the three of us boiled bottles. Brother Eustace looked very upset when I told him there would be no tea today."

Dominic opened the box and removed one of the twenty small square glass bottles with brown rubber nipples that he had ordered directly from a factory in Bristol. He held the bottle up in the air and looked at it. In his mind he pictured the three monks in the kitchen, bending over the huge stainless-steel cauldron as steam filled the room.

Thomas pointed to the cord snaking on the stone floor. "What is this?"

Dominic put the bottle back into the box. "A line for the baby's wash."

Set side by side on a tile counter that ran the length of the wall were two large washbasins. Above them were bay windows overlooking the manicured monastery lawns. Dominic washed the soiled linen diapers by hand by filling one basin with scalding water and soaping and scrubbing the linens on the washboard until they frothed. In the other basin he rinsed each linen individually with cool water. He squeezed out the excess water in the sink, then hung them over the sides of the basins. In his mind he saw the small squares hanging from the newly erected clothesline to dry, like so many tiny white flags.

Thomas eyed the diapers folded over the basins. "You're doing all the wash yourself?"

"Yes," said Dominic.

"Why can't Gregory do it?"

Dominic picked the line up off the floor and stared up at the ceiling. "Didn't want to bother him. He's got enough on his plate with us lot. Perhaps in due course . . ."

Thomas sighed. "Nobody is set up to handle a child in this place." He looked around the laboratory. "Where do you intend on putting all these?" he said, nodding toward the box of milk bottles. "You hardly have room as it is."

Dominic scratched his head. Most of his medicine preparation work was done on the counters next to the basins, so storing anything there was out of the question. The wall opposite the door had the fireplace; it was only common sense not to store anything near fire. Plants and flowers bordered the walls of the room. The shelves on the wall that ran floor to ceiling opposite the basins were filled with books, jars, bottles, vials, tubes in wooden racks, and beakers of medicine—all different sizes and shapes, with handwritten labels. A stepladder stood nearby.

Tapping one of the wooden shelves with his hand, Dominic said, "I'm going to have to make room here."

Both men heard a rustle and turned toward the baby's crib, which sat near the long table in the middle of the room.

"It's changing time," said Dominic. "I'll need your help." He crooked his index finger, and Thomas followed him over to the far end of the table.

"There needs to be more than one person around here who is proficient at changing diapers," Dominic told him. "Now we can practice the technique I've been teaching you." He opened a brown wrapper, revealing a book. "It's a book on child rearing. I ordered it from Foyles in London."

In his thick Welsh accent Thomas muttered, "I hope it has diagrams."

Dominic smiled.

"What would you like me to do?" Thomas said with a sigh.

"Help me clear off some of the table."

The long rectangular walnut table that dominated the room was cluttered with charts, books, medicine vials, and pestles and mortars. The two monks carefully cleared bottles and notebooks from one end of the table and put them on the counter near the sinks. Dominic unfolded a white towel and spread it out over the cleared area. Lifting the little bundle from the crib, he laid him on the towel. The two monks looked down at him. The infant wore a cloth diaper that was wrapped around his body several times and fastened by a safety pin at either end.

"This doesn't look right, the way you've put it on," said Thomas.

Dominic brought the child-rearing book closer and turned to a dog-eared page. He put on his glasses and pointed to a diagram.

"This is the way it's done," he said, tapping the page.

"And what have we been using for diapers, then?" Thomas said.

Dominic pointed to a stack of white linen squares on the table. "Our sheets."

"You tore up our sheets?"

Dominic nodded. "Just until we get some proper diapers."

"No wonder Gregory has been complaining of a sheet shortage."

"Don't tell anyone, will you?"

Dominic unwrapped the baby. Thomas made a face. "Good heavens! Not exactly spring roses, is it?" He held his nose.

"Right," Dominic said. "You hold up his legs, and I'll slip off the diaper."

Still holding his nose, Thomas held up the infant's legs with his free hand. Dominic removed the diaper and took it over to the sink, where he examined the moist brown patch on it. He rinsed it off under cold running water then left it in the sink. Fetching a fresh cloth, he moistened it with warm water and returned to the table. He wiped and cleaned the infant's bottom with the cloth, then tossed it into the sink from where he stood. He took another fresh diaper and folded it.

Brother James came into the laboratory, looking for Dominic. He stopped in his tracks and stood in the doorway, head tilted to one side, watching. "I'll come back later," he mumbled, and was gone.

"Lift his legs," Dominic said to Thomas.

Thomas did so, and Dominic slipped the clean diaper underneath.

"While I hold the two sides, you pin him up," said Dominic.

Thomas pointed to the book. "But the diagram clearly shows to fold it this way. Look."

"No, it doesn't," said Dominic. He elbowed Thomas out of the way. "Here, let me do it!" Holding the sides of the diaper, he said, "Now please just pin him where I'm holding him."

"But what if I miss?"

"You won't miss because I'm holding it. Now will you please, for the love of God, get on with it?"

Thomas ran the first pin through the cloth where Dominic's fingers held it and did the same with the second.

"Done," said Dominic. Relieved, he carried the infant back to the crib and covered him up again.

Thomas did not look happy. "How long are we going to have to do this?"

"As I understand it, about a year or two." Dominic walked over to the basin and washed his hands. After drying them with a towel hanging on a nearby hook, he returned to the table and picked up the volume once more. "Let's see what the book says."

"Ah, yes," said Thomas. "The book, the book. We don't have a clue what we're doing, so a ruddy book is going to tell us. What were we thinking, taking in an infant? It's sheer madness. We don't have the facilities or the experience. Not to mention the disruption in our lives. We all came here to get away from this sort of thing."

Thomas walked over to the crib and looked in. "I just don't think it's too late to give the child to the proper authorities—you know, someone who knows about this sort of thing."

Dominic yawned heavily. The baby had kept him up all night with frequent feedings.

"You're starting to sound like Immaculus," he said.

WITHOUT BEING asked, the abbot raised his hands above his head as Thomas and Dominic slipped the crimson cassock over him. The robe cascaded down his body and over his undergarments, falling softly to the floor like a curtain. The two monks smoothed out the vestment with their hands all the way to the abbot's ankles. As they worked, the three monks kept bumping into each other in the cramped vestry, but no one said a word. The only sounds were the rustling of garments and a fly that buzzed in the room. Folded on a small wooden table in the corner were stacks of white linens, from altar coverings to Communion napkins. On the wall was a plain wooden crucifix.

Thomas held out the virgin-white surplice in front of Immaculus. The cook's disheveled red hair looked as though it had not been combed in days. As the abbot threaded his arms through the sleeves, the monks pulled the garment over his shoulders. Behind the abbot, Dominic methodically buttoned it up. One button was missing.

At eight in the morning, the intense sun lit the room through the only window, near the door. It reflected off the light wood of the vestry walls, illuminating Dominic's tired face as he placed a large gold chain over the abbot's head and adjusted it on his shoulders. Attached to it was a spectacular gold pectoral cross with a depiction of the Savior nailed to it. Dominic fumbled with the cross as he attempted to pin it to Immaculus's vestments.

"You're nervous," the abbot said.

"Yes."

"Me too. This is the first time I've said Mass in as long as I can recall. Ah, the things I miss. Running this place and keeping you lot in order leaves me little time to indulge in the things I enjoy. But saying a Mass in honor of someone we are about to call our own . . . now that is special. That needs to be celebrated."

Dominic finished pinning the cross to the abbot's chest and anxiously looked over his shoulder at the crib tucked away in the corner of the room. The infant was sleeping peacefully.

A FEW evenings earlier, the abbot had summoned Dominic to his study. "What are we going to name the boy?" he said, looking up from his desk.

"Steven," Dominic said.

The abbot rearranged the few thin strands of hair left on his head. "And a surname?"

"St. Francis."

"I see. And how did you arrive at this name?"

"I wanted to name him after the man whom I have modeled my life after, St. Francis of Assisi."

"A splendid choice," said the abbot. "I just want you to know that Brother James combed through the archives in search of any record of a child baptism that had taken place here. In our entire recorded history he could not find a single entry, not a one. This is the first child baptism to take place here."

IN THE vestry Thomas put the tippet around Immaculus's neck and placed on his head the simple box miter that matched the color of his cassock. Dominic handed the abbot his ornate gold staff. He then carefully lifted the sleeping infant, who was wrapped in a warm quilt. The baby held out his arms to Dominic.

Thomas opened the door to the chapel. The abbot entered first, followed by the two monks. Butterflies fluttered in Dominic's stomach. In his excitement he stumbled coming out of the vestry but recovered, clutching the infant even more securely to his chest.

The chapel was magnificently lit by great rows of candles that flickered by the altar. The acrid smell of incense was everywhere. Every monk watched as the procession slowly moved toward the altar.

When Mass ended, Dominic removed the baby from the quilt. The abbot motioned him to come forward and hold the naked infant over a bowl that Thomas held beneath the baby's head. Immaculus gently poured lukewarm water from a tiny silver cup onto the child's forehead. Immediately the child began to cry.

"Your name is Steven St. Francis," said the abbot. "May the Almighty grant thee eternal happiness and preserve thee from sin always. I baptize thee with the power vested in me through Jesus

Christ our Savior, in the name of the Father, and of the Son, and of the Holy Spirit. Amen."

The abbot anointed the tiny forehead with holy oil and took the child from Dominic's arms. He looked down into the baby's face and made the sign of the cross over his fragile body. In a clear, distinct voice over the child's crying, he said to his congregation, "Steven St. Francis, you are now one of us."

Forgetting himself, Brother Andrew rose from his pew and began clapping energetically. Three others did the same. Within moments the entire chapel was on its feet, engulfed in an ocean of applause.

Immaculus looked up. Even he could not restrain himself. Handing the child back to Dominic, he joined in himself.

3

DOMINIC KNOCKED ON THE abbot's door.

"Yes, come in," came the answer from the other side.

Dominic popped his head around the door. "Abbot, a moment, please?"

Immaculus waved him in. Once comfortably seated, Dominic said, "I've been told that the people in the village are in desperate need of medicine."

The abbot raised his eyebrows, urging him to continue with an almost imperceptible nod.

"Because of the attack on Coventry," Dominic said, "the entire countryside is running short on supplies."

Immaculus suddenly sat forward. "Are you suggesting we send medicine to the village? Our medicine?"

Shifting in his chair, Dominic watched the abbot's eyes narrow. "There's a war going on, Abbot," Dominic said. Immaculus didn't interrupt, so he continued. "We need to deliver badly needed medicines to the villagers whose supplies have been limited due to wartime rationing."

Dominic knew the abbot did not approve of monks offering their services beyond the abbey, but he believed a response was necessary. "The abbey has a very well-stocked supply of medicine," he continued. "We would not be dangerously depleted; we have more than enough. I wouldn't have to leave the abbey. I could give the supplies to Dr. Cotter, the town's physician, who would distribute them accordingly."

Immaculus rose and walked over to the window. He stared out at the green lawns in silence for what seemed like whole minutes.

"Yes," the abbot said finally. "Yes, this is important."

Dominic saw the abbot wipe a tear from the corner of his eye.

A MONK lived by the order's rules and diligently followed its teachings. They became part of his skin. There was nothing luxurious or glamorous about a monk's chosen way of life, for it was not meant to be comfortable or pleasurable. It was a world consumed by spiritual meditation and thought, religious exercise, repentance and prayer, abstinence and fasting, contemplation, the pursuit of solitude and silence, scholasticism and learning, penance, poverty and chastity, obedience and observation of the rule, and retreat from the outside world. Aside from personal time, every waking hour of the day was spoken for. A monk's life, in large part, belonged to his abbot, to his community of brothers, and to God.

There were many special benefits to this lifestyle. Apart from the fulfillment earned through hard work, there was peace and tranquility. Many cherished the solitude, and at the abbey that solitude could be found in many places. The monastery was situated on fifty acres of land. The buildings consisted of a chapter house, infirmary, laboratory, dormitories and latrines, granary and mill, cellars, chapel, cloister, kitchen, refectory, a large larder, and a library that housed a vast repository of knowledge, including the Greek and Latin classics, sacred and secular writings, and volumes on medicine, science, and monastic history. The grounds themselves consisted of massive lawns, vegetable gardens, a greenhouse, an apple and pear orchard, and a graveyard.

A flower garden was nestled in the middle of the cloister grounds. As large as any medieval marketplace, half of the garden was planted with rows of rose bushes, all of different colors. At the center was a small pond, home to a group of chattering ducks. In summer and autumn the monks were fond of feeding them, but in winter the pond froze over and the ducks flew away. A gravel footpath circled the garden, following the inside of the high stone walls that were covered with ivy and provided privacy. In each corner of the garden was a tree-shaded bench.

Brother Eustace planted different bushes and flowers that exploded into a rainbow of colors in spring and summer. During hot spells, especially after long intervals of strenuous religious exercises, the monks took refuge on a bench under one of the huge linden trees. There, a cup of lemonade in hand, shaded from the sun by the enormous umbrellas of branches and leaves, they admired a bee shaking a clematis blossom or a blackbird racing across the lawn or a red admiral butterfly opening and closing its wings.

While the garden was a place where they could be alone to reflect, it was also a place where they could stroll arm in arm in conversation. When prayer failed, a few peaceful hours sitting together under the shade of a tree calmed their spirits. In a world of tremendous self-discipline, the garden became a retreat, one in which they stole time out of each day to enjoy.

On Sundays especially, the brothers enjoyed moments of recreation. In summer they played badminton in the garden, croquet on the front lawns of the cloister, or a round of tag or blindman's bluff in the courtyard. Sometimes simply going for long walks around the estate was enough to replenish the waters of the soul. A tree-lined drive began at the main gates and ended at the monastery front doors. During warmer months, the monks, all of whom were voracious readers, would stroll, book in hand, under the elm trees, whose branches and leaves formed a canopy over the long, serpentine drive. If it rained, they played indoor games such as chess and checkers. Many loved singing and looked forward to choir practice.

This was life until Steven arrived. Dominic's daily routine, once governed entirely by prayer and the practice of medicine, became filled with diaper changes, laundry, warming up milk bottles, and mending garments. Each of the monks, in his own way, helped to raise the child. Thomas boiled bottles in the kitchen, and Gregory washed diapers and baby clothes in the laundry. Christopher built a succession of cribs and toys in his workshop, while Brother Samson stitched clothes.

To many, Steven was a reminder of an outside world they had once known, a reminder of what it felt like to touch and love another human being. In his presence, all discipline, all self-control melted away. Steven was a burst of sunlight in the dreary monastic routines and years of solitude. Even the strongest will evaporated at the sight of him, for none could resist lifting him up and kissing him.

As the child grew, the monks would play blindman's bluff with him in the courtyard and zoom through the most sacred parts of the cloister with him on their backs. Squeals of joy echoed through the ancient corridors. Whatever their activity, whether rapt in prayer or in some office duty bound by silence, if they felt his gentle tugging at their robes calling them to play, they obliged without a moment's hesitation. When Steven laughed, everything brightened. When he cried, they dropped whatever they were doing and rushed to him.

Dominic took Steven with him wherever he went, whether it was making his rounds of the fields in search of medicinal plants or tending to the monastery garden. When Steven was an infant, Dominic wrapped him in a blanket and transported him in his wicker basket. As Steven grew older, they would walk hand in hand through the same fields. Every night at bedtime, Dominic sang Steven a lullaby. Once the child was fast asleep, Dominic would say, "Holy Father, bless my son. Give him the strength he needs to survive in this mortal world. Fill his life with light and happiness, always."

A SMALL, stout Welshman, Brother Thomas stood barely five feet two inches tall, with a warm, freckled face and a head of wiry red hair. His chubby hands and fingers possessed remarkable strength and dexterity. No one could slice and chop food like he could. As a youth he had dreamed of becoming a chef in one of London's fine restaurants. Whenever a monk made an appearance in the kitchen, Thomas, out of force of habit, gave him something to eat. He was always badgering some poor soul into trying something he had just made. Thomas was a jovial, gregarious, lighthearted man who, above all, loved his kitchen. He would stand in front of the woodfire stove, ladling out soup and taking pleasure in its aroma, and he could never keep quiet while he cooked. If he wasn't barking orders to his staff, he was quietly talking to the food as he prepared it. He was the first one in the kitchen in the morning, praying aloud over his pots and pans for divine inspiration.

Thomas also loved to sing, especially Italian opera, which he frequently sang in the bath. Once he got so carried away with an aria that his big toe became stuck in the bathtub spout. The fire brigade was called. When they arrived, they applied a grease that gently eased the toe out as, much to Thomas's embarrassment, half the monastery looked on.

Brothers Ignatius and Matthew were Thomas's faithful assistants. While Thomas was an extrovert who sang and talked to everyone and everything, Matthew, by contrast, lived in a shell of shyness. This was not helped by a slight lisp, which made him all the more self-conscious.

Many aspects of the monastery distinguished it from others of
its kind. To some monks it was the vast fields and surrounding
countryside. To others it was the sheer weight of the abbey's history and tradition, the closeness of the unit, the challenge of the
discipline, the transcending of the temporal, and the embracing
of the spiritual. But the monastery was best known, in England
and, some even said, in the farthest reaches of the European con-
tinent, for its bread. Baked fresh daily, it was one tradition that
had survived all religious changes and monastic reforms. The
recipe remained relatively unchanged throughout the centuries.
The only thing that did change was the way it was made.

Seventy-five years earlier a waterwheel was used to harness the
power of the stream that ran alongside the east wall of the cloister.
This propelled the machinery that ground the wheat and millet
into flour. That practice had long been abandoned. Now the abbey
bought its flour from the village and had it delivered weekly. The
dough was placed in trays and baked in the abbey's large ovens.

The smell of baking bread in the morning permeated every
part of the monastery. Its effect on the monks was powerful. One
whiff of the hot, fresh loaf at the breakfast table, and their eyes
would roll back in their heads, followed by a collective sigh of
pleasure. Whether laboring in the hot fields of summer or praying in their cells, their minds would inevitably wander off to
mealtimes and to the bread that would be served. Often it was the
only thought that got them through their rigorous day. There
were even those who considered their bread a sacrament, not
unlike Holy Communion.

Thomas's cooking was just as well loved, but the one cloud
that hung over the otherwise satisfying mealtimes was Tuesday
supper. Hardly a monk looked forward to it. That was the time
Thomas presented his new creations. His efforts often emerged
charred and overdone, or so overspiced that they were inedible.
It was not unheard of for the kitchen to fill with thick black

smoke, requiring all the kitchen doors and windows to be opened. Tuesday supper was an experiment for everyone.

One night Thomas introduced a new stew. He stood proudly in the corner of the dining room, watching silently as each monk at the long table of nineteen sniffed and cautiously brought their spoons to their lips to sample the concoction.

Brother Lawrence, who lived by a vow of silence at mealtimes, was the first to speak. "Really, Thomas," he said, "this has gone too far. What are you trying to do, poison us?" He rose from the table, threw his napkin down, and stormed out.

Brother Andrew watched him leave and leaned over toward Benedict. "I would rather eat the weeds in the garden than this muck," he whispered.

The next day Thomas stood in front of the abbot, who was leaning back in his chair behind his desk.

"I like experimenting," said Thomas. "Variety in diet, I think, is a good thing."

"Yes," Immaculus said. "But many do not consider your experiments delightful, Thomas, as the display last night by Lawrence illustrates. No one disputes the quality of your standard menu. It is when you deviate from your carefully chosen culinary map and drift into the dark, uncharted waters of the unknown that you run aground. Carry on with your regular menu instead."

Disheartened, Thomas followed the abbot's orders. He prayed to God for inspiration daily and sang softly in the kitchen while he stirred the great cauldrons of hot potato soup. Several months later Thomas felt he had received his inspiration. On a Tuesday evening he presented his brothers with a new soufflé. The abbot, who sat at the head of the table, said to him, "I thought we agreed you would stop your experimenting."

Thomas gushed with childlike exuberance. "I sought divine guidance, and I had an intervention. I wanted to share the result with all of you."

"Divine intervention, indeed," mumbled Lawrence to Christopher, who sat next to him. "Here we go again."

Hesitantly Lawrence put a forkful of the soufflé into his mouth. Immediately his eyes closed and a look of ecstasy came over him. His mouth still full, and breaking his rule of silence for the second time, he said, "Thomas, you have outdone yourself! This warrants a special Mass!"

ONE MORNING during Steven's fourth year, Thomas found a golden Labrador retriever scavenging out near the refuse. The dog was scruffy and cadaverous, his fur matted and falling out in places, revealing unhealed wounds. Thomas approached the dog and reached out a hand in a gesture of affection. The animal only snarled at him.

Thomas went into the kitchen and returned with some stew from the day before. He put the bowl down on the ground and slowly backed away. Cautiously the dog approached the bowl and sniffed. Then it began to eat voraciously. Thomas stayed with the dog long enough to win its confidence. He led it to his cell, where it curled up on the small square of carpet next to his bed. There he quietly nursed it back to health, with a little help from Dominic, and in a few weeks' time it had metamorphosed into a handsome animal. Its dark eyes sparkled, and its coat shone with a soft, glossy radiance in the sunlight. Everyone was astounded by the animal's remarkable transformation, save for Brother Gregory.

"It's your stew," he said. "That stew of yours could raise Lazarus from the dead!"

Thomas named the animal Cain, after one of his favorite biblical characters. Practically everyone knew of the dog except the abbot. He would have called for the animal's immediate removal if he had found out. Two years earlier Thomas had lobbied for a guard dog. The monastery was a vast complex of buildings to which anyone could gain access with little difficulty. He had explained to Immaculus that a dog would alert them in the event of danger. But his pleadings fell on deaf ears.

Ironically, a short time later they were burglarized. Brother Ignatius, one of the lightest sleepers in the abbey, heard noises coming from the chapel late one night while the rest of the monastery slept. He went to investigate and spotted an intruder fleeing through an open window. Nothing was missing, but the incident did expose their vulnerability.

It was inevitable that Immaculus would find out about Cain. One afternoon he came looking for Thomas, and when he swung open the door to the monk's cell he was met by the growling dog.

"I'm giving you one hour to get rid of that animal!" the abbot said to Thomas, whom he found in the kitchen. "Remove it and we shall forget the matter entirely."

Thomas looked down at the sink. "But Your Grace, we could use a good guard dog around here," he said. "Remember the burglary we had two summers ago? We were all fast asleep and didn't hear a thing, except for Ignatius."

"You have one hour, Thomas," the abbot said.

By this time eighteen monks had quietly filed into the kitchen.

"The animal will be no trouble," said Brother James. "We've all agreed to look after it."

"A dog will keep the rabbits away from our vegetable garden," chimed in Brother Eustace. Each monk took his turn saying something in the dog's defense. Going against the abbot was such a blatant act of disobedience that had it not been for their numbers, any one of them could have received severe punishment.

The abbot was stunned. Clearly outnumbered, he said, "Alright, we'll keep the dog."

After that, Cain guarded the monastery as if the buildings belonged to him. He was playful and never tired of games. And, true to his breed, he was also an expert retriever; no matter what was thrown to him or where it landed, he always found and returned it. Brother Christopher built a kennel for him outside the back door of the kitchen so Cain could have shelter and warmth all year round.

Steven came to love Cain with all his heart. Every morning he would wake up, scurry into the kitchen, and throw open the back door. Finding Cain, he would lock his arms around the dog's neck as though it had been lost for a week.

"If I didn't know better," said Brother Matthew, observing the two, "I could swear that God had joined the two of them together by the umbilical cord."

During summer Cain and Steven roamed the nearby woods and forests on hunting expeditions. Cain always took the lead, sniffing and panting, inspecting every tree trunk, every shrub, ferreting out creatures only he could see. As the day wore on, his tongue would roll out, covered with saliva. At dusk, Dominic would ring the bell for supper, and the two friends would hurry home through the fading twilight.

4

ONE MORNING IN STEVEN'S tenth year, Brother Thomas went to the kitchen to start work for the day. Normally when he opened the back door Cain would bound in, greeting him with licks and pants of appreciation, pouncing and jumping all over him, hungry for food and affection. But this day, the dog was eerily quiet. Curled up inside his kennel, he shivered, responding to neither affection nor food.

Thomas fetched Dominic and Matthew. The three of them moved Cain indoors and made a space for him on Dominic's laboratory floor, next to the fireplace. Dominic found a patch of rug and placed it underneath him. Cain lay listless, refusing all food. Dominic's knowledge of animal husbandry was limited, and so the brothers decided to take Cain to the village veterinarian.

Matthew and Dominic placed Cain on the veterinarian's examining table and watched as the dapper doctor, who wore horn-rimmed spectacles and sported a neatly trimmed mustache, carefully tended to the sick animal. There was complete silence for several minutes while he worked. He looked into the dog's mouth, checked his ears, and ran a hand firmly along the animal's spine and neck. He felt his paws and legs and parted the fur to examine the skin underneath.

"I am satisfied he has a disease," he said finally. "But I cannot identify it or its source."

"Source?" Dominic said.

"Where it was contracted." The veterinarian opened his black leather bag and began preparing a syringe. "Had he been bitten by another animal—a tree rat, or perhaps another dog—there would be wounds, lesions, puncture or incision marks. None are apparent. This leaves an insect, perhaps a flea or a tick. They too can transmit disease. But I cannot be sure. There are also canine diseases, of which we know little, much less how to treat them."

The veterinarian gave Cain an injection on the nape of the neck. "If there is no sign of improvement in three days," he said, "call me."

Except to sleep, Steven did not leave Cain's side. By the warmth of the fire in his laboratory, Dominic dabbed the animal's hot, dry nose with a cool, damp cloth and tried unsuccessfully to get the dog to eat and drink.

Early on the morning of the third day, Dominic found Cain as he had left him the night before, curled up by the fire, appearing to be asleep. But when he bent down to touch him, the dog was cold and stiff as a November morning. With help from Thomas and Matthew, he carried Cain's body outside to the woodshed and covered it with an oilskin tarpaulin.

It was not long before Steven found them. The boy knelt down and gently pushed his hand through Cain's shiny fur. No movement, no breathing came from his faithful companion. Steven ran from the shed and disappeared for the rest of the day. That evening he did not come to dinner.

Dominic found Steven in his room, lying on his bed, face buried deep in his pillow, which softly muffled his weeping. His body shook from long, stuttering sobs. Dominic sat down on the bed and stroked the boy's head. His heart ached too. Dominic wished he could trade places with his son, but he knew that no one was immune to life's losses.

It snowed that night, and a soft white blanket covered the ground and trees. Standing in the cold, tranquil morning air the next day, Dominic, Steven, and five monks stood by as two brothers lowered Cain's body, carefully wrapped in a white linen sheet, into the dark mud of a shallow grave. At Steven's request, Cain was buried in his favorite place, under the linden tree in the garden where on hot summer afternoons the dog would lie in its shade to escape the heat.

Dominic opened his Bible and began reading. "The Lord is my shepherd: I shall not want. He maketh me to lie down in green pastures; he leadeth me beside the still waters. Yea, though I walk through the valley of the shadow of death, I will fear no evil; for thou art with me; thy rod and thy staff will comfort me."

He closed the Bible and added, "Of dust we are made, and of dust we shall return."

After they had buried Cain, Dominic took his son by the hand, leading him through the mists of the overcast morning through the frosted fields until they arrived at the stream. At the water's edge, amid a stand of tall trees, Dominic stood completely still. He removed bread from his pockets and handed some to Steven.

"Break it into crumbs," he said. "Put the crumbs in your hands and hold them out, like this."

Dominic held out his arms at shoulder level, palms up, as Steven looked on. Steven copied him, holding the bread in his open palms as if it were some offering in an ancient pagan ritual. He felt embarrassed and stupid. *The rigors of monastic life have finally robbed my father of his senses,* he thought. *Could all the years of strenuous repetition, both in manual labor and in prayer, have finally taken their toll? Is this the ultimate price one pays for constant devotion to God?*

Without warning, a single sparrow fluttered out of the mist. It circled Steven, beating the air with its wings as though unable to decide if he were a tree or a threat. It circled again before landing on the boy's shoulder. Immediately it was joined by another. In tandem, the two tiny creatures strutted down to Steven's elbow and paused before fluttering off into the air. They circled his body and perched on his hand. Nervously they looked around, then cautiously pecked at the bread. Suddenly they flung themselves wholesale into their feeding.

Within moments, birds of all kinds flocked to Steven's body, covering every available inch of his head, shoulders, and arms, and that of Dominic's as well. The noise of fluttering wings was everywhere. Steven had an almost irresistible urge to reach out and pet one, just once, but was afraid to break the spell. He knew these were not domesticated birds privately trained by his father.

Then Steven noticed something else. His sadness had lifted.

When all the bread was gone and the birds had flown away, Dominic brushed off the remaining crumbs. He bent down and put a hand on his son's shoulder. "The answer to everything lies inside us. It is up to you now. You must find your own answers."

His father had performed a kind of exorcism that had chased away his sorrow—not with holy water and prayer, but with nature. From that moment on, Steven regarded his father no longer as a solitary figure roaming the countryside, but as a wise enchanter so in harmony with nature that he could summon its powers at will.

As Steven matured, he helped the monks with their daily tasks. It was a rare day when Steven did not pay a visit to Brother Thomas to help prepare the daily meals. Brother Basil, the monastery chaplain, allowed Steven to help him clean and maintain the chapel and sacristy. Brother Christopher taught the boy how to look at any drawing and build a bookshelf, chair, and many other things out of wood. With Luke and Lawrence, Brother Gregory's helpers, Steven delivered fresh laundry to their brethren. Brother Aloysius, who at ninety-two was the eldest and most devout of all the monks, had been the monastery librarian before passing the torch to Brother James. All his cataloging from memory was passed on to his younger successor, who recorded everything. In his youth Aloysius possessed a remarkable memory. He could tell you where any volume was, on any subject, without looking it up. He also had a keen recall of events and dates. Steven spent several hours each week in the library reading and helping to catalog the books.

Brothers Andrew, Benedict, and Richard were in charge of all monastery maintenance. At thirty-three, Richard was the youngest monk. Their duties entailed cleaning the abbey's communal areas, from scrubbing the stone floors with buckets of hot water and soap to dusting the pews in the chapel and the benches and long dining table in the refectory. (Each monk was responsible for cleaning his own cell.) No one could wash walls like Benedict could. Under his scrubbing brush, grime and dirt magically dissolved. A small, humorless man, Benedict took his work and duties quite seriously. He was hard of hearing, and often the others had to shout at him in order to be heard. Steven was a little fearful of him, and sometimes hid when he was called on to help with the monastery cleaning.

Brother Eustace, the chief gardener, sometimes allowed Steven to help him and his assistants, Samson and Innocent. They planted and maintained the magnificent tapestry of flowers and blooms in the garden year round as well as attended the larger vegetable gardens. No one was more devoted to the cloister's outdoors than Eustace. If anyone wanted to find him, all he had to do was look in the garden. The monks referred to the garden as Eustace's. He felt it rightfully belonged to him, and all others were there by his unspoken invitation only.

STEVEN'S FORMAL tutoring in Latin and his religious studies were undertaken by the abbot himself, whose scholarship in these areas was without peer. Dominic schooled Steven in the art and science of medicine, teaching him about its history and philosophy. He also taught him how to identify a plant by its characteristics and peculiarities, its curative properties, where it was most commonly found, and in what season. Steven learned how to preserve and grow herbs during winter and autumn and how to store them in jars. Dominic also taught Steven the proper preparation of medicines. As tedious as it was, Dominic insisted that his son be able to describe every plant from memory and know its Latin derivation.

"Latin is God's language," said Dominic early one morning when they were out in the fields searching for medicine.

Now twelve years of age, Steven was a round-faced youth with wavy hair. His keen mind eagerly absorbed everything around him.

"How did all these remedies come to be known?" Steven said.

Dominic put his arm around the boy as they strolled through the fields. "Someone discovered them."

"How?"

"That's a good question. Trial and error, I suppose. Apothecaries a thousand years ago combed this land in search of medicine, gathering herbs and plants at random and consuming them without regard to their properties or what effects they produced. Those that were beneficial, they kept. Those that were not, were discarded. If the apothecary died, another took up the search."

"In other words," Steven said, "they were their own experimental subjects."

Dominic bent down to pluck a plant from the ground. He shook the dirt from its roots and stowed it in his basket. "Precisely," he said. "That's how our science evolved. Some in the past even believed that the Devil himself could be fought with the right combinations of herbs."

Steven looked all around. "Why do you have to do this so early, anyway?"

"You mean search for medicine?"

The boy nodded.

"During spring and summer I make my rounds of the countryside, collecting supplies to last through the other two seasons when the weather makes collecting impossible."

"Yes, but why so early?"

"During summer I like to get an early start. By nine in the morning, the intolerable heat of the sun makes working uncomfortable."

"You have a perfectly adequate greenhouse, though."

"The greenhouse is only functional once I supply it with the things we need to sustain us through the two harsher seasons. Although I have its added advantage, it is still necessary for me three times a week during spring and summer—summer especially— to search for herbs and plants to replenish my stock. In many cases this entails finding new, healthy specimens to replace those that either have died or are no longer potent."

Steven picked up one of the plants in his father's basket and looked at it. "And how do you do that?" he said.

"I take entire plants or cuttings from mature plants and replant them in the greenhouse, where we can have access to them during autumn and winter."

Steven was still perplexed.

"You see," Dominic said, taking the plant from Steven's hand and putting it back in the basket, "I don't ever want to run out. Years ago Brother Bartholomew died from a high fever brought on by influenza. I could have successfully treated him during a different season, when the plants I needed were readily available.

But it was winter. I had no extra plants, and a heavy snowstorm had cut off telephone communication, denying us outside help. The day after we buried Bartholomew, we began constructing the greenhouse we have today adjacent to the vegetable gardens. It was unfortunate that it took a tragedy for that to happen."

Dominic stopped to pluck another plant from the earth. He held it under his nose. Eyes closed, he inhaled deeply. A look of ecstasy came over him.

"You must never forget that nature is the face of God," he said to Steven, stowing the plant in his basket. "And nature is magic. It can create bliss, even rapture. Although there are some who would instead call these drugs."

Steven knew the countryside was his father's life and nature his true religion. Everything Dominic needed, he found there. In troubled moments it consoled him. The outdoors could relieve mental anguish, dissolve distress, and soothe anger. As an inspiration, it never failed to uplift.

"Nature has the power to cure," Dominic said. "It's a miraculous healer. But you must know that all life is on loan. In the end, nature reclaims everything it so generously gives us in the first place."

Many times Dominic used nature to illustrate a point. A bird or a plant, even a passing cloud, became part of a lesson. He frequently quizzed the boy on his medical knowledge.

"Where does a headache come from?" Dominic said.

"A headache is a clear sign of toxicity," Steven replied. "It's an allergy. Identify its source and the pain vanishes."

"Very good," Dominic said, patting him on the back.

Once, when Dominic himself was bedridden with influenza, he gave Steven a list of medicines to collect and sent him either to the laboratory or out to the fields. From his bed he instructed his son on how to prepare them. Steven learned a tremendous amount doing it himself. From then on he helped

Dominic regularly in the laboratory and accompanied him on all sick visits.

THE RAIN fell in heavy sheets as the friars prepared for the funeral. Inside the chapel two large stainless-steel bowls normally used for making bread dough now served as catchbasins to catch the water. One was near the foot of the altar and another on a pew. Matthew, who had scrambled to the kitchen to collect the bowls, got up periodically from his pew to monitor them. The electricity was out. Although it was midmorning, the skies were dark, and the chapel had to be lit with every candle that could be found. At certain moments lightning lit up the room with blinding flashes followed by a deep-throated rolling thunder that shook the windows in their casings. At times the downpour was so fierce it drowned out the monks' recitation and song.

Near the altar, Immaculus lay in a plain pine coffin. He was dressed in a virgin-white habit and clutched a wooden crucifix on his chest. Six large white Mass candles on bronze stands flanked the coffin, and the acrid smell of incense filled the room. Steven sat in the front row, close to the open coffin. All around him monks knelt in their pews, their brown cowls up and their heads lowered.

After the ceremony, six brothers acting as pallbearers led the procession out to the graveyard in the back of the monastery. Despite umbrellas and protective clothing, they were soon soaked from the downpour. They had all wanted a graveside eulogy and readings from the abbot's favorite biblical passages. Instead, as the rains beat down even harder, Brother Basil, the chaplain, loudly and hastily read the Twenty-third Psalm from the wet pages of his Bible.

As the pine box was lowered into the ground, one monk lost his grip. The wet rope slipped through his hands, sending the coffin plunging headfirst into the muddy bottom of the grave with a thud. The impact sprayed the monks with mud that quickly washed away in the rains. Seeing there was no dry earth to throw on the coffin, each monk scooped up a handful of mud and slung it onto the wooden lid before returning to the warm, dry shelter of the cloister.

A week before, Steven had been quietly reading in his room when Dominic paid an unexpected visit. Steven rose to his feet, as he had been taught to do out of respect when one of his elders entered the room.

"The abbot wishes to see you," Dominic said.

Steven did not know why he was being summoned but felt that to ask would be disrespectful. He followed his father through the monastery until they reached the abbot's cell. Brother Vincent, one of the abbot's assistants, sat outside the door. Dominic put a hand on Steven's shoulder and nodded to Vincent. Vincent opened the door and ushered the boy inside. Then Dominic left.

Save for a single candle burning in the corner, the room was devoid of light. The air was hot and stale, and Steven found it difficult to breathe. After a moment, when his eyes had adjusted to the dark, he recognized the abbot's living quarters. Although spacious, it was sparsely furnished, like the other monks' cells. A desk and a chair faced one of two windows that overlooked the manicured lawns. A favorite reading chair was positioned near the fireplace, which was lit in winter. The heavy maroon fabric of the chair's armrests and back was now threadbare. Tucked in the far corner was the abbot's bed and wardrobe, and not far away were the table and washbasin he used every morning. A small, overcrowded bookshelf graced the opposite wall.

Steven moved to the abbot's bed and found Immaculus on his back, motionless, his eyes closed. Steven did not recognize him at first. The once striking profile was now lined like a road map, his complexion a pasty white.

For nearly two months the abbot had been absent from cloister life. Steven often saw pairs of monks standing outside the abbot's quarters, patiently awaiting admittance. Rumors concerning his declining health abounded. Now they were confirmed.

Steven slowly bent over the sleeping abbot and, with great reservation, planted a light kiss on his forehead. A repulsive smell emanated from the abbot's wrinkled skin.

"Good evening, Immaculus," said Steven.

The abbot's eyes flickered open. He lifted a frail hand and touched the boy's cheek. As he did so, a wan smile broke across his old face and his eyes sparkled. He took the boy's hand. "Sit down," he said.

Steven sat in the chair next to the bed. There was a long-drawn-out pause as the old man collected his thoughts. After what seemed like an hour, the abbot spoke.

"I'm dying," he said. "Do you understand?"

He spoke with great effort, fighting for every breath. His chest rose and fell rapidly, forcing a fetid halitosis through his cracked lips. The deep, resonant voice that had dominated the abbey for more than a quarter of a century had now dwindled to a pathetic, almost inaudible sandpaper whisper. There was resignation in his voice, but it rang with a tenderness familiar to Steven.

"Yes," said Steven.

The abbot looked straight at him. From the dark recesses of his hollowed orbs, his stare seemed to penetrate the very depths of Steven's soul. While death was slowly claiming his body, his most formidable characteristic remained intact.

"I shall miss you," he said, his voice growing more hoarse.

He struggled for breath. Without warning he suddenly released Steven's hand. His eyes closed, and he turned his head away. He whispered a few phrases in Latin—lines from a prayer—then said nothing more. Steven saw tears glide down his sunken cheeks.

Three days later, after eighty-eight years of life, the abbot passed away.

5

DANIEL, THE MONASTERY'S NEW abbot, tapped his water glass with a fork. Everyone stopped eating and looked in his direction except Benedict and Aloysius, who couldn't hear the sound. Aloysius turned around only after Brother James gently squeezed his shoulder.

"Brothers," Daniel said, "Immaculus's final wishes, written shortly before his death, included that this letter, which I am now holding, be read aloud."

At fifty, Daniel was considered relatively young to be the new prior. But Immaculus had chosen Daniel to succeed him, and the monks abided by his decision. Daniel was already showing himself to be quite talented at working with the brothers and overseeing the abbey's operations.

Daniel held up the letter, showing it to everyone present, then began reading:

My dear Brothers,

There is something that has been on my mind for a long time. We have had sixteen wonderful years with our beloved Steven. But now, more than a decade after the end of the war, there are many young souls who may still be displaced and orphaned because of it. One of the duties of this monastery is to offer hospitality and sanctuary to those in need. Is it not time we consider opening our doors to other orphaned boys? Delude yourselves not into thinking this undertaking will be easy. No doubt it will present many challenges. I implore you to consider this issue carefully and put it to a vote. This is something that should not be foisted upon you. You must feel strongly about it yourselves. I believe, however, that this will be the best way for our community to grow and remain vital in the rapidly changing modern world.

I am counting on you to make the correct decision.

God be with you.

Immaculus

Daniel looked up and surveyed the faces of the men sitting at the long table. "Any questions?" he said.

James was the first to speak. "How would we teach them?"

"To the best of our ability," said the abbot.

"But how will it affect our duties?" said Matthew. "Our days are already full. How can we carry out our responsibilities and still attend to the needs of these boys at the same time?"

"We don't know," said the abbot.

"How many children are we talking about?" Gregory said.

"Twenty, perhaps. Immaculus does not say."

"Twenty children?" said Gregory. "Doesn't that seem a bit excessive?"

"How many do you think we can handle?"

"Abbot," said Lawrence, "the number is not the issue. More, it is a question of space. Where are we going to find the room to accommodate a single one of them?"

"Well, we could refurbish some of the old storage areas into sleeping quarters. Also, we all have single cells. Perhaps some of us could share."

Christopher was flabbergasted. "What, refurbish all this our-selves?"

"Immaculus apparently considered the past decade and a half of raising Steven as some sort of trial period," Daniel said. "In the back of his mind, he had a plan. That is what he wanted us to discuss now. Clearly it is his final request. These are merely thoughts for the moment. I suggest we contemplate them over-night and tomorrow cast our votes, as Immaculus prescribed."

The abbey was not accustomed to democracy. The monks had never made a collective decision before. All dictates came from the abbot. They finished their meal in silence. That night every monk went to bed wrestling with Immaculus's proposal.

JUST BEFORE his routine pre-dawn excursion to gather herbs, Dominic stopped at the kitchen. He watched as Brother Thomas stretched to reach one of the large iron pots hanging on hooks above the stove. Retrieving the pot, he placed it on a nearby counter, then turned around to fetch the grain to make the breakfast cereal. His eyes registered mild surprise when he saw Dominic.

Dominic smiled and stepped closer. "Now that we've all slept on it," he said, "what is your opinion of Immaculus's plan?"

Deep in thought, Thomas poured oatmeal from a large can-ister into the pot and added water. "Crusty old Immaculus. He continues to lead us in spirit, even now. All along he was planning to bring us into the modern world. We just didn't know it yet." He chuckled. "I support it."

Dominic paused for a few moments as his friend put more in-gredients into the pot and placed it on the stove. "I am afraid this move will have repercussions on Steven most of all," Dominic said. "He has been exposed only to adults, monks no less, not to boys whose unfortunate circumstances might have hardened them in ways we cannot even imagine."

Thomas put his arm around Dominic's shoulders. "Well, if that is the case, we shall have to ask the Lord to show us the way to help them." He patted Dominic's shoulder and smiled. "Steven will more likely than not teach those boys a thing or two now, won't he?"

That evening at dinnertime, the brothers took their places at the long table. Before grace was said, the abbot stood up. "It is now time to vote. We have all had the opportunity to think about it and meditate over what Immaculus suggested. If we vote in favor, we will find the strength and perseverance to work through the obstacles. I'm sure we will receive divine guidance. I am posing the question to you once again: Should we open an orphanage for boys? Those in favor, raise your hands."

There was a moment of hesitation, but in the end, not a single monk refused his hand.

"It's settled, then," said the abbot. He sat down, grace was said, and the meal was served.

TIRED AND weary, the monks hammered and sawed. The abbey's old pigsties and stables were converted into two dormitories. Each was divided into two rooms that would in turn house five boys each. Another two would room with Steven.

Steven finished tidying up his corner of the room that until today had been his alone. His dresser and shelf now flanked his bed on either end. Against each of the two other walls stood one dresser, shelf, and bed in similar configurations, waiting for their new occupants.

Having been the only youth for so many years, Steven felt lucky and unlucky. He wasn't sure he liked the way things were changing, but he was trying to accept it. In truth, he was looking forward to a little companionship from someone his own age. But some of the boys scared him. They seemed so rowdy, a rag-tag bunch. There was skinny, pimply-faced Shelby, who could not sit still, and boisterous, loud, heavyset Chris. He hoped his new roommates, due today, at least settled down at night.

The new boys, as everyone called them, needed to do some academic catching-up. All but one. Michael Warren was a brash and arrogant sixteen-year-old who possessed an intelligence that distinguished him from the others. Although Michael was academically without equal, he was also a rebel, a free spirit who marched to the beat of his own drum. Many monks marveled at his academic wizardry and admired the sharpness of his intellect. Yet they found his lack of humility and his radical, even heretical views on Scripture—which he knew as competently as any of them—grating. They struggled to find answers to his endless, searching questions. A few even felt his constant challenging of their beliefs, traditions, and doctrines was the last straw.

Brother Richard taught far more classes than any of the other monks and thus was the spokesperson on education issues. The abbot met with him in the library to discuss the problem the monks had with Michael.

Daniel said, "According to previous school records, he has a reputation for being difficult, unruly, and uncooperative. Oddly enough, his academic scores remain exceptionally high despite his afflicted circumstances."

"Afflicted circumstances?" said Richard.

"At the age of five he was sent to the countryside to live with an aunt. During that time, both parents perished in the bombings."

Richard leaned against a bookshelf and sighed.

"Most of the boys here," the abbot continued, "have been orphaned by the Blitz. Some have adjusted better than others. Michael Warren has not. It's clear that his deeply troubled nature and subsequent psychological problems stem from losing his parents at a formative age.

"I dismiss his questionings as a childish ploy to seek attention and test our patience. Nothing more."

"But others see it differently," said Richard. "They feel threatened."

"You are overlooking Michael's academic talents and branding him a troublemaker with no redeeming qualities. You are quick to dismiss him as a poisonous influence. Are you suggesting he should be separated from the others?"

Richard did not reply.

"I think not," said the abbot.

Later, in the privacy of his study, Daniel voiced his concerns to the newcomer. "I'm simply advising you to tone your views down a little, Michael."

"Am I not here to learn?" said Michael.

"Yes. But some feel you take great relish in intentionally annoying your tutors."

Michael smiled. "Is not questioning the very foundation of learning, of education, of knowledge itself?"

"Yes, it is."

"And knowledge the concrete of civilization?"

"There would be no civilization without knowledge, that is correct."

"Then it stands to reason that questioning is an integral part of the academic process. Is that not so?"

The abbot coughed into his hand nervously. "Academics is not the issue here. The rules of this abbey are. I have no doubt that in your view they are in grave need of reform. But they are what you must follow."

Daniel rose from his chair. "We will be making adjustments regarding your sleeping arrangements. That will be all, Michael."

ONE OF Steven's roommates was unexpectedly assigned to another room, and Michael Warren moved into his place. To Steven, Michael was just another face. He had no opinion of him.

Steven was on his bed reading quietly when the handsome, dark-haired sixteen-year-old walked through the doorway. He glared at Steven and tossed his bag on the bed that just one day earlier belonged to Steven's roommate Edward. The other roommate, Tobias, came in two minutes later followed by Brother Luke.

Brother Luke plopped a pile of fresh sheets on Tobias's bed.

"Fresh sheets," said the monk. He left with his arms still full of sheets to be delivered to other boys.

Tobias buried his face in the clean linens. "Mmm, these smell good."

Michael was indignant. "Get your fat face out of my sheets and toss them over."

Tobias started walking them over to Michael.

"Just toss them," Michael said.

Tobias threw the sheets. They unfolded in midair and came cascading down on Michael. One slipped through his grasp and fell to the floor. Michael picked it up and, without beating the dust off it, dropped it on his chair. He tore the old sheets off his bed and flung them across the room, where they hit the wall and were deposited in a corner.

Michael began haphazardly making his bed.

"So, Steven," he said, "explain to me again why you're supposed to be a such a positive influence on me."

Steven just looked at him.

"Are you some kind of saint or something?"

Tobias laughed out loud.

"Have you ever been with a girl?" said Michael.

"No!" said Steven. "And we're not allowed to talk about that."

Tobias stopped the game he was playing—throwing a ball from one hand to the other. "You've never been with a bird?"

"No," said Steven, softer than before.

Michael finished his sloppy efforts at tucking in his blanket. "I bet you've never even kissed one, either."

"No."

"Never even held hands with one?"

"No."

"Never touched one?" said Tobias.

Steven was beginning to feel desperate. "Look, can we stop talking about this?"

"You really are some kind of a saint!" Michael said. "Were you taught that women are from the devil or something?"

"Look here, you don't get to see too many girls around this place, if you get my meaning."

Tobias and Michael exchanged knowing looks. Michael said, "Doesn't the whole idea of sex make you curious?"

Steven looked straight at his tormentor. "Have you ever had sex?"

"Yes."

He switched his gaze over to Tobias. "And you?"

"Yes, I have," said Tobias.

"So tell me what's so fantastic about sex? What is it that makes the both of you so crazy about it?"

"Mate," said Michael, smiling, "until you've had it you'll never understand."

And with that, Michael turned his back to both his new room-mates and began unpacking his bag in silence.

Steven was fascinated by this wordly boy, yet regarded him as much too rough around the edges to become friends with. A week later, however, Steven made a discovery that made him view Michael in a completely new light.

Steven was studying in the common room late one night after lights out, without permission. To escape detection, he worked in the dark by the light of his pocket torch. Thinking he had accidentally thrown away a sheet of notes, he began rummaging through the wastepaper basket. He opened up one wadded sheet, thinking it was his discarded notes. Ironing it flat on his thigh, he looked at it. It wasn't his notes, but a pen-and-ink drawing of a tree that stood next to a stream. Steven recognized the tree and its location immediately. The drawing was so vivid he could almost hear the sound of the wind rustling through the leaves.

Searching deeper in the basket, Steven found more discarded drawings. He examined every one. Almost all were of the monastery buildings and landscapes of the surrounding countryside. But some were obscene drawings of some of the monks and the abbot. They shocked Steven. Others made him laugh. The majority, however, moved him in a way he had never been moved before. Without spilling a single drop of blood, they ripped through the fragile lining of his consciousness. They were a knife wound that left no trace. That the person who created these drawings had extraordinary talent was not the issue. The question was, who made them? It seemed unlikely it was any of the boys with whom he shared the common room.

Steven opened his desk drawer and stuffed them on top of his exercise books. For the next three days he kept an eye on the wastepaper bin in the study. By the end of every evening it was full of discarded drawings, sometimes overflowing to the point that they littered the surrounding floor like drifts of autumn leaves. But by morning, everything was gone. While the boys slept, a monk emptied the contents of the bin into the incinerator.

Secretly, Steven began to collect the drawings. Many times they were sketched on the back of a schoolboy's essay. By saving the drawings, he was able to compare the handwriting on the back of the papers with that of the seven boys in his common room.

One boy's writing matched perfectly. While others in the study toiled over essays on eighteenth-century British sea power or scribbled away in their exercise notebooks on how to interpret the Sermon on the Mount in the New Testament, Michael Warren quietly drew on the backs of discarded assignments. To all appearances, he looked like any other student silently working on his classroom assignments. But when prep ended, he nonchalantly dumped everything into the waste bin.

Unable to keep this discovery to himself, Steven brought some of Michael's drawings—those depicting the monastery buildings and landscapes—to his father's laboratory.

Dominic scrutinized them. "Where did you get these?" he said.

"I found them in the wastepaper basket."

"Where?"

"In the common room."

Dominic looked horrified. "Are there more?"

"Tons."

The words rang in Dominic's ears. "Tons?"

"Every night. Last thing. The bin is chock-full."

"Are you sure they're his?" said Dominic, rubbing his forehead as he looked at the drawings.

"Positive."

Dominic paused, then reached into a cabinet and pulled out a canvas bag. "This is what we must do. Every night after prep, as soon as the others have left, you will put the entire contents of the bin into this bag and bring it directly to me. If someone asks what you are doing, simply say you are running an errand for me. Do you understand?"

Steven nodded.

"If trouble brews, send for me immediately. And not a word to anyone." He put his arm around Steven. "I'm proud of you. You had the option of saying nothing to me about this. I am grateful that you have."

Steven did as he was told. Every night after everyone had left the common room, he dumped the entire contents of the rubbish bin into the canvas bag and delivered it to Dominic. But one night when he dropped off the bag, he noticed a gray-black ash filling the grate of his father's fireplace. The smell of freshly charred paper hung in the air. Peering closer, he saw an unburned portion of one of Michael's drawings among the ashes.

The boy could not contain himself. "Why are you burning them?"

"I'm taking precautions," Dominic said.

Steven was stunned by this answer. "But aren't you going to show them to Abbot Daniel? They might change his opinion."

"That is precisely what I'm afraid of," Dominic said. He told Steven to sit down. "The contents of a rubbish bin are the community property of the universe. In the past, prying monks dug through the abbot's trash after collecting it from his study, hoping to peek inside his mind, to gather advance information about plans and changes within our small community, and to know who was in favor and who was not. When the abbot learned of this intrusion, he took to burning his own refuse in the fireplace of his study.

"There is the possibility that had I not seen these, I too would have continued to view Michael in much the same manner as many of the others do, as an arrogant upstart. In a sense they confirm what I already know—that Michael Warren is not one of us.

"You see, we are all angels, but we are reluctant to admit that there are those who are more gifted, more advantaged than we are. While the rest of us struggle just to stay in the air, some can fly higher and faster, it seems, with the greatest of ease. They soar effortlessly through the skies. Faced with this sobering fact, our admiration melts in the furnace of our jealousy. We are no longer awed by their talent but have become blinded by our own envy.

"In the wrong hands, these drawings could be devastating. They could permanently jeopardize Michael's chances of ever leading a peaceful life with us here. I'm not prepared to take that risk."

In his mind Steven pictured his father as the loving curator of Michael's work, carefully preserving them until they were presented to the outside world. Steven had been taught that good always prevailed, no matter what the odds. By his actions, however, his own father was demonstrating that he too felt threatened by Michael.

Steven realized he had made a dreadful mistake. Despite his father's eloquent explanation, Steven refused to believe that the majority of these haunting drawings—apart from Michael's obscene depictions of some of the monks he hated—could be so horribly misconstrued and damaging. Hurt and angry, he vowed never again to confide in his father.

Out of two large pieces of cardboard taped together on three sides, Steven constructed a portfolio. He slipped it between the wall and the settee in the common room. Every night after sifting through the rubbish bin, he removed the drawings he wanted to keep and hid them in the portfolio before delivering the remaining ones to Dominic.

6

In the room they shared, Steven often saw Michael sip from a small vial while he lay in bed either reading or sketching. From its strong smell, Steven knew it was spirits. While other boys at the abbey read or did puzzles before bed, Michael got quietly drunk.

Steven knew Michael kept the vial hidden in his mattress. He had bored a hole into the side that faced the wall, out of sight of the monks' probing eyes. What mystified Steven was where he was getting the alcohol. A bottle was stashed away somewhere, but Steven knew Michael wasn't stupid enough to hide it indoors.

One afternoon Steven secretly followed his roommate from a distance down to the stream and watched as Michael crouched beside the water. Slowly he drew up a cord from the water, and a dark green bottle appeared dangling on the end of the line. The other end of the cord was tied around an elm tree that stood by the water's edge. Michael refilled his vial, sealed the bottle, and lowered it back into the cold water.

A few days later, in the library, Steven overheard a conversation between two monks in the next aisle. He could make out only parts of their conversation, but he did hear that a surprise inspection was to take place sometime that afternoon. Normally inspections occurred on Fridays. Steven knew that Michael removed the vial from his mattress on Friday mornings and hid it someplace outdoors. With no time to warn him, Steven raced back to their room and shut the door. Frantically he tore the sheets off Michael's bed and found the hole. Removing the vial, he thrust it into his pocket. He then plugged the mattress hole with a few socks he haphazardly grabbed from Michael's drawer. After quickly remaking the bed, he left.

Just after five that afternoon, the bell sounded and a monk yelled "Inspection!" at the top of his lungs. Boys dropped whatever they were doing and scrambled to their rooms. Once there, they stood silently at attention in front of their beds.

Steven, Tobias, and Michael stood stiffly at their beds, waiting. Several pairs of footsteps echoed down the hall. As they approached, Steven's insides churned. The door to their room was flung open, and Brother Richard marched in, followed by two boys who were prefects. One was Peter Saunders, the head prefect. Bypassing Steven and Tobias, Richard walked directly over to Michael and stood in front of him as Peter and the other prefect began searching his bed, wardrobe, and bookshelf. Michael's bed was unceremoniously yanked from the wall and the sheets pulled away from the mattress.

"Over here!" said Peter.

Steven watched, a blank expression on his face, as Richard approached the bed. Peter indicated a hole stuffed with socks. The monk crouched down and pulled out the socks one at a time, revealing an empty cavity. Michael made no attempt to look at him.

Richard rose and stood before the boy, inches from his face. "What's a hole doing in your mattress, Warren?"

"It's always been there, Brother Richard," said Michael.

"You use it to store alcoholic beverages, don't you?"

"Absolutely not, Brother Richard."

The monk pointed an index finger menacingly at Michael's nose. "You're lying. I'm getting you a new mattress. I'll personally make sure there's nothing wrong with it. If I come to find so much as a pinprick in it, I'll have you caned so hard you won't be able to sit down for a fortnight. Do I make myself clear?"

"Perfectly," said Michael.

"Perfectly, what?" the monk shouted back.

"Perfectly, Brother Richard."

Abruptly the monk turned on his heel and marched out, followed by the two prefects. After what seemed an eternity, the bell rang. Inspection was over.

As Michael began searching his bedding for the vial, Steven left the room and returned a few minutes later. Tobias was gone. Steven shut the door.

"Looking for this?" he said, dropping the vial on Michael's bed.

Michael stared at it, astonished. He grew pale. "Where did you find it?"

"I hid it in the bushes."

Michael's eyes closed, and a trembling wave of relief flooded his body. He sighed and smiled. "I suppose I ought to thank you."

From that moment the boys bonded. Steven felt Michael's earlier mistrust toward him evaporate.

"LET'S GET plastered," Michael said.

"You mean get drunk?"

Michael nodded.

"We're bound to get into trouble," said Steven. "And where do you find the money to buy spirits, anyway?"

"From the collection plate at St. Vincent's."

"You stole money from the village church?"

Michael shrugged. "It's for a good cause. Coming or not?"

"It has trouble written all over it," said Steven as he followed his roommate.

"Life was designed for getting into trouble."

Steven shook his head.

Michael put a hand on Steven's shoulder. "Many things are forbidden, young soul," he said, playfully impersonating the abbot. Then he returned to his normal tone. "That doesn't mean they're not meant to be explored. Everyone convinced Columbus that his idea of sailing across the ocean was sheer lunacy. Remember, this was a time when people believed the earth was flat and the planets revolved around the earth. People reminded Columbus that the earth was flat and that he would fall off its edge if he sailed too far from land. If Columbus really had believed all that cow shit, he would have never followed his instincts and stepped foot outside his front door. If you want to live the rest of your life sheltered from the beauties, marvels, and wonders of the world, fine. That's your choice."

Steven sensed trouble but was too intrigued to say no.

They slipped down to the stream and sat on the grassy bank, their backs against the bend of an elm tree that arthritically hunched over the water's edge. Michael reached for the cord and brought the line up a hand at a time. The same green bottle Steven had once seen from a distance now emerged from the waters. Close up, Steven noticed Michael had cleverly tied two stones to it to weight the bottle down.

Michael opened the bottle and took a long swig, then passed it to Steven, who brought it up to his nose. He grimaced at the smell. Indulging in alcohol flew against everything he had been taught: that drinking was in league with the Devil. Nonetheless, he held his breath, took a swig, and passed the bottle back to Michael.

The boy took another hearty swig and held it out to Steven, who made a gesture of refusal with his hand. Shrugging, Michael began guzzling the liquid like water.

"What happened to your parents?" said Steven.

Michael belched loudly. "Killed. Pummeled. Reduce to oblivion, to rubble."

"What do you mean?"

"They were buried in our house amongst the rubble and ruins."

"They died in the Blitz?"

Michael belched again. "'Fraid so, old man."

He looked at Steven to see if he was listening. "Then I went to live with my Aunt Fiona. She was Beelzebub's imp! Medusa in the flesh!"

"What do you mean?"

"She beat me. She beat me for everything from dropping a crumb on the table to looking at her the wrong way."

"What about your uncle? Didn't he stop it?"

"No uncle, old boy. The witch lived alone. No children."

"Didn't you tell anyone?"

"Mate, I ran away all the time. All the time! I was expelled from more schools than I care to mention. Finally one enlightened local authority intervened after seeing my bruises. It eventually led to her losing custody and legal guardianship. That old witch! I was given over to the care of the state in 1949."

"What happened to her?"

"Who knows. Probably died, nobody found her and her cats ate her."

"Sorry," said Steven.

Soon after, Michael fell into a stupor. Steven could see the alcohol taking possession of his friend. Michael's speech became slurred. He laughed deliriously for no reason. With every hiccup, a thin streak of whiskey ran down his chin. His eyes wandered sluggishly and his eyelids were half closed. He rolled in the wet grass in fits of laughter. At one point he stood up, yanked down his zipper, and without embarrassment or conscience urinated into the stream as he sang to the fields. In one breath he swallowed a fly and began violently coughing and choking. He staggered, lost his balance, and fell backward into the grass, and in a fit of uncontrollable coughing wet himself.

Steven sat him up and thumped him on the back.

"Keep your mouth shut," Steven said as Michael hacked. "The moment you talk to nature, she talks back."

He helped Michael pull his pants up. Within half an hour Michael had passed out, the green bottle between his thighs. Steven, feeling the effects of the one taste of alcohol, dozed off by his side.

St. Martin's bell echoed across the fields. In Steven's half sleep he counted every chime. There were five. It was the call to supper.

Steven sat bolt upright, his insides churning in terror. Frantically he shook Michael awake. "Let's go or we'll be late for dinner!" he said.

With great difficulty Michael sat up and rubbed his eyes. He got to his feet, staggered, and collapsed again. Steven quickly recorked the bottle and lowered it back into the water.

Struggling to help his friend up, Steven said, "Come on. Let's get going."

"Damn dinner bell," Michael slurred.

They got back to the dining hall and sat down just as the pea soup was being served. Their tardiness did not escape the abbot's attention.

"AND WHERE were you two before dinner?" the abbot said in his study after the meal.

Michael propped himself up unsteadily against the side of Daniel's desk. "In the fields, Abbot," he slurred.

Daniel reeled from the blast of Michael's breath. "Have you, now. Conducting a nature study, I suppose?"

"Quite correct, Abbot." Michael hiccuped and then violently broke wind.

"That's enough!" boomed the abbot. He shook with rage, a fault line creasing his forehead. "Alcohol is the nectar of Satan and shall not be tolerated within these walls. Do I make myself clear?"

"Yes, Abbot," the boys replied in unison.

"I will inspire you both never to follow this path again. Your punishment will be meted out in the morning."

As they walked to their room, Michael said, "You would have thought we killed someone, the way he went on."

With little sleep and monstrous headaches, Steven and Michael were placed on bell-ringing duty the following morning. They were responsible for ringing the bell for all offices and lessons for the entire day. The noise was excruciating. The horrific clanging, the echoing and reverberating inside the colonnaded gallery made Michael's head throb in pain. Whenever he pulled the rope to ring the bell, the noise made him release the rope and grab his head. Eventually he resorted to pulling the rope with one hand and holding his head with the other. Michael motioned to Steven to ring the bell more softly. But when they did, Brother Richard rushed into the gallery.

"Louder, louder!" shouted the monk. "The community of brothers will never be able to hear their call to office, and the boys won't know when their lessons begin!"

Steven never drank again after that. He still kept his friend company down by the stream, but he would fish quietly while Michael shared a bottle with himself and serenaded the cows in the neighboring fields. When Michael passed out, Steven would always save him from certain trouble by reviving him and getting him back safely to the monastery.

The two boys were as different as night and day. While Steven thought everything out carefully before he acted, Michael was impulsive and spontaneous. In contrast to Steven's shyness and boyish naïveté, Michael was bold and arrogant, subject to sudden outbursts of temper and inspiration. It was this bravado and daring to which Steven felt drawn. Steven was conscientious and methodical. Discipline guided him. His schoolwork was always done neatly and on time. Michael merely glanced at the assigned texts. His work, although brilliant, was sloppy and incomplete.

Michael's audacity was constantly getting him into trouble. He had few friends, but for some reason it never bothered him. Little did. And while Michael viewed the cloister as a prison, Steven, who did not possess a rebellious bone in his body, saw it as his home. He embraced asceticism and the teachings of the church. He also loved singing, and sang at every available opportunity, especially at Mass, where he could sing with a full choir. There was something about music that transported him in a way other things did not.

Singing and praying were not Michael's release. Art and alcohol were. His gods were pen, paper, and his imagination. When he drew, nothing else mattered.

AT FIRST Steven found it difficult to embrace his friend's carefree philosophy, but Michael could be persuasive. He had a way of putting things that made it difficult for Steven to refuse him. Michael also had a wicked sense of humor. His impersonations of the monks, especially the abbot, both shocked and entertained Steven. But there were times Steven considered Michael's actions crude and tactless. Every Friday morning the entire monastery assembled in the chapel for Mass. After the congregation replied "Amen" in answer to the chaplain, there was a moment of silence that Michael promptly shattered by delivering the most rancorous fart, setting the schoolboys snickering in their pews.

Steven knew Michael did things to get attention. One day in class, Brother Richard asked, "On page two Hamilton is born. By page fifty-five he is dead. What does that tell us?"

Michael blurted out, "It tells us he had a very short life."

The class erupted in laughter.

Many of the monks did not like Michael. Some viewed him as an aberration in their midst. Others, for the most part, left him alone. There were two, however, who waited for him to set a foot wrong.

Brother Basil was the monastery chaplain. There were a few brothers—Basil among them—who had sought the monk's life for the security and sustenance it offered. He was offended by Michael's heretical theological views and his outspoken criticism of the Bible. Peter Saunders, the head prefect, was Basil's apprentice. Peter detested Michael for entirely different reasons. For Peter, achieving merely satisfactory marks required extreme effort on his part. Michael, however, showed little interest in his studies and frequently dozed off during lessons, yet still excelled academically. The sight of Michael sleeping with his face pressed flat on the pages of an open book made Peter's blood boil in envy.

Peter had two goals. One was to become the abbey's favorite, and the other was to make Michael Warren's life a living hell. His plan was simple: find ways to divert Michael's attention away from his studies. When this occurred, Michael's academic failure would be imminent. The obvious way to accomplish this, Peter felt, was to punish him. Most punishments were carried out in the form of manual labor, from scouring the bathrooms to working in the kitchen.

The prefect began by concocting false incidents of misconduct, which he duly reported to the abbot. As a result, Michael was sentenced to orderly duties, which meant he had to serve everyone's food at meals and clean up afterward. He also had to help out in the kitchen washing and drying the dishes. On another occasion he had to mop the hall floors, which took several afternoons. But all these failed to put a dent in Michael's academic performance.

When Peter began stealing Michael's textbooks, Michael found access to others, from either fellow students or the library. No matter how much punishment was heaped upon him, no matter how much he was deprived of his academic tools, Michael always prevailed.

For his part, Michael knew who was tormenting him. He would have liked nothing more than to settle matters between him and Peter with his fists. But that was out of the question. Fighting was strictly forbidden. Also, striking a prefect was tantamount to striking a monk. With his record, Michael would have been expelled. And although Michael hated the abbey, the thought of being expelled and going into foster care or to another orphanage was something he wasn't prepared to risk at that moment. For a long time he had secretly held a plan. He would remain at the cloister until he was eighteen. On his eighteenth birthday he would leave. Legally he would be an adult. No one could do anything to him.

MICHAEL AND Steven were spending an afternoon hour strolling together along the perimeter of the monastery wall.

Michael thought aloud. "I wish I had an answer. What to do about bloody Brother Basil and that boy of his, Saunders. Particularly Saunders. What can I do to get that turd off my back without me getting chucked out?"

"Leave it alone," said Steven.

"I feel cornered. I need to put an end to this. But I've no ideas."

"Stay away from it. It's more trouble than it's worth. There are those who would be delighted to see the back of you. Don't give them that chance."

"I'd like to put mud down his mattress," said Michael.

Nestled among the vines of ivy, a lawn snail slowly inched along the wall. Michael picked it up and examined it. He snickered.

"What are you going to do?" Steven said.

"I've got an idea," he said, as he put the moist creature into his pocket.

That night Michael was on orderly duties. At dinner he served the first course to Peter, a bowl of leek-and-potato soup. Peter took a spoonful and crunched into something. He spat the soup out onto his spoon. Dangling from the crushed shell was the snail's twisted body. The boy whitened in shock. His body stiffened and froze before becoming wildly animated. He choked and convulsed, then dashed outside, where he could be heard retching.

Michael beamed with delight. But just as Steven anticipated, the prefect quickly retaliated. Suspecting Michael was the perpetrator, Peter redoubled his efforts to make Michael's life miserable at every turn. Michael needed something to embarrass Peter so thoroughly that he would leave him in peace.

Aside from prefect, Peter was also head altar boy. Every Friday morning he assisted Michael's other nemesis, Brother Basil, at Mass. Such a combination, Michael reasoned, was a gift from heaven.

IN THE dark bathroom, Michael uncorked the bottle of Mass wine. He turned on his pocket torch and trained it on the sink. With a steady hand, he poured half the bottle down the drain.

It was past midnight. Everyone had been in bed for hours. Hearing footsteps, Michael turned off his torch. The moonlight that strayed through the window bathed the bathroom in a tranquil glow. The figure stopped at the door.

"What are you doing up?" said a voice.

Michael recognized it and turned his pocket torch back on. He opened the door. "Keep your voice down," he whispered.

Shielding his eyes from the light, Steven wandered in to use the toilet. When he was finished, he tied his belt around his bathrobe and came to the sink. He rubbed his eyes. "What are you doing?" he said.

Michael handed the bottle to Steven. "I'm adding spirits to this."

Steven squinted at the label under the light of the torch. "This is Mass wine. Where did you get this?"

"From the sacristy."

Steven handed the bottle back to Michael. Michael poured the spirits into the half-empty wine bottle.

"I thought the cabinet was always locked," Steven said.

A sinister grin crossed Michael's face. "You're right. Christopher Morgan showed me how to pick the lock on the wine cabinet. It was a trick I never had much use for until now. A few nights ago I sneaked into the sacristy and pinched a bottle."

"Christopher Morgan. Yes, of course. What do you intend to do?" said Steven, looking down into the sink.

"It's time to clip their wings."

"Who?"

Michael hesitated for a moment. "Basil and Saunders."

Steven was dumbfounded. "Are you mad? But why add spirits? Mass wine is already alcoholic."

"Barely," Michael said. "It's low proof. Wouldn't get an ant smashed."

"I never knew that," Steven said. "I always thought normal wine was drunk at Mass."

"If that were so, no Mass would ever finish. By the Offertory, the chaplain would be passed out on the floor."

Steven knew that both chaplain and congregation were required to fast for twelve hours before receiving Communion. He also knew that pure spirits on an empty stomach would make anyone pass out.

During the Mass, it was the altar boy's duty to make sure that the chalice remained full at all times. Before the service, it was Peter's duty to transfer some of the wine to be used in the service into a small vessel. When that was done, he was responsible for locking up the bottle again. Michael guessed that the chaplain never saw the bottle from which the wine was poured.

When the wine bottle was full, Michael recorked it. "Done," he said. Satisfaction rang in his voice. "Now I'll just return this, and we'll be set for the festivities on Friday."

HIS HEART pounding with anticipation, Steven joined the group of choristers. The boys hurried across the cloister lawn, like so many white butterflies, to the chapel, which was already filled to capacity. Steven took his place in the choir loft with the others as bells rang out and Mass began.

Brother Basil drank from the chalice handed to him by the unsuspecting Peter Saunders. Within minutes Basil fell into a stupor. He stood at the altar, swaying like a cobra. His speech became slurred, and he chanted prayers out of sequence. He skipped an entire section of the Mass. At one point he made a wide sign of the cross in the air, clumsily knocking over the chalice and spilling wine onto the white altar cloth. Snickering erupted from the congregation. Horror-stricken, Peter looked to the abbot for help. The abbot frantically signaled from his pew, and the drunken monk was hurriedly ushered back to the sacristy. Another friar quickly took over at the altar.

Michael kept his head bowed reverently, feigning prayer until Mass ended. Back in the safety of his room with the door closed, he rolled on the floor, howling with such laughter that Steven thought for a moment he might be having a seizure.

The next day when Basil was sober, the abbot questioned him.

"Of anyone," said Daniel, "you are the last person I would have suspected to have a drinking problem."

The abbot sat at his desk and played with his glasses in his hands. Basil sat in a chair, rubbing his forehead. The headache had been with him all morning.

"Abbot, I do not have a drinking problem. You have never seen me drunk before, and you will never see it again."

"Yes, but how did you become so intoxicated?"

"I do not know. I drank the usual amount that I do when saying Mass. That is all."

"Maybe you've developed a reaction to the wine. That is possible. And if that is the case, you know I will have no option but to relieve you as chaplain. I'm sure you understand. I cannot have a chaplain who becomes intoxicated when saying Mass."

"Again, Abbot, I do not have a drinking problem. And I'm not prepared to believe I can no longer tolerate Mass wine."

Daniel leaned back in his oak chair, which creaked. "Let's put this matter to rest, shall we?" The abbot got up from his desk. "Follow me."

Basil trailed behind the abbot. When they arrived at the sacristy, the abbot took out a set of keys from his pocket. They jangled as he opened the wine cabinet. The bottle of Mass wine sat right in front. Daniel uncorked it and put it up to his nose. He shook his head and passed the bottle to Basil. "Now tell me if you think this is Mass wine."

Basil sniffed and grimaced. "Good heavens," he said. "This is spirits."

The abbot took back the bottle and put it on the floor near his feet. Then he began shifting some of the bottles in the cabinet from side to side, not knowing what he was looking for. Within the first row he found a half-empty gin bottle. The abbot removed it and opened it. Smelling it, he said, "Yes, this is what's in the Mass wine."

Basil immediately grew defensive. "It wasn't me, Abbot. I mean, I had nothing to do with this. This is some prank, someone's idea of a joke."

"Who else has a key to this cabinet?" said Daniel.

Basil vigorously rubbed his head and thought. "There's you and I and Peter Saunders."

"Let's go back to my study." Locking the cabinet, Daniel took the two bottles with him. On their way they found Peter. "Follow us," Daniel said to the boy.

In the abbot's study Basil sat down while Peter stood at attention. The abbot pointed to the two bottles on his desk. "I want you to smell these," he said to Peter. The altar boy opened one bottle, then the other, and sniffed them.

"Well," said the abbot, "what do you think? There's a bottle of spirits and a bottle of Mass wine that smells exactly like the spirits. Do you have any theories?"

Peter was so dumbfounded he could hardly speak. "No," he finally said, "I have none. This wine," he said, pointing to the one bottle, "was the one I served Brother Basil yesterday."

"I'll make it simple," said the abbot. "There are only three who have keys to the wine cabinet. All of us are here now. I certainly did not get drunk yesterday at Mass, so that leaves the two of you. I admit that this might have been some kind of prank. Perhaps there's some quarrel or disagreement between the two of you." He looked at Peter. "Perhaps you wanted to pay back Basil in some fashion. I don't know. Whatever the reason, the two of you are responsible for the contents of that cabinet. And I'm holding both of you accountable. Basil, I'm suspending you as chaplain for six months. Saunders, I'm stripping you of all altar boy privileges and demoting you as prefect. You've been a model boy, but this is such a grave offense that it warrants only the severest punishment."

STEVEN AWOKE in the middle of the night to a rustling sound. He could see Michael perched on his bed, peering out the curtainless window.

"What are you doing?" Steven whispered.

"Look," said Michael. "The first snows of winter."

Steven rose from his bed and joined Michael on his. With the sleeve of his nightshirt, Steven palmed a circle in the frozen windowpane next to Michael's and pressed his nose up against the cold glass. He watched the gentle snowfall come down in thin, hesitant flakes, caught by the light of a full moon that suffused everything. There was no sound; the world had been silenced by the snow.

So captivated by the sight, Steven was unaware of Michael's hand on his back. Before Steven realized it, Michael had slid his arm all the way around his waist. The next thing he knew, Michael was drawing him down onto the bed. Steven did not resist. Michael ran his fingers through his roommate's hair, then lowered his lips to his. As he did, he unbuttoned Steven's nightshirt and slowly ran his hand over his hairless chest. Steven lay in a terrified stillness as Michael's inquisitive hands explored him. He was unsure of what Michael was doing, yet his curiosity electrified him.

Michael's hand traveled down the length of Steven's body, stopping at the waistband of his pajama bottoms. Michael untied the drawstring and slipped his hand underneath, where he was greeted by Steven's member, bowed hard in an arc. Gingerly Michael encircled his fingers around it and began gently kneading it. Steven wanted Michael to stop, yet felt compelled to let things continue. Michael's touch stirred a restless whispering from him that rippled into heavier and more intense breathing. He feared the excitement would overpower him. His heart raced, and he broke into a hot, fleshy perspiration that drenched his body. He became weak to the point of fainting. His body suddenly became rigid, then began quivering uncontrollably. He tried to stop Michael, but it was too late. He was seized by a series of convulsions that caused his face to contort and his body to tremble and jerk like a berserk marionette. His body throbbed and pulsated. Unable to restrain himself, hot fluid gushed from him in long, explosive streams, spilling onto his chest. Spent, Steven slumped back into the mattress, embedding himself there. He panted heavily, fighting for breath. Lightheaded and dizzy from lack of oxygen, he released the last fluttering breath of air lingering in his lungs. When he regained his strength, he rose from Michael's bed and staggered over to his own, where he flopped down and within moments was devoured by sleep.

AT BREAKFAST the next morning, Steven avoided eye contact with Michael and was careful to stay away from him all day, for fear his secret would somehow be revealed to the others. It was difficult for him to concentrate on his lessons, and he hardly felt like eating. His mind continually wandered back to the night before. He had become physically aroused by Michael. Feelings he had never known before had been evoked. These dizzying emotions were foreign to him, their unfamiliarity terrifying.

For the past five years Steven had been curious as to why he felt certain sensations. When he asked Dominic what they meant, his father told him, "Save doing anything about them for the sacrament of marriage. For now, ignore them. They will pass."

It was then Steven realized that sex was the abbey's forbidden topic, the one subject never taught or brought up in conversation, not even by his own father. At first Steven equated his feelings with demonic possession, but he soon dismissed that. *How could something so wonderful be so evil*, he thought. The only term he could think of to describe the way he was feeling was *ecstasy*. But that, he had been taught, was akin to the cardinal sin of lust, and the Bible reminded him that such thoughts and behavior were forbidden. What he had done with Michael was wrong, and that hung heavy over his conscience.

Haunted by his feelings, he confided in his old friend, the library. He could find no books on human sexuality and reproduction. But he knew these volumes existed somewhere, probably in some damp storeroom. Steven knew that no matter how much a topic was forbidden, knowledge was sacrosanct to a monk, and destroying it would be sacrilegious. By chance, he found a treatise on love written by a poet centuries earlier. The poet's symptoms dovetailed with his own: the endless thoughts about the object of his affection, the throbbing pulse, the irregular breathing, the lack of appetite, and the tormented wanting to the point of embarrassment.

Late that afternoon Steven and Dominic were collecting strawberries in the greenhouse. The boy held the wicker basket as his father dropped strawberries into it.

Steven's insides churned. "What is love, Father?" he said, out of the blue. After the incident with Michael's drawings, Steven had vowed against consulting his father. But now his feelings compelled him to do so.

"That's a curious question," Dominic said. He sat down to rest and scratched his head. "Love is the first commandment of Christianity. It is the greatest gift one can give or receive. Monks take vows to serve God above all else, but most men and women experience love as the human fulfillment of creation. More than any other thing, it penetrates and fills every part of us. Nothing else binds us so completely as love does. It captivates the heart and, like the heart, it always chooses sides. We know things better through love than through anything else."

"Is that why we feel the way we do about doing certain things?" Steven said.

Dominic pondered the question. "You do certain things because you feel them, and you do them for no other reason than the fact that you love to do them. Love is the same. In order to truly love, you must surrender to it. You must be willing to give up everything for love."

Steven had never heard his father say such things before. Dominic was describing exactly what Steven had done. And at that moment, he was finally forced to acknowledge that he was in love with Michael.

"Is that wrong, to love?" Steven asked.

"Heavens, no! It's nature's way. We must love. It's essential. Life without love would be unimaginable."

Reaching a hand into the basket, Steven pretended to examine the fruit. "But is it wrong to love too much?"

The question caught Dominic off guard. "There is no such thing as loving too much. But there is a reason why you are asking all these questions."

Embarrassed, Steven said, "Just curious, Father."

Dominic put a hand on his son's shoulder. "Love is the most precious commodity in the entire universe. As a healer, it has no rival. It is the greatest remedy of all. We still don't know how it works." He chuckled. "If I could only bottle it, what eminence I would achieve!"

Dominic picked another strawberry and dropped it into the basket. "True love is perennial and as fragile as the wind. It casts a spell that only time can break. It is everlasting and can flourish anywhere. And when you least expect it, it finds you, even on a street corner."

"Have you ever been in love, Father?"

"Yes," said Dominic, "yes, I have."

"What happened?"

"It was wonderful."

"No, I mean what happened to the relationship?"

Dominic frowned and wagged an index finger at Steven's nose. He chastised jokingly, "That is a different story, young man, one that I shan't repeat to you, at least not today." Smiling warmly, he ruffled the boy's hair. "Besides, it's nearing teatime, and I'm getting hungry."

THAT NIGHT after lights out, Steven trembled as he felt Michael slide beneath the sheets of his narrow bed. He lay quietly, again surrendering to Michael's curious, probing hands as they delicately groped and explored his body. Like the prior evening, Steven became rigid at his friend's touch. But when he reached the point where he felt he was unable to contain himself, he said, "Michael, I can't do this. It's wrong." He pulled away and turned over.

Michael was surprised but said nothing. He got up and wandered off to his own bed.

7

ALTHOUGH HIS CONSCIENCE AND religious conviction would not permit the contact to continue, for the next two nights Steven lay awake, his mind playing over and over again the symphony of creaks and groans that came from his bed as Michael climbed into it. On the third night, racked by anguish and weakened by yearning, a kind of sleep—though shallow and broken—finally came.

But two nights of this had taken its toll. In a change of heart, he decided he wanted to be close to his friend again. The next evening Steven went over to Michael's bed. When he drew back the covers, however, he found the bed empty; it had been stuffed with a dressing gown, pillow, and other articles of clothing cleverly molded to resemble a slumbering shape.

For the next few nights Steven, pretending to be asleep, observed his friend closely. He watched as, shortly after lights out, Michael got out of bed, stuffed it with clothes and his pillow, and left. When Steven awoke just before sunrise, Michael was back in his bed, sound asleep.

One morning the two were alone in their room. Steven was stuffing his book bag, getting ready for the day's lessons. Michael was making his bed.

"Where do you go at night?" said Steven, pretending not to be overly curious.

"None of your bloody business," Michael said.

Steven was not rebuffed by his answer. He still wanted to know where Michael disappeared to after lights out. Again, pretending to be asleep, Steven watched that night as Michael got up, arranged his bed, and left. Steven waited ten minutes and then followed, tiptoeing from one room to the next. In one room he found one of the five beds empty. Listening in the quiet, he heard sounds like a soft groaning coming from the closet.

Quickly exiting the room, Steven waited outside the door. After a few minutes, he heard the closet door open and someone get into bed. He waited until all was still before quietly opening the door and peeking around it. There, his arm draped over Simon Robert's slumbering body, was Michael, fast asleep.

Steven was unable to move or speak. His head spun and he felt nauseous. His entire body broke out in a cold sweat. He rushed back to his room and leaped into bed. Shocked, scared, confused, he desperately wanted to talk with someone but did not know who to turn to. He remembered his father mentioning on several occasions that if he was ever troubled, he should come and see him, regardless of the time. Steven hesitated. Again he remembered Michael's drawings and his vow never to confide in Dominic again.

Nevertheless, Steven found himself creeping into his father's cell. Dominic was snoring in a deep autumnal slumber, lost in the snowstorm of his bedclothing, a sleeping cap pulled low on his forehead. Steven gently nudged him awake.

"Who is it?" said Dominic.

"It's Steven, Father."

Dominic slowly sat up and in the dark struck a match. He lit the candle by his bed. The light flickered on his features.

"What is it, my son?"

"I can't sleep."

"Come. Sit down."

Steven sat down in a chair near the bed.

"Any particular reason?" said Dominic. In the candlelight he could see the torment on his son's face.

"I'm . . . I'm in love, Father."

What should have been a proclamation of joy was instead a voice choked in sorrow. "Are you—are you certain?" said Dominic.

"Yes, Father."

"Have you thoroughly questioned your feelings about this?"

"Yes, Father, I have."

Dominic did not ask Steven to name the object of his affections. That much was obvious to him.

"One thing is certain," said Dominic, "your feelings never lie. Trust them. They will never lead you astray. Every one of us knows when we are in love. We don't need anyone to tell us. At the same time, we mustn't be afraid of it."

He stroked his son's cheek with his warm hand and kissed him on the forehead.

NOT SINCE Cain's death had Steven known such heartache.

After lessons the following afternoon, he closed the door to his room and got down on his knees. He closed his eyes and folded his hands on the bed. As he prayed, he hoped that repeating the words he had said so many times before would make the turmoil inside him magically disappear. But the prayers, faithfully said, did nothing.

Perhaps the answer lay in confession. Steven considered rushing to his father and telling all. More than ever, he yearned for the security and tranquillity of Dominic's wisdom. But the thought of revealing more than he already had seemed far worse than what he was going through now.

He could feign illness. Steven knew Dominic would give him medication. But that would bring only temporary relief; the twisting knots in his stomach would still be there the moment he opened his eyes the next morning.

Maybe he could find the answer in nature, as Dominic did. In times of difficulty, his father had always sought solace in the outdoors. Steven rushed into the woods just as the late afternoon sunlight broke through the bare branches of the midwinter trees. But as he looked around, the happy playground of his youth had been transformed into a forbidding skeletal jungle. He thought of feeding the birds but had no bread. Regardless, he went to the water's edge, hoping to lure a flock down to his outstretched arms. A solitary sparrow circled him twice and flew away when it found the boy's palms empty.

No matter where he turned or where he went, his world throbbed in pain. His prayers had gone unanswered. He had tried plunging himself into his studies, to no avail. He had tried communicating with nature, but like God, the forest too was silent.

Returning to his room, Steven searched for an instrument sharp enough to cut his wrists in the warm waters of the bathtub. Everything was either too blunt or too large. The sheets of his bed could be easily tied and knotted together into a noose, but there were no rafters to hang them from.

Then, like a lightning bolt, it came to him.

Belladonna.

He recalled his father's tutorial years ago. They had sat together at the table in his laboratory, studying a drawing of the plant in a large botanical reference book. The illustration depicted it as menacing and evil.

"*Atropa belladonna,*" his father had said, "is a member of the potato family, which includes tomatoes and sweet and hot peppers. Throughout history, especially during the Middle Ages, it has been associated with magic and religion. It is well known as a tool in witchcraft. Combined with other compounds, it can treat stomach disorders, even ulcers. But accuracy in dosage is crucial. A minute dose can induce sleep. A moderate one can cause severe delirium. A high dose can result in vomiting and convulsions." Dominic tapped a finger on the picture. "An excessive amount causes brain damage and even death from heart failure. Usually the root is eaten. But other methods can be used. Every part of the plant can be brewed into teas. It has even been ground up, put into fat, and rubbed on the skin. The safest part of the plant is its roots. They have the lowest concentration of poison. The most dangerous part is the seeds. They have the highest concentration and must be used with extreme caution."

Steven made sure the laboratory was empty before he entered. He walked over to an enormous bookcase lined with jars and volumes on medicine. The top shelf was devoted to containers of poisonous plants and books on poison.

Quickly Steven pushed a chair up against the bookcase. Scanning the rows of jars, his eyes stopped at one. It had a white label with the name inscribed in black ink in his father's hand. Belladonna. He pulled the jar down from the shelf and slid it into his coat pocket.

Only one question remained. Where could he go to be alone? The answer sprang instantly to mind.

The tree next to the stream.

Steven maneuvered through hallways crowded with shouting boys. At one point a monk called out to him. Steven turned, but the monk was already talking to another boy. He hurried outdoors and down the familiar overgrown path to the stream, finally plopping himself at the water's edge, next to the tree that was Michael's and his secret hiding place.

His body shivered in the wintry cold. The clouds of his breath hung in the air. Steven removed the jar from his pocket and with

his cold hands unscrewed the lid. There, ready for use as medicine was the dry, crushed plant. Steven carefully touched some of
the flakes. Dominic's words echoed in his mind.

"Provided they are taken in the appropriate doses, nature's
most powerful poisons can be extremely beneficial in treating
certain illnesses." As a postscript the monk had warned, "Excess,
however, can prove fatal."

Steven scooped up a palmful of the dry flakes and furiously
crammed them into his mouth. Its sharp and extremely bitter
taste was repulsive, but that did not deter him. He was glad because he knew the end was in sight. Within minutes his plight—
where he was and what he was doing—was completely forgotten.
Everything had receded into a dull, intoxicating numbness.

In the distance someone called his name. Glassy and warm,
the voice jolted him. Instantly he sprang to attention. His heart
raced. Over the sound of the stream he heard familiar laughter.
It was Michael. He was coming to stop him. He was coming to
tell him that he was sorry, that he had made a terrible mistake.
Weak with relief, Steven sobbed uncontrollably. Then, without
explanation, the voice vanished. Anxiously Steven looked around,
but no one was there. It had been a hallucination.

Spasms of pain stabbed at his stomach. He felt feverish and
disoriented. His vision blurred. Gradually he became aware of the
abrasive cold again. With manic energy, he shoveled handfuls of
the plant into his mouth until he could remember nothing else.

Dominic had not seen Steven since early morning. Usually he
spent time in the garden in the afternoon, but he was not there
today. He also wasn't at supper that evening. Steven's middle-of-
the-night visit to his room haunted the monk.

Thomas and Matthew were washing the dinner dishes when
Dominic burst into the kitchen. "I haven't seen Steven. Have
you?"

Thomas looked up at Dominic from the sink. He finished drying a plate with a cloth. "Sorry, I haven't. Something wrong?"

"He wasn't at supper. I've asked if anyone has seen him since lessons, but nobody has. I need your help. I just need to know where he is."

The three friars searched every building they thought Steven might be in. Finding nothing, they returned to the kitchen.

"Just as I feared," Dominic said. "I think he's outside. Each one of us, grab a torch. I'll meet you at the back entrance."

A fine mist enshrouded the countryside. The three monks crossed the dark fields armed with torches and entered the forest along the narrow path. It had been a long time since Dominic had been in the forest at night. He had forgotten what a hazardous place it could be in the dark: the ground was riddled with twigs, dry bark, and a myriad of other obstacles. They split up in different directions, the light from their torches their only visual contact. Intermittently they called out Steven's name.

Three quarters of an hour passed. Frustrated and bitterly cold, Dominic returned to where the forest began. He stopped and looked back at the wandering mists that snaked through the trees. He had combed the woods as best as he could. Far off, the monastery bell sounded the start of study hall. Then he heard Thomas's call. "Over here!"

"Where? Where?" Dominic shouted back.

"Here! Over here by the stream!"

Guided by the beam of Thomas's torch and his echoing shouts, Dominic made his way through the misty darkness to where Thomas and Matthew stood. Lying at Thomas's feet, curled up, was Steven, appearing to be fast asleep.

Dominic crouched down and tried to wake the boy, but without success. He checked for signs of breathing and a pulse and was relieved to find them. The beam of his torch then fell onto an open glass jar next to Steven. He picked it up and read the label. His heart sank. Unnoticed by the other monks, he screwed the lid back on and slipped it into his habit pocket.

Carefully they picked Steven up and carried him back to the monastery. Dominic carried Steven by the shoulders, and Matthew carried his feet. Thomas led the way, navigating them through the dark fields. They spirited the boy undetected through the back entrance and down the empty hallways and corridors. Fortunately the boys would be in study hall for another half-hour before lights out.

In the infirmary Dominic pointed to an empty bed. They gently set Steven down. As they undressed him, Thomas said to Dominic, "We must tell the abbot."

"You two go," said Dominic. "I'll stay here." Then he nodded for them to leave.

Dominic finished undressing Steven and tucked him under the fresh sheets. He lit three candles by the bed to give himself enough light. With a soft, damp cloth, Dominic dabbed the feverish perspiration off his son's face. He tried not to make any noise, but the wooden chair he sat in creaked slightly as his weight shifted when he bent over Steven.

You forgot to do what I showed you, didn't you? he thought to himself. *Why? You knew what to do. Why did you forget? Feeding the birds would have taken your daunting sorrow away. Dear sweet creature, why did you forget?*

Steven was a bright boy. He had always paid close attention during his lessons. Dominic had tried instilling in his son the knowledge that nature had the power to bring all things to an end if the warnings were not heeded. But when it came to taking his own life, Steven had chosen a formidable instrument.

But I know. I know that when your world is ringing with pain everywhere you turn, it is all you can do to turn it off any way you can.

In his mind Dominic reviewed every sentence Steven had uttered to him in the past month until fatigue and endless self-questioning made clear thinking impossible. He knew this had everything to do with his son's love for Michael.

Why didn't you tell me? But then, where was I? Where was I before all this happened? Had I only heeded the signs, you never would have known any of this.

Dominic dipped the cloth again in the bowl of warm water on the table next to the bed, pressing it to Steven's face and lips. Since Steven was not conscious to drink or to take medication, this was the best he could do at the moment.

Oh, my son, my son! I'm so sorry. I should have known. Forgive me. If I only had the power to wipe away your suffering with this cloth, how happy I would be! How I would gladly trade places with you if I could!

Matthew, Thomas, and the abbot appeared at the infirmary door. Dominic rose from his seat when the abbot entered, but Daniel motioned him to sit down. The glow from the candles shimmered on Steven's face.

The abbot's voice was anxious. "What does he have?"

"I don't know yet."

"Where was he?"

"By the stream near the woods."

"He didn't fall, did he? Have an accident?"

Dominic shook his head. "I don't think so. There are no wounds."

"He could have eaten or been bitten by something, perhaps. Is he running a fever?"

Somberly Dominic replied, "Yes, he is."

"That in itself could be a sign of some kind of poisoning," said the abbot. "But you would know more about that than I."

Smart man, the abbot. His deductive powers were not leading him astray.

Dominic's conscience would no longer allow him to remain quiet. He pulled the jar of belladonna out of his pocket and handed it to the abbot. "He took this."

The abbot brought the jar over to the candles and adjusted his glasses as he read the label. "How much?" he said.

"Judging by what's left, quite a bit."

Heaving a long-drawn-out sigh, the abbot muttered grimly, "Belladonna." Even his limited knowledge of the plant told him the gravity of the situation. In the waning candlelight, he looked into Dominic's troubled face. Then he leaned over the bed to study Steven more closely. He placed a hand on the boy's sweat-drenched face. When he touched his cheek, he felt the burning heat emanating from his skin.

"It appears he's being visited by severe toxemia," said the abbot. "What shall we do?"

As the candlelight dimmed, so did Dominic's hopes for Steven's recovery. He realized he was unable to cure the very person he cherished most. Dominic felt betrayed and abandoned by his gifts as a doctor. Yet as much as Dominic feared hospitals, he did what was needed.

"Call an ambulance," he said.

It had snowed a little, which delayed the ambulance's arrival. Close to an hour later it raced up the gravel path, its clanging siren waking most of the monastery. Old Aloysius, confusing it with the bell for office, dressed and went to the chapel.

Dominic looked on helplessly as two ambulance attendants placed Steven's limp body on a stretcher and carried it out to the vehicle. A few boys, awakened by the commotion, stared from the windows of their bedrooms. Dominic climbed in next to Steven, and the doors were shut behind him. Nothing could have kept him from going. Monastic obedience and allegiance to his abbot and to God paled in the face of his precious child's life.

ALTERNATELY PACING and praying, Dominic did little else in the three long days he stayed by Steven's hospital bed, except beg

God to spare his son. As Steven lay in a coma, Dominic barely slept or ate. He did not bathe. Nervously he wrung and yanked his habit until it was wrinkled. The hospital room overlooked green lawns, and if he was not staring into Steven's face, searching for any sign of life, Dominic sat staring out the window. At night he prayed for hours, holding Steven's hand.

On the morning of the fourth day, the coma lifted.

In the hallway outside Steven's room, the doctor gave Dominic the news. He was a short man in a long white coat, his hair pressed neatly against his scalp as though it had been ironed into place.

"I don't have to tell you," the doctor said, "that belladonna is usually lethal in these doses. The fact that he survived at all is what you in your line of work would call a miracle."

The doctor cleared his throat. "In extreme cases, such as this one, there is usually some degree of damage to certain vital organs, which can be permanent. It appears there has been some damage to his liver."

Dominic felt weak. He placed a hand against the wall to steady himself.

"He can still live a normal life," the doctor continued, "provided he watches his health. No alcohol, no physical exertion or strenuous activity of any kind. He needs lots of rest." Then he added in a lowered voice, "I will, of course, have to file an attempted suicide report. Standard procedure, you know."

STEVEN WAS released from the hospital and brought home in a wheelchair. Dominic kept a constant vigil over his young patient as he drifted in and out of consciousness in the quiet isolation of a small, private room.

When Steven woke, two nights after he had come home, he was disoriented and groggy. "Where am I?" he whispered.

"Home," said Dominic.

Steven recognized his father's voice. He also recognized the sound of a match being struck against the sandpaper strip of the box. There was a burst of flame as a candle was lit.

Dominic was watching him. "How do you feel?" he said.

"Tired," answered Steven. His father appeared out of focus.

"I can imagine."

Dominic excused himself and returned a few minutes later with two steaming mugs of cocoa. He sat Steven up in bed and put a mug in his hand. Dominic sat down in the chair by the bed, lifted his mug in the air, and said, "To strawberries."

Steven smiled weakly and sipped his drink. To Steven, the cocoa tasted better than anything he had ever tasted before. He was more grateful to see his father than he could have ever imagined.

Dominic began recounting a humorous story told to him by one of the other brothers, but the cocoa and the soothing warmth of his father's voice soon made Steven so drowsy that his eyes closed once more. He felt Dominic remove the mug from his hand and heard him place it on the nightstand.

Then he felt something he had not felt in a long time. Gently Dominic gathered up Steven in his arms and held him. It was like this that the boy fell into a deep, healing sleep.

8

WHEN STEVEN FINALLY WAS strong enough to get up from his sickbed, he saw that he had been moved to a private room in the isolated east wing. Instead of a view of the sprawling monastery lawns, he now looked out onto a tiny yard enclosed by high walls. That night Steven lay in bed, listening to the icy November rains tapping on his window. Although he had been given no reason for the move, he knew just the same. Rumors that he needed to recuperate from the pressures of his academic studies had been allowed to circulate. But in the eyes of the church, attempting to take one's life was something that could not be easily forgiven. He understood all too well. Yet, when he examined his conscience, the only real crime he had committed was that he had given his heart to someone else. As he lay there, he vowed never again to love someone as much as he had loved Michael.

Once Steven had recovered enough to resume his studies, he had two ways of dealing with Michael. Either he avoided him, or when that wasn't possible, he treated him like a stranger. If Michael walked into the library while Steven was studying, Steven got up and took his books elsewhere. At meals, if they sat near one another, Steven communicated only when something needed passing.

MICHAEL RETURNED after lunch to his too quiet, too empty room. An envelope was on his pillow. He opened it. It was a letter from the Royal Academy of Arts, in London, thanking him for his "impressive submission" and inviting him to an interview. The letter, signed by the head of admissions, went on to say that financial assistance in the form of a scholarship was available to him if tuition was a problem.

Two things piqued Michael's curiosity. First, the letter had arrived unopened. That in itself was surprising. It was common practice for the abbot to censor all incoming mail for the boys. Second, and far more perplexing, was the fact that Michael had never sent any samples of his work to anyone, let alone the prestigious Royal Academy.

That night, when he was sure everyone was asleep, Michael made his way through the darkened corridors to the east wing. He entered Steven's private room and shook the letter in the dark.

"What's this about?" Michael whispered loudly. "Is this some kind of joke?"

There was a rustling of sheets. A candle was lit. Steven sat up in bed. He rubbed the sleep from his eyes and took the letter from Michael, reaching for his glasses.

"You've received a reply," he said, studying the letter. "They really must like your work." He removed his glasses and handed the letter back to Michael. "Congratulations."

"I suppose you had something to do with this?" Michael said.

Candlelight flickered across their faces. Steven still looked gaunt from his illness.

"A long time ago I badgered you without success about applying for a place there, remember? So I took matters into my own hands. I wrote to request an admittance form. They posted one back to me. I told them you were eager to attend but couldn't afford the tuition. I enclosed some of your work, forged your signature, and posted it off."

Michael sighed. "But the drawings . . . where did you get the drawings? I thought I threw them all away."

"You'll find plenty behind the settee in the common room."

Steven blew out the candle, turned toward the wall, and pulled the bedclothing over him. Michael wandered out and headed toward the stash of drawings.

DOMINIC WATCHED as Steven began to indiscriminately shut out everything and everyone, including him. Hurt by his son's silence, he knew better than to interfere. He watched as the boy became withdrawn. The bright light of his enthusiasm faded, and so did his appetite for learning. He became a mannequin, performing lessons and chores without zeal. He no longer rambled in the woods, no longer hungered to sing in the choir. On several occasions Dominic tried enticing him to go strawberry picking, but Steven always declined, using his academic studies as an excuse.

MICHAEL FOUND Dominic in the laboratory, making notes at his long table. When he entered, the monk looked up and smiled. It was a smile as familiar and warm as the hills in summer.

"What is it, my son?" said Dominic.

"I need to speak with you," said Michael.

Dominic indicated the chair next to him and the boy sat down. In typical fashion, Michael wasted no time.

"I'm leaving," he said.

Dominic was stunned. "What will you do? Where will you go?"

Michael handed him the letter from the academy. Dominic picked up his glasses and put them on. As he read, the monk's face brightened and his lips broadened into a smile.

"Congratulations, my boy." Dominic took off his glasses and peered unwaveringly into Michael's eyes. "Tell me, is this what you want to pursue?"

"I think this is a golden opportunity."

Dominic nodded. "It certainly is."

"I came to say good-bye. I'll be leaving tomorrow morning."

"So soon?" The monk noticed the determination in the boy's eyes. Michael said nothing more.

"Well, perhaps it's for the best," Dominic said, and sighed.

THE PALE gray dawn crept through the bare window. Michael got up and noticed a wicker basket by the foot of his bed. He recognized it immediately as Dominic's plant-collecting basket. A note was pinned to the white linen cloth draped over it.

> *My son,*
>
> *It is difficult to conceal my sorrow at your leaving, but in my heart I am glad for your new opportunity.*
>
> *Enclosed you will find a few provisions until you have reached your destination. There is something else I've included. Despite how you feel about the Holy Trinity, I would like you to have it anyway. I acquired it on a pilgrimage to the Holy Land many years ago. It has always brought me luck. May it furnish you with the same.*
>
> *Please remember you are always welcome here.*
>
> *God be with you.*
>
> *Dominic*

Michael would miss the monk. He was one of the few who had understood him and accepted him unconditionally. His quiet words of encouragement had seen him through more difficulties than any number of theology lessons or prayers. Aside from Thomas, Dominic was the only monk Michael was fond of.

Removing the white cloth, Michael found in the basket some cheese, sausage, and fruit. There was also a loaf of brown monastery bread, still soft and warm—probably baked early that morning—and a candle and matches. Ever the doctor, Dominic even included some medicine. At the bottom of the basket was a hard-shelled box, not more than four inches square, bound by an old violet ribbon. It rested on top of an envelope. Inside the box was a solid gold crucifix and chain pinned to a bed of deep-blue silk. The envelope contained a five-pound note.

Michael folded the note and pushed it into his pocket. He took out the food and medicine to pack into his canvas knapsack. The box with the crucifix he placed back into the basket.

Of his own personal belongings, he was taking only what he needed: a few books from the shelf near his bed, a few articles of clothing, and basic toiletries. Michael had made a careful selection of his drawings from the large cardboard envelope Steven had secretly kept. He had rolled them into a tube and tied them. He left his school uniform—black trousers and purple jacket with a white cross embroidered on the breast pocket—hanging in the closet.

When Michael reached the top of the monastery drive, he saw a white carpet of fresh snow blanketing the countryside. He turned to look back at the abbey. The scene was peaceful. The snow had muffled and silenced the world around him. It was as though the entire countryside had fallen asleep and could not be awakened. A wisp of smoke from a chimney dissipated into the winter sky. As the first breath of freedom filled his lungs and the clouds of his breath grew thicker and he grew colder, he realized that it was time to go. The train station was more than seven miles away, and in the snow it would be an arduous journey.

"Is it true?"

Dominic stood in awkward silence in front of the abbot's study. "It is," he said.

"Then why the devil was I not informed? I had to hear of it from Matthew, who told me Michael had missed the morning meal."

Dominic shrugged, his face solemn.

"Well, on the one hand," the abbot continued, "we are rid of Michael Warren. I shan't be losing any more sleep over him."

The abbot sat back in his chair and removed his glasses. "But on the other hand, I am at a loss. In the eyes of the law, Michael is still a minor and therefore bound to remain under our custodial wing until the age of eighteen. What would you do, if you were in my shoes?"

Dominic chose his words carefully. "While you and the others see him in one light, I see him in another. He is one who does not see as we do. He has his own vision, lives in his own world. It would be tantamount to plucking a tiger from the wild and trying to domesticate it. Michael is destined to live in a world only he can govern, not one that is governed for him.

"To survive, he has had to enclose himself in his own personal cloister, one he has erected to shield an overt sensitivity. His unruly behavior is merely a defense. And although there are those, I grant, who would argue to the contrary, he is harmless. He is a soul who is trapped not only within himself, but within our very own walls. Beneath that chain mail of false bravado lies a shipwrecked soul, delicate and fragile as an autumnal zephyr, tormented by neglect and robbed of affection. Under that troublemaker's skin lurks a tender, vulnerable soul."

The abbot was silent for a moment. "You have never let me down, Dominic. I have always known you to be of sound judgment." He waited.

"Let Michael Warren go," said Dominic. "Release him. Give him his freedom. It's simply not in his character to blindly follow a set of rules as we do. He is a free spirit who cannot conform to the rigors and confines of this institution any more than we could adopt his ways. He belongs in an art college, not a cloister."

"I cannot permit that," said the abbot.

"He will be eighteen in just a few months," Dominic said.

"Why not let him go?"

The abbot sighed. "Alright. I'll not interfere."

MICHAEL STOOD uneasily in the wood-paneled office as the principal sat quietly, reviewing his work and notes from Michael's interview.

"Why don't you take a seat," he said. Relieved, Michael sank into the chair.

The principal was a thin man and almost completely bald. As he talked, he smoked a cigarette. "I've good news," he said. "The academy has decided to accept you. You'll be granted a scholarship. The review board was very impressed with your submissions, which I also feel are exceptional."

"Thank you," said Michael.

"Now, term commences the twenty-first. That's next week. Have you secured lodgings yet?"

"No, sir. I was hoping the college would be able to help me. I've no money."

"Of course," said the principal, running a hand across his bald head. He opened his desk drawer and pulled out a sheet of paper. Then he scribbled a note on a piece of stationery, and handed both papers to Michael.

"Here is a list of our approved boardinghouses, and my note to the bursar. He will give you a chit. The scholarship pays for your tuition and accommodation. It does not, however, cover living expenses. I can provide you with a position here, if you wish. We are in need of janitorial assistance. Would this be agreeable to you?"

"Yes, sir," said Michael.

"Good. I'll have a word with Mr. Duncan in our maintenance department." The principal rose from his desk and shook Michael's hand firmly. He smiled. "Let me know how you're getting on, will you?"

THE FIRST place he looked at on the principal's list was smaller than his room at the monastery; it had a thin excuse for a bed that sunk radically in the middle. An unpleasant odor like rotting vegetables hung in the air. The rotund matron, wearing a frayed bandanna around her head and slippers with holes in them, stood at the door as Michael looked around the room.

"No excessive noise," she said. "Main doors are locked at ten. No visitors after nine. No overnight guests. No members of the opposite sex allowed. Ten pounds a week. Meals included." She stretched out her hand, expecting payment.

"What happens if I come in late?" Michael said.

"Then you sleep outside, luv." She puffed on a cigarette and used the palm of her hand to catch the falling ash.

As Michael walked away, she shouted after him, "You won't find better!"

It had started to rain. Michael hurried through the wet streets to the second address, a house in Ladbrook Grove. He was met at the door by a portly man sporting suspenders and chewing on an unlit cigar. The man unlocked the door, pushed it open, and stood under its frame as Michael inspected the room. It was large, with a bay window and a view of the street. Despite the window, the room was quite dark. Michael guessed it saw little natural sunlight. As a painter, natural light was a valuable commodity.

"Nice, ain't it?" grunted the man in a thick Cockney accent. He hooked a thumb under one suspender.

When Michael was done, he said, "I have a few other places to look at. I'll let you know."

The man lit his cigar. "It's gonna go quick, laddie. These places always do."

Michael thanked the man and stepped out into the rain, pulling his coat over his head. The next address was a tall, pencil-thin Georgian house on a side street off Queensway. It stood in a neat row of similar houses on a quiet, tree-shaded lane. Michael was taken by the tranquility. When he rang the doorbell, he was greeted by a man in his early fifties wearing a white open-collared shirt, gray flannel pants, and a pair of house slippers.

"I've come about the room," Michael said, showing the piece of paper in his hand.

"From the academy?" the man said.

"Yes."

"Come in," said the man. "The name's John Bain. I'm the landlord."

He ushered Michael up three flights of narrow carpeted stairs.

"It's not the Taj Mahal," he said, "but the room is comfy, and you'll have free use of the kitchen and bathroom. The rest of the house is off limits. It's my private residence."

They arrived at the top landing and walked down a corridor. At the end of it, the man pushed back a door. A spacious room was dominated by two large windows. On a sunny day, Michael could tell that the room would be flooded in pools of natural light. It had a bed, a wardrobe, and an armchair. An area rug covered part of the wooden floor. A small washbasin was mounted on the wall next to a single towel railing. Close by was a shilling gas meter.

"I'll take it," Michael said.

"I gather you are on scholarship, so the school will pay. I'll need a chit from the bursar then."

"When do you need it by?" Michael said.

"Week's end."

Michael shook the landlord's hand warmly. "I'll have it for you by then," he said.

THE ACADEMY was an enormous place, teeming with life. Props, from unfinished canvases to human skeletons hanging from mobile stands, lined the corridors. When classes were recessed, the halls came alive with students.

Each studio was a high-ceilinged room with wooden beams, as large as a small warehouse. A uniformed porter guarded the main entrance and greeted every student in the morning. Local women posed nude for life classes.

Michael spent the first week becoming acquainted with the school and its routines. In contrast to the monastery, which adhered to rigid structure and discipline, at the academy it felt as though time did not exist. His classes and job started and ended at appointed times, but for Michael the hours and days ran together in a single, happy blur. He got up every morning and did the very thing he loved. And when he sketched and painted, nothing else mattered.

Every morning Michael yawned heavily and stretched himself awake by six-thirty. He threw on his bathrobe and tied it, then lumbered down two flights of stairs to the kitchen, where he made himself a cup of tea. He took the cup back upstairs with him and climbed back into bed, where he read for an hour. Then he got up and washed his face in the small basin. After he shaved and dressed, he sauntered down to a small French patisserie on Queensway that had a tiny service area with a few tables and chairs. He sat down and ordered the same thing he ordered every morning, a steaming café au lait and three freshly baked shortbreads. He picked up each one and inhaled its aroma before taking a bite. Their freshness reminded him of the monastery bread. It was one of the few things he genuinely missed about the abbey. By nine he was headed toward the Queensway tube station, and by nine forty-five he was sitting in front of his easel at the academy.

At lunch hour he often strolled to a nearby vegetarian café, where he devoured a jacket potato with all the trimmings and a small bowl of soup. For dessert he treated himself to a honey-and-wild-oats flapjack that scrumptiously melted in his mouth. Then he returned to the academy.

Michael resumed his place in front of his easel and worked right up until three o'clock, when the dismissal bell sounded. Wasting no time, he packed up his things, walked to the Piccadilly Underground stop, and took it to Queensway. He exited the station, going left on Queensway and walking to Westbourne Grove. He turned left on Westbourne Grove, and a few short blocks down turned right on the street where he lived. When he arrived at his front door, he twisted the key in the lock and gave the door a nudge with his shoulder. The door shuddered open.

After climbing the stairs to his room, he dropped his knapsack at the door and removed his shoes. He made himself some tea, then sat down with a sketchpad and pencil and drew for two hours while listening to the strains of classical music on the BBC. He had purchased a radio from a secondhand store; its wooden cabinet was battered and stained, but it had become a faithful friend, keeping him company while he worked. He had originally bought it to drown out the sound of the bells from the church down on the corner. Instead of languishing in their rapturous chimes, Michael recoiled. They were an everyday reminder of the monastery bell that had once summoned him at all hours. Now the soothing music blotted out that world.

When he finished for the evening, he cleaned his paintbrushes and dusted the eraser crumbs from the coffee-stained sketchbooks that littered the floor. He went downstairs to the kitchen to prepare his dinner. The menu was the same every night: tinned baked beans on a slice of toast, and a large jacket potato. Potatoes were the cheapest food at the open-air markets, and he enjoyed watching the brown dirt roll off their skins as he scrubbed them clean under the flowing water of the basin before baking them. He ate his dinner slowly and deliberately, savoring every bite.

After dinner he collapsed in his armchair and rolled himself a cigarette using tobacco from a dented tin that he always carried with him. Once he finished his smoke, he was back on the tube to Piccadilly to start his janitorial work at the academy by seven in the evening. He swept the long, empty corridors with a large broom and emptied the dustbins in each studio into a large rubbish bin at the back of the building. Then he cleaned the lavatories, sweeping up the cigarette butts off the floor around the toilets. Students were not allowed to smoke in the building, but they did so in the bathrooms. After making sure there was ample toilet paper in each stall, he left the academy at ten, switching off all the lights and locking up.

Back in his room, he brushed his teeth, washed his face, and crawled between the sheets of his unmade bed, where he read for an hour. When he finally turned off the light, he would lie on his back and watch the shadows cast by the streetlamps as they danced across his white ceiling and down the walls.

One obstacle dogged Michael after he fell asleep: the cold. The shilling gas meter in his room provided the only heat during icy winter nights. A single coin bought three hours of warmth. By 3 a.m. the meter ran out, and Michael would stumble out of bed, drop in another coin, and twist the knob to deposit it. Then he would nose-dive back into bed. He kept two quids' worth of shillings neatly stacked on top of the meter for just that purpose.

ON FRIDAYS after he returned home from school, Michael cleaned his paintbrushes and arranged his canvases and drawings, then straightened up the rest of his bed-sit. He ran a hot bath and languished in it for half an hour before making dinner. Friday was his day off from work, and so after dinner he crawled into bed, read a few chapters of a book, and went to sleep early. On Saturdays and Sundays he made the rounds of the museums and galleries in London.

He loved museums. He wandered through the halls and salons, some as large as a house. Inside them he lost all track of time. He was unaware of the other visitors and their whispers, or the guards standing in the corners like statues, or the muted thundering of a jackhammer on the street outside. Whenever he stood in front of certain paintings, he was transported to a different universe, one where he felt like he was floating a few feet off the wooden floors of the gallery. Standing before a Renaissance Madonna and child, Michael was awestruck at how the artist could manipulate his emotions using only a flat, one-dimensional surface. When the guard wasn't looking, Michael reached out and touched the painting that breathed such vibrant life. But all he could feel was the cool surface of the canvas.

At these moments he was reminded of how great art could uplift the human spirit. Certain paintings moved him to contemplate his own existence. The paint-splattered canvases of conceptual art did nothing for him. It was realism that gripped him. Michael was spellbound by the Dutch painter Vermeer and his ability to capture his subjects with photographic quality. There was also the Italian Baroque master Caravaggio, whose religious depictions inspired a spirituality in Michael that he was reluctant to acknowledge. And Michael was not ashamed to be sexually aroused by the sight of the French artist Bonnard's nudes.

But his true religious experience came when he gazed upon the Turners at the Tate Gallery. Filled with mystery and wonder, these masterworks cast a spell over him. They possessed colors and light Michael had never before seen. Turner's summer sunsets of burning oranges and weeping pale blues made Michael rethink the use of color in his own work. Sometimes, without realizing it, he would spend as much as an entire hour studying a single painting. He often laughed at the thought of living in a museum just to be close to the art he so loved.

A guard once noticed how enraptured Michael was with one of the Turners. He approached and said, "It's magnificent, isn't it?"

Without looking away from the canvas, Michael said, "Just put a bed in the corner for me, will you? I promise to lock up and turn off the lights after everyone's gone."

The guard chuckled.

One Saturday after leaving a museum, Michael was famished, as always. He was also exhausted from the intensity of his visit. Making his way to the nearest café, he treated himself to a steak dinner heavily dusted with pepper and washed down with hot coffee, followed by a rolled cigarette. As he relaxed, sated, he reflected on what he had seen. Suddenly an idea came to him. He searched for something to write on. Finding a few pieces of crumpled paper in his pocket, he scratched the idea down. Within days he had attempted dozens of sketches and drawings, which littered the floor of his bed-sit.

Over the next few weeks Michael constructed three massive canvases that fanned out in a zigzag fashion across his room, dominating it like an enormous Oriental partition. The work was to be modeled on a medieval triptych, but instead of depicting religious scenes from the Bible, the subject would be the monastery buildings and the surrounding countryside. For months the paint flowed from Michael's inspired brush, slowly covering the stark white canvases.

9

THE LIGHT OF DUSK cast the laboratory in shadows. Glasses perched on his nose, Dominic sat at his table, grinding herbs with a pestle and mortar. Steven stood in the doorway, watching. After a few silent moments, he said, "I want to take my vows."

Dominic didn't even know Steven had been standing there. The monk almost lost his balance and fell off his chair. Regaining his composure, he took off his glasses.

"How did you come to this?" he said.

"After my . . . you know. I've decided that I want to take my vows."

Dominic put a hand on his son's shoulder. "I'm not so sure you're doing this for the right reasons."

"I've thought it through thoroughly, Father."

Dominic was skeptical. "You will have to be approved by the community and then serve as a postulant before even entering the novitiate. Do you understand that?"

"I know what's involved."

"Alright, then. I will go to the abbot and inform him of your wishes."

MOST DAYS MICHAEL STAYED in and painted during his lunch hour instead of going out. The studio was empty, and he liked the quiet. For several days in a row, a girl with long, curly brown hair and emerald eyes had appeared at the door.

"Is John Mantle around?" she said.

Michael looked up from his easel and over at his neighbor's empty easel. "Don't think so," he said.

"How about Simon Owens?"

Without looking up he said, "No, haven't seen him either."

"Stephen Maynard?"

"Suspect they've all gone out for lunch."

And with that she promptly left.

Michael recognized the girl as Suzanne Wright, another first-year student at the academy. Her studio was all the way down at the end of the corridor. At first Michael thought nothing of these daily visits and questions. Students regularly came to the studio asking the whereabouts of someone else. But with each passing day her identical questions became irritating.

As lessons drew to a close one afternoon, the studio was full of chatting students packing up their work for the day. Some were in clusters, talking among themselves. Michael was the only one still working.

Suzanne walked in and joined some of the other students. She sat atop one of the vacant desks near Michael. Intermittently she kept looking at him out of the corner of her eye, hoping he would notice her. But Michael remained buried in his work.

When she could no longer contain herself, she got up and stood next to Michael's easel, partially blocking his view. "Don't you like anyone here?" she said.

Michael became indignant. "Can't you see I'm busy?" he snapped. "I'm here to do my work, not to win a bloody popularity contest."

The room went quiet. Suzanne stood frozen in place, stunned and embarrassed. Then she ran out of the studio. Michael tried regaining his concentration, but it was futile. Exasperated, he tossed a few things into the frayed leather satchel that had been with him since his earliest school days and left.

THE NEXT day Michael spotted Suzanne on the stair landing as he began to climb up. She stood looking at some of the work by other students that was on exhibit. Seeing her brought back the incident from the day before. He caught up to her.

"Sorry I was a bit short yesterday," he said.

Suzanne ignored him and stood looking straight ahead at a watercolor. Michael positioned himself next to the painting, a seascape. "I was rather caught up in my work. Please accept my apology."

She continued staring straight ahead. Michael got the message and left.

At lunchtime Michael was working alone in his studio. He heard the door open and footsteps approach, but he kept on working.

"Apology accepted," a voice said behind him.

Michael turned around, paintbrush still in hand.

"I'm Suzanne Wright," she said, extending her hand.

Michael put down his brush and shook her hand. "I'm Michael Warren."

"I know," she said.

"Let me make it up to you," Michael said. "Have tea with me after college."

"What, today?"

"Yes."

She paused, and her lips formed a smile. "Alright, then."

When the bell sounded for dismissal, Michael went to Suzanne's studio. "Just let me collect my things and we'll go," she said.

While she hurriedly packed her bag, Michael walked over to her easel. Bits of paper—sketches, drawings, notes she had hastily

scribbled to herself—were pinned to its sides. On the easel itself
was a pencil drawing held in place by four pins, one on each corner. It was a nude from life class. The reclined nude met the
viewer's gaze with such sensuality that it physically aroused
Michael.

As Michael pondered it, Suzanne blurted out, "I'm thinking
of turning it into an oil. I haven't decided yet."

She hefted the heavy leather bag onto her shoulder and the
two left, walking out into the crush of Piccadilly Circus rush hour
as people poured out into the streets.

"You take your work very seriously, don't you?" she said as
they wove through the crowds.

Normally a fast walker, Michael made a conscious effort not to
outpace her. "Concentration and focus are important, I believe."

"My God, every time I come into your studio, your nose is
buried in your canvas. Mr. Watson says you're terribly dedicated.
Your work is highly praised by all the teachers, even the head-
master. You must be very proud."

It was the first time he had ever heard anyone talk like that
about him. *If only the monks could have been present for that comment,*
he thought.

As they strolled to the Piccadilly Circus tube stop, they talked
about the college, about which teachers they liked and disliked,
and shared their mutual distaste of anatomy class. Michael was
enjoying himself. It was refreshing. He had forgotten how much
he missed companionship. But he also felt a pang of guilt that he
was not going straight home to do his work.

They arrived at Michael's house and passed through the poorly
lit foyer. Michael guided her up the flight of worn, carpeted stairs
to the first floor. Taking Suzanne's coat and bag, he placed them
on the sofa. He then ushered her to the kitchen and showed her
to a circular wrought-iron table next to a huge French window
overlooking the street below.

"Take a pew," Michael said. He filled the kettle from the tap and placed it on one of the burners. He struck a match and the burner flamed to life. "Hungry?"

Suzanne nodded. Then she looked at him and said, "Where are you from?"

"Surrey, originally." Michael measured enough tea in the strainer for two cups.

"Is that where your parents live?"

"Originally, yes." He opened a cupboard and removed a tin of biscuits from a high shelf. From the metal container he selected an array of different shapes and sizes and placed them on a tray.

"Where do they live now?" she said.

"They're deceased." Steam burst from the kettle, making the metal lid bounce and rattle. Michael turned off the flame.

"I'm sorry," she said. "How, if you don't mind me asking?"

"Car accident," Michael lied. "On holiday." He carefully poured the hot water through the sieve and into the teapot.

"How old were you?"

Michael picked up the tray and put it on the table. "I was ten."

"Do you have brothers and sisters?"

"No." Michael sat down and poured the tea into two mugs that gave the appearance of always looking dirty; one had a permanent brown ring near the top of the inside, marking the usual level of the beverage.

Suzanne picked up a biscuit and took a bite. "Where did you go to school, then?" she said.

"At a monastery orphanage."

With her mouth full, she said, "Were you going to be a monk or something?"

"At the time of my parents' death, I was entrusted into the custody of this orphanage. Milk and sugar?"

"Please."

Michael passed her a small pitcher of milk and the sugar bowl.

Suzanne rhythmically chewed on the biscuit. "Why did you leave?"

"In the first place," said Michael, "I was old enough to leave. But being there was suffocating me."

After he left the monastery, Michael had promised himself never to talk about his past. And yet, now there was a part of him that yearned to speak to someone with complete abandon. He wanted to open up and tell her everything, get it off his chest, all that he had carried around for so long. Deep down inside, he knew that talking about it would be the best thing. But he couldn't bring himself to do it. Instead, he was guarded and careful. He remembered how Steven on occasion had questioned him about his past. It had always made him feel uncomfortable. Dodging Suzanne's questions brought up that same trapped feeling.

Michael turned and gazed out the window. "Suzanne, I really don't feel comfortable talking about this right now."

Suzanne fell quiet, sipping her tea in nervous silence. Sensing the awkwardness, he said, "Let's go upstairs. I've something to show you."

They finished their tea and climbed the steps leading to the third floor. At the end of the corridor, Michael swung the door open. Suzanne walked in and stopped in her tracks, staring at the massive canvases that dominated the small room and the paintbrushes lined up on the windowsills. Nodding, she sat down in the armchair.

"This is exactly how I always envisioned a dedicated artist's abode to look like," she said.

Michael noticed his unmade bed. Embarrassed, he straightened it up. Smoke curled from a cigarette Suzanne had just lit. Michael knelt down and pulled out some sketches from under his bed. He spread them on the floor and moved aside to let his visitor have a look.

"These drawings and sketches," he said, "refer to the large canvases you see in front of you."

Suzanne glanced at them briefly. They were drawings of monks in various forms of activity, working out in the fields, making bread, and praying.

"I'm modeling it on a medieval triptych. It's going to be a series of three large oils."

He saw she was looking instead at the pencil outlines on each canvas, but she said nothing. Perhaps she's overwhelmed, he guessed. Gathering up the sketches, he stowed them under the bed again.

Michael sat on the bed and rolled a cigarette. He could see that Suzanne was visibly anxious. Her effervescent talkativeness had vanished. She got up from the armchair and walked over to the window. The last rays of the late afternoon sun fell on her, highlighting the river of wavy chestnut hair that cascaded over her shoulders in tiny brown ringlets. Roses filled her alabaster cheeks. As her eyes searched the street below, her hair tumbled forward into her face. Barely five feet tall, Suzanne had a seductive figure and ample breasts camouflaged beneath loose clothing. But her hands were short and stubby. *The hands of an artist*, Michael thought. He found her attractive.

Nervously Suzanne tried lighting another cigarette. She fumbled with the matches, then looked over at Michael. "I can't seem to light it," she said.

Michael removed the box of matches from her hand and, in one smooth movement against the sandy strip of the box, ignited the stick. Suzanne bent down but stopped just before her cigarette met the flame. The match began burning down. Michael touched her hand as he quickly blew out the match.

"What's the matter?" he said.

Dropping the cigarette, Suzanne threw herself into his arms and wildly kissed his neck.

"I love you, Michael," she said. "From the moment I laid eyes on you, I loved you."

Taken completely by surprise, Michael did not know what to think. He felt sorry for her, as though she were afflicted with some terrible disease.

"How did all this come about?" said Michael.

"I was attracted to you the moment I saw you. You work constantly, like a madman, as if the outside world did not exist. You never notice me. You never notice anyone, for that matter. And so I became attracted to this obsessed soul, this man of mystery who worked to the exclusion of everything else, who hardly ever spoke to anyone. You've become something of an enigma at the college. I came to your study every day at lunchtime because I knew I would find you alone, but I could never drum up the courage to actually talk to you."

Their lips met, and they reclined on the bed. Michael had never kissed a woman before. The deep-tongued kiss was sexual and salacious. Michael ran his hands over her body, edging them between her legs. She sat up suddenly and looked at her watch.

"Good God!" she said. "I've got to go. I'll be late getting home."

She fetched a brush from her handbag and began brushing her hair. "Can I tell people at college we're going together?"

This is rather abrupt, Michael thought. "Whatever you like," he said, calmly rolling a cigarette.

"Can we have lunch tomorrow?"

"Of course."

Michael walked her to the tube station and kissed her good-bye.

The hour with Suzanne had been a delightful intrusion into his well-ordered life. When Michael returned home and opened the door to his room, he was met by a wave of stale cigarette smoke infused with Suzanne's perfume. It made him smile.

SUZANNE DID not let Michael forget what he said. The next day she bounded into his studio at lunchtime and stood between him and his painting. This time Michael found the intrusion charming. They ambled to his favorite vegetarian restaurant, where Michael had his usual jacket potato and Suzanne a small bowl of pea soup and a salad.

On their way back to the academy they passed a florist.

"Wait here a second," Michael said.

He disappeared into the shop and reappeared hiding something behind his back. "Close your eyes," he said, "and hold out your hand."

Suzanne did as she was told. Michael placed a single red rose in it. "Alright, you can look now."

When she opened her eyes and saw the rose, she threw her arms around his neck and planted kisses on every part of his face.

For two weeks they ate every day at the vegetarian restaurant and had tea after college in a small, sweaty café near the academy. The windows were fogged up from the heat of the espresso machine and the cold outside. They sat across from each other at a corner table, hands joined. They kissed in alleyways. On weekends they frequented art galleries and exhibits and, provided the weather was favorable, painted together in the park.

At first Michael found it awkward being with Suzanne; he did not know how to react to all her demonstrative displays of affection. The attraction he felt toward her was undeniable. She had a strong, outgoing personality, and at times Michael found her domineering. Popular at the academy, she was chatty and made friends easily. But she could also be moody. Her intoxicating effervescence was marked by periods of girlish pouting. Having spent so little time with the opposite sex, Michael was not accustomed to a woman's moods and whims.

One afternoon after college, Suzanne and Michael leaned against a tree in Green Park, kissing.

"Why don't we carve our initials in this tree?" she said. "We'll make it ours."

Michael ran his hands along the tree, then pulled out his pocketknife. For twenty grueling minutes he hacked away at the sappy bark until he clumsily carved their initials, connected by a plus sign and encircled by a lopsided, arrow-pierced heart. By the time he finished, it was already dark.

They strolled the cold streets, the frosted streetlights sparkling in the crystal-clear winter air. Michael bought a pack of hot chestnuts from a street vendor and shared them with Suzanne.

"Do you realize," Michael said, chewing on a nut, "that we haven't spent an entire night together?"

"What are you suggesting?" said Suzanne.

"Why don't you come and spend the night this Saturday? That way you won't have to get up and leave."

She hesitated a moment. "I work at a fashion boutique on Saturdays. I get off at three. I could be your way at four."

All week long Michael's insides twisted in anticipation. That Saturday he tidied his room in preparation for her arrival, stowing away canvases and paintbrushes. He made his bed and dusted everywhere. He bought food for dinner and some fresh fruit from the small store around the corner.

While he waited, he sat in his armchair and tried to read, but he couldn't concentrate. He turned on the wireless and tried listening to music. When that failed, he felt like going out for a long walk but was afraid she would arrive while he was out. Unable to quell the butterflies in his stomach, he paced the floor of his room in endless circles until he grew weary. Lying down on his bed, he stared up at the ceiling. He could not calm his nerves. He kept getting up and glancing out the window, hoping to catch a glimpse of her walking up the street. Every time the doorbell rang, he leaped to his feet and charged down the three flights of stairs to the front door. The first time it was a tenant who had locked herself out. The second time, an hour later, it was the postman with a special delivery for Michael's landlord.

Four o'clock came and went. By the hour it grew darker and colder. There was no sign of Suzanne. At six, exhausted and convinced she was not coming, he glumly prepared dinner and ate it in front of the fireplace in the living room. He stared into the flames until the fire expired.

At seven thirty the doorbell rang. Breathless, as though she had been walking fast, Suzanne greeted him with, "Sorry I'm late. Had to close the store."

Michael took her coat and escorted her up to his room. They sat on the floor, smoking cigarettes and talking. Hours flew by.

Suzanne looked at her watch and panicked. "I've missed the last train!" she said. "I have to find some way of getting home."

"But I thought you were going to spend the night," Michael said.

"Well, I wasn't sure. My father would be furious. I thought at least we could spend the majority of the evening together. I was late coming from work. I apologize. But if I don't get home, there'll be hell to pay."

Michael leaned back against the bed and scratched his head. "Can't you make up some kind of story?"

"I suppose I could tell my father I'm sleeping over at a girl-friend's."

Michael wasted no time. He led her to the downstairs phone in the living room. While she dialed the number, Michael raced back up to his room, switched off the light, and lit a candle by the bed. From down below he could hear Suzanne's voice.

"I'm sorry, Daddy, I didn't realize the time. I'll spend the night here at Sally's."

Michael arrived downstairs just as she was hanging up. To-gether they walked upstairs, hand in hand. They entered his darkened room and Michael closed the door behind them.

"I'm going to undress," Suzanne said. "I want you to turn around."

Michael obliged and faced the blank wall. He could hear the rustling of garments and the creaking of his bed. "Can I turn around now?" he said.

"Yes, yes."

Michael undressed and slithered between the cold sheets of his creaky bed. They lay trapped in the valley of the mattress, shiver-ing as their bodies warmed each other. Michael kissed Suzanne. After a moment she guided his hands to her breasts. He licked her nipples and her breasts, which were like ripe melons to him.

"I've never done this before," he said.

"Here, let me show you."

Taking his hand, she gently placed it on her crotch. It was a forest of thick hair, wet to the touch, almost as if she had gone to the bathroom and not wiped herself.

"Touch me there," she said. "Yes, there, there . . . like that . . ."

Suzanne began moaning. She maneuvered herself underneath Michael, and awkwardly Michael mounted her. He was hard and slipped easily inside her wetness.

Suzanne's cheeks flushed red and her eyes closed. "Make sure you pull out," she said.

Michael moved slowly.

"Oh, it's heaven!" Suzanne said. "It's heaven!"

She reached down and began kneading his testicles. Michael felt the tension in his body rising and radiating out until he began to quiver and shake. In a final moment of panic, he fumbled and removed himself. His face contorted as he let out a muted cry. He was seized by a momentary convulsion, then a series of quick, spasmodic jerks, his body throbbing and pulsating with each one.

When he had emptied himself, he collapsed on top of Suzanne. She coiled her arms and legs around Michael, and within moments both drifted into a sound winter sleep.

THE WINDOWPANES magnified the light streaming into the room. Groggily Michael opened his eyes and found the room stifling. For a moment he thought he was in Dominic's greenhouse.

He looked over at Suzanne, who was still asleep. Michael quietly got out of bed and crept downstairs to the kitchen, where he prepared some tea. He brought a tray upstairs and gently woke Suzanne with a kiss. She sat up and rubbed her eyes. Michael handed her a mug and watched as she sipped.

"Sleep well?" Michael said.

Suzanne was still drowsy. "Like a stone at the bottom of the ocean."

Glancing dreamily around, she noticed a poetry anthology on the bookshelf and pulled it down. She took a sip of tea. "Have you ever read Coleridge's 'Rime of the Ancient Mariner'?"

Michael shook his head.

"Get back into bed. I'll read it to you."

She read the poem eloquently, as if she had written it herself. When she finished, she closed the book and looked at Michael. He was fast asleep. She returned the volume to the shelf and snuggled up next to him.

FOR SIX weeks they met regularly at his flat, taking off their clothes and climbing between the wrinkled sheets. For six weeks Michael ran his hands over the curvy geographic contours of her body. For six weeks he told her how much he loved her. For six weeks the strong smell of her perfume lingered in his room. Nothing else mattered but her. Suzanne read him poetry in bed, and on weekends they set up their easels in the park and painted side by side.

"Why do you have a job cleaning the college?" Suzanne asked him one afternoon as they took a break.

"That's how I make my living money," Michael said. "My scholarship funds my tuition and rent." He finished the biscuit he was eating. "You've never invited me to your home."

Suzanne nodded, looking somewhat embarrassed. "We have to do something about that now, don't we?"

A few days later she sneaked him into her house. "I had to make sure my parents are out," she said. "They disapprove of me bringing boys home."

It was an enormous home—a palace, Michael observed—overlooking Regent's Park, with high ceilings and majestic chandeliers. A grand staircase swept up to the second floor. "What's up there?" said Michael.

"My parents' living quarters. Can't show you that, I'm afraid. If they found out, they'd kill me."

Michael walked through halls lined with paintings and drawings by famous artists. He recognized a Bonnard, a simple painting of a woman bathing. A drawing by Matisse caught his eye. But what really took his breath away was a Turner, down at the end of a corridor. It was a train racing across a bridge against a fiery sunset.

Michael felt a stab of pain at the divide between them. For the most part, he had always known poverty. It was clear to him that Suzanne had never wanted for anything.

AFTER MICHAEL'S visit to Suzanne's house, things began to change. Over the next two weeks Suzanne made excuses every time Michael suggested they get together after college or spend the weekend at his place.

On Wednesday of the third week, he caught up with her in her studio and asked if she was free the coming weekend. "I'm sorry," she said, nervously twirling a length of her hair around her index finger. "I can't. I'm going to my aunt's in the country."

Saturday night Michael called Suzanne's house from a call box. "Is Suzanne in?" he said.

Michael recognized her mother's voice. "She's gone to the movies with a friend, I'm afraid. Shall I tell her who called?"

"No, thank you," Michael said and hung up.

That Monday Michael waited to see if Suzanne would even bother trying to find him in his studio.

She never came.

Concealing himself in an alcove, Michael waited until classes ended. He saw Suzanne exit the building with a crush of other students, and from a distance he followed her. Rain had begun to fall. She walked and chatted with two other girls, then descended into the tube station alone. Michael kept his distance from her on the platform. When the train arrived, he got into the carriage adjacent to hers. Being rush hour, the train was crowded, and she didn't notice him. Seven tube stops later, Suzanne got off. This was not the area where she lived. Michael followed her.

It was five o'clock and already dark. The street lamps were lit. Unseen, Michael trailed Suzanne through the rain-washed streets. For ten minutes she walked through a myriad of streets, finally stopping in front of a redbrick house with a brass door knocker. Michael hid in the darkness of an alley across the street. Suzanne knocked three times. The door opened. Michael saw a man take her into his arms and kiss her. The door closed behind them.

MICHAEL DID not remember how he got back to his flat. From his rain-drenched clothing he assumed he had walked the entire way. He hung his soggy coat on a nail behind the door. He turned off the light and lit a candle, then sat down on the corner of the bed and rolled himself a cigarette. In the darkness he sat, staring at the flame until the candle had completely melted away and only the melted wax remained, gradually hardening from a warm, smooth pool to a cold, shapeless mass.

Early the next morning he left his flat and bought a bouquet of blood-red roses on his way to college. He arrived before most of the students and strategically placed the flowers on Suzanne's chair in front of her easel with a note that read, "Would love to see you this weekend."

He heard nothing from her for the rest of the day.

The bell rang for dismissal, and students herded out in a massive exodus. After the great emptying out, Michael went into Suzanne's studio but found it empty. The flowers were gone too.

That evening, having returned to do his janitorial duties, he decided to clean Suzanne's studio last. The heavy rains outside thudded against the windowpanes. He was about to empty the bin in her studio when he noticed flower stems jutting out of it. He put the bin down and pulled them out.

They were his roses.

The delicate buds had been smashed from being shoved in first. At the bottom of the bin, wadded up in a ball, was the note. Without thinking, Michael shut his eyes and squeezed the stems as hard as he could. He did not feel the thorns driving into his palm as the rains poured down harder outside.

EVERY COFFEE-STAINED notebook, every sketch pinned to Michael's walls, no longer belonged to him. Michael sat in his armchair chain-smoking. He looked around his room at the books on his shelves, some standing upright, others lying flat. He stared at the sketchpads and notebooks that lay in piles in the corners, at the half-finished canvases that leaned against the walls, at the paintbrushes that stood at attention in empty coffee cans on the windowsills. Suzanne had invaded the room and stamped herself on everything. Every breath she had taken was sealed within his walls that now exhaled all the memories of their laughter and lovemaking, replaying them over and over like a broken record.

He wanted to hide everything connected with her. *If only it would all fit under my bed*, he thought. *Out of sight, out of mind.* He could start with the books. Every line from every book of poetry she had read to him could be crammed into his already over-stuffed closets and under the bed. Then there were the nude drawings of her hanging on his walls. They too could be rolled up and stored under his bed. Likewise, the sheets they had slept in could be folded and put away. But what about the bed itself? Where could he hide that? He caught himself and realized how ridiculous the idea was. Throwing away everything that was a re-minder of her would leave him with an empty room. There had to be a simpler solution.

What if there were something that could remove the memo-ries but leave the room intact? The monks believed that the burning of incense had the power to expel evil spirits. It was late, and all the stores that sold incense were closed. Maybe there was something similar he could buy that could expunge the memo-ries, like a spray that removes unpleasant odors. Could he find that at the all-night Pakistani food store just around the corner? His mind raced. And if he couldn't, what about a magic spell? He recalled that medieval alchemists were renowned for allegedly turning base metals into noble ones. Maybe a wave of a magic wand could make the memories disappear.

He caught himself again. The whole notion was ridiculous. The truth was simple: his sanctuary had become a prison he now shared with a ghost. And he knew that when he returned to his room every night after cleaning the college, he had to face her.

As the heavy rains pounded against his windows, he stubbed out a cigarette and rolled another. He tried convincing himself that his love for Suzanne hadn't been real. But that wasn't true. He had never before told someone that he loved them.

Michael clenched his teeth, his eyes narrowing. The truth was Suzanne was just a spoiled rich girl. To her, his mystery and aloofness had been a challenge, and once she had won him, he became her plaything. And when that thrill was gone, she discarded him with no more thought than one would give a piece of used tissue paper.

As hard as he tried, he could not escape her. Every time Suzanne glided by him in the hallway at the academy, he felt weak. It was as though all the life had been sucked out of him and replaced by an aching emptiness. Sometimes he did not even have to see her. All it took was the sound of her voice above the din in the corridor or the smell of her perfume in the air for his body to start to shake. Not even his art kept frustration and grief at bay. Whether in his studio or in his flat, he stared blankly at the canvas. The brush in his hand refused to lift itself to paint.

Only at night did he feel safe at the academy. As he swept the hardwood floors of the empty corridors, moving his broom mechanically, he could hear echoes of the day—the clatter of students in the hallways, Suzanne's liquid laughter ringing in the background. He was relieved to be alone but always dreaded the next day.

Sleep came with great difficulty. As he lay in bed on his back staring up at the ceiling, he revisited every memory of Suzanne in painful detail. On those nights when he couldn't sleep at all, he got dressed and walked aimlessly around the city. He wandered along the Thames and watched the barges and boats drifting by on the tide. He meandered through parks at night in the chilly rains, oblivious to the cold and wet. After going for miles, he felt as if he had not walked at all. He continued until he was too tired to stand, and it was all he could do to stagger home and pass out fully clothed on his bed.

Whenever these nights of insomnia occurred, he would sleep through the next morning, missing classes and tutorials. By mid-afternoon he awoke. He did not change his clothes or bathe, and numbly he made himself something to eat. But instead of going to the college where he could still make an afternoon tutorial, he would go out walking again until it was time for his work shift to start.

One afternoon while he was walking in the rain, he passed a poster of a Turner painting in a shop window. He stood in the pouring rain without an umbrella, staring at it. In the past he had always found refuge in the artist's bright landscapes and radiant skies, which blazed with triumph and glory. The painting before him flared and raged with color, yet to him it was merely a picture stuffed with brilliant, swirling colors all chasing each other in a frenzied confusion. The artist who had once filled him with awe and inspiration meant nothing now. He walked on.

Michael remembered Brother Thomas telling him that whenever one felt vanquished in spirit, one should allow the body to feast. Proceeding to the nearest restaurant, Michael ordered several items. But when the food came, all he could do was stare at it. He bought some fruit from an outdoor vendor at the Berwick Street market but could neither taste the tartness of a fresh apple nor choke on the sweetness of an orange. He tasted nothing.

Dust clung to every corner of his room. Cigarettes were piled high in ashtrays, like the corpses of dead soldiers. Sheets were disheveled. Books once neatly stacked on their shelves were strewn everywhere. He had tried numerous times to clean up but could muster neither the strength nor the inspiration.

Unable to face even the prospect of bumping into Suzanne on a daily basis, he stopped attending all his classes and tutorials. One night after he finished cleaning the college, he removed every trace of himself. He collected all his books, paintbrushes, and canvases from his studio and took them home. From then on he entered the building only when he knew he would be alone.

Michael borrowed a hammer and nails from the maintenance closet at college and bought some heavy black cloth and thick black tape. He decided that he did not want to see daylight when he awoke. After applying a generous coat of glue to the frame of each of his two windows, he covered both windows with the dark cloth and nailed it to the wooden frame. Just before gluing and nailing down the last portion of cloth, he glimpsed outside. The sun bathed the entire world in a golden mantle of warmth. He could feel a breeze on his face that gently stirred the leaves on the trees. Except for a few birds and a lone cyclist, the sunlit street was quiet.

As he shut the window and quickly sealed it off, the room was plunged into darkness. He turned on the lights and trimmed the overlapping cloth around the edges of the window with a pair of scissors so that it was uniform with the frame, then taped it down.

It took a few days to adjust to the darkness that flooded his room like black ink. The sun neither rose nor fell, because all his days began and ended in darkness. Since night had become indistinguishable from day, only by his watch did he know the true hour. And knowing that, only under cover of night did he go out to work or to buy food.

Darkness befriended him. It made no demands. At long last, Michael had found the forgiveness he had been craving.

A COLLECTION of student artwork—the winners and honorable mentions from the academy's annual art competition—hung on a wall in the main foyer. Michael wondered if he would have been awarded a place here, had he submitted anything.

Studying each entrant carefully, he moved from one to the next, until he finally reached the first-place winner. It was a fragile watercolor depicting a park scene on a spring day. People sat on lawn chairs on the green grass. A woman walked a dog. The lawn was shadowed by a tree, and a partially hidden lake lured the eye off into the distance. The setting was tranquil and serene, locked in a moment of time. It was a familiar landscape.

He looked at the signature. It was Suzanne's.

His heart sank. He felt weak and leaned against the broom in his hand. He touched the cold glass that protected the watercolor and remembered the day she had painted it. That Sunday they had taken a hamper with some ham-and-cheese sandwiches on an outing to Hyde Park. Suzanne had erected her easel so that it faced the south side of the park. Michael sat on a blanket with his sketchpad, munching on an apple, and sketched the same scene. It was a simple pencil sketch he would later turn into pen and ink.

He dropped the broom and ran from the hallway as fast as his legs could carry him.

10

A FEW SOLITARY DRINKERS were scattered among the tables under a haze of blue cigarette smoke. The barman methodically dried tankards by hand. Despite the muffled sound of the downpour outside, the loud ticking of a wall clock behind the bar could be heard.

Michael did not complete his janitorial duties after seeing Suzanne's watercolor. *I'll return later,* he thought, *after I've had just a few drinks.* It would give him the courage to finish up for the night. He bought a pint of ale and sat down in a booth near the heater to keep warm. *Need to find myself a full-time job,* he thought, *away from the academy.* He cursed his own weakness, knowing he didn't have the energy to go out and seek work.

By the time the publican called closing time, Michael had knocked back six pints and four whiskies in between half a dozen cigarettes. Under the awning of the pub's front door, he stood looking out into the rain as a chill searched through his clothes for his bones. Finally, after mustering the courage, he turned his collar up and stepped into the pouring rain.

Unable to recall where the academy was, he began wandering aimlessly. Each street seemed to point the way there, every turn offered a glimmer of familiarity. In his stupor he clung to lampposts in desperate attempts to regain his equilibrium and perspective. Still, he kept losing his footing. He stumbled and fell again and again. Each time he felt the cold, wet pavement against his cheek. Each time he considered leaving himself there, but he pried himself off the ground and carried on.

Frustrated and exhausted, he turned down an alley and searched for someplace where he could rest for a while, perhaps even sleep. He spotted a portico. As he staggered toward it, his foot caught on something. There was the momentary sensation of falling, the helplessness of tumbling uncontrollably through the air. Then his head struck something cold and hard, and everything went black.

IT HAD not been a particularly busy night. The heavy rains had chased away her regular customers. As she approached the back entrance to her flat, the dull glow of the alleyway light revealed a man lying in the rain, blocking the portico steps.

Another tramp, she thought. It was happening more frequently now. At least once a fortnight she found someone, usually a drunk or a vagrant, sleeping in the doorway.

"C'mon," she said, impatient to get inside. "Time to go!"

When he failed to respond, she shouted, "Don't you have someplace to go?"

She tried to nudge him awake with her shoe, but there was no reaction. Pushing him to one side was out of the question; he was too heavy. Holding on to her umbrella, she turned him over with her free hand with some effort. A thin rivulet of dark fluid running down his forehead was quickly erased by the rain. She bent down for a closer look. It was blood.

He's dead, she thought. *Just what I bloody need.*

She thought of leaving him there. She could use the front entrance to her flat to get in. Instead, she bent down and felt his wrist. There was a pulse.

He was young, and oddly enough she found him attractive. The vagrants she booted away from the door were older, decrepit, their faces and bodies eroded by alcohol and life on the streets. Although the young man reeked of liquor, he wasn't dressed like a vagrant. She decided he was probably the victim of a mugging or a fight.

She slapped his face hard and in her heavy East End accent said, "C'mon, luv, time to wake up."

It had no effect.

Sheltering in the portico, she lit a cigarette. She stubbed it out on his hand and heard the sizzle as it made contact with his wet flesh.

Still nothing.

She stepped over him and unlocked the back door, then disappeared into the building. A few minutes later she returned with a bottle of liquid ammonia and a hand towel. She unscrewed the lid, pressed the towel to the open nozzle, and turned the bottle upside down, dousing the towel. She stuck the towel underneath Michael's nose. Coughing and hacking, Michael was jolted back into consciousness. She helped him sit up. "Just relax a moment," she said.

He looked around, dazed, and instinctively raised a hand to where the concrete had met his forehead.

"Take hold of my arm," she said.

Slowly she helped him up. He reeked of alcohol. "Careful, now," she said. "We're going upstairs."

Unsteady on his feet, step by step Michael struggled up the stairs. Relieved to be out of the rain, he passed out on the floor of her flat the instant he felt carpeting beneath his feet.

Wasting no time, she swiftly dressed and bandaged the wound on his forehead and plugged his bloody nostril with tissue. She undressed him where he lay and toweled him off, then wrapped a blanket around his naked body and positioned a pillow under his head. After hanging his rain-soaked clothes to dry over the chairs in her kitchen, she checked on him one more time before going to bed.

THE BRIGHTNESS of the sun streamed through the windows and woke Michael. Shielding his eyes from the blinding glare, he looked around. He did not know where he was. A strange woman in a pink bathrobe and a white towel wrapped around her head stood over him.

"Feeling better?" she asked.

"Feel . . . terrible," Michael croaked.

"Sit up," she commanded. With her help he sat up slowly. Suddenly he grabbed his head as a searing pain sliced through it. He groaned, his face screwing up in agony.

"Here," the woman said, "give me your hand." She dropped two pills into his palm.

"What are they?" he said, his eyes closed.

"Aspirin."

He popped the pills into his mouth. Placing a glass of water in his hand, she guided it to his lips. He sipped the water and swallowed the pills with great effort, then handed the glass back. He sank down to the floor and fell asleep again.

DOMINIC WAS hunting everywhere for two medicines. After combing through his shelves, he recalled that Steven had collected these recently but probably stored them in a place in their shared laboratory where Dominic wouldn't think to look. Steven's own filing system, of a sort.

Dominic went in search of Steven and found him kneeling on a rug in a corner of the garden, digging the soil with a trowel. He handed him a mug of cool lemonade.

Steven stopped what he was doing and rose to his feet. He retrieved a handkerchief from his pocket and brushed the dirt from his habit, then wiped the sweat from his brow.

"Come, walk with me," Dominic said.

He took Steven's arm. They walked the gravel path to the corner of the garden and sat on a bench under their favorite linden tree. In the shade they sat, admiring the garden. A cloudless blue sky hung above them. Intermittent patches of bright sunlight broke through the trees, signaling the coming of spring.

"Something is preying on you," said Dominic.

Steven looked at his father quizzically.

"Your excessive gardening is betraying you."

Steven looked down at his lemonade.

"It's Michael, isn't it?" Dominic said.

Steven said nothing.

"You miss him, don't you?"

"Yes, Father," Steven said, "I do."

"Very much?"

Steven nodded.

"You loved him, didn't you?"

Steven took a sip of lemonade. "I never told you."

"You didn't have to. What happened?"

"I'm afraid it might shock you."

Dominic chuckled. "Nothing shocks these old bones any longer."

Breaking his silence, Steven told him how he and Michael became friends, and about that fateful night that led to their division. After he finished, he felt much lighter.

"Michael's path has been troubled," said Dominic. "I have a feeling he will return here someday and ask us for help. Should he ever do so, you must help him."

Steven looked at Dominic, accepting his demand.

"You asked me once if I was ever in love," Dominic said. "Do you recall?"

"Yes, Father."

"I'll give you my answer now. Not only was I in love, but I was married."

"You were married?" Steven said.

"Very happily. Rachel was everything to me. She was pregnant with our child. Toward the end of her term she developed influenza. It turned into pneumonia. She and the baby died in childbirth."

Dominic focused his tear-filled eyes on a spot in the distance. "Maybe I could have saved them both. Who knows? She should have recovered, but she didn't. Complications stemming from that, I think. She was so young." He paused. "And so it was my grief that brought me to these doors. Here I discovered my calling as a doctor. I was powerless to save my wife and child. Perhaps I could save others."

"Why didn't you remarry?" Steven said.

Dominic looked straight into his son's eyes. "No one could ever replace her, that's why."

From the folds of his habit, Dominic produced a bread roll. Silently he opened Steven's hand and closed his fingers around it.

"There are those," Dominic said, "who have never known love. Feel lucky that you have."

MICHAEL BECAME aware of the distinct scent of perfume swelling around him. It was not Suzanne's. Opening his eyes, he saw the same young woman from before. Michael noticed her slender face and dark blue eyes. This time her hair was done up, and she wore heavy eye makeup and red lipstick.

"Where am I?" he groaned.

"In my flat," she said.

"Where?"

"Kensington."

"Who are you?"

"Amanda. Amanda Lerner. What's your name?"

"Michael Warren. How did I get here?"

"I found you," she said. "You were passed out in the rain last night just outside, near the steps. You've got a nasty bump on your head. You must have fallen hard. Been asleep all day, I'm afraid."

Lightning-bolt recollections of what had happened the night before flashed through his mind. "Thank you," he whispered hoarsely.

"How does your head feel?"

Michael rubbed his forehead. "The pain's gone," he said.

"Good. I'll fix you something to eat."

She put a white bathrobe around him and helped him thread his arms through the sleeves. It was far too small, but Michael was too weak to be embarrassed. She helped him to the kitchen and sat him down at the table.

Within a few minutes she served him a plate of two fried eggs, two slices of toast, and fresh brewed coffee. Sitting across from him, she watched as he slowly ate in silence. When he had finished, she removed the dishes and put them in the sink.

"You've got to leave now," she said. "I'm headed off to work."

He drained the last of his coffee and eased himself uncomfortably into his dry clothes. "Thank you," he said again.

Unsteadily he worked his way down the stairs, clinging to the railing. It was dark when he stepped outside. He was relieved that it wasn't raining. Feet heavy as lead, he made his way into the night, sober this time.

MICHAEL WOKE up the next morning in his own bed. He wanted someone to talk to, but he was alone. He tried doing normal things like cleaning up his bed-sit, but he could not muster the inspiration. Everything became a chore. After an hour's deliberation, he decided to go back and visit the strange woman who had helped him.

Walking the streets, he tried to remember where she lived. He had not paid much attention when he made his way home the evening before. Determined, he went on a hunt for her flat. After two hours of searching and retracing his steps, he stood under the portico of a familiar doorway in the alley. But there was no doorbell.

He went around to the front of the building. There were four buttons to the right of the front door, two above and two below, with a surname next to each one. Michael knew the woman lived on the second floor. He rang the top right-hand button, with the label Lerner.

Footsteps could be heard coming down the stairs. The door opened just enough so that he could see a face. It was the young lady, wearing a dressing gown.

"I need to talk," he said after an awkward pause.

Amanda stood in contemplation for a moment, then swung the door open.

"I want to thank you again," he said when they were in her flat. "You probably saved my life."

"You'd do the same for me," she said. "Hungry?"

Michael nodded.

"Come sit down in the kitchen."

Amanda cooked him the same breakfast as the day before. Again, she deliberately did not make conversation with him while he ate.

He's good-looking, she thought. She could not put her finger on it, but there was something about him that was different. She had developed an instinct about men. Without knowing why, she felt sorry for him. He brought out the caring side in her, a nurturing instinct. Usually whenever that instinct raised its ugly head, she quickly fought it back down with her hard side.

After breakfast they sat on the floor in the sitting room and Michael rambled on aimlessly. He let everything spill out.

Previously he had always been cautious about revealing the details of his life. But Amanda was a total stranger. He felt he could unburden himself to someone who knew nothing about him.

Amanda listened quietly. At one point she excused herself and returned a minute later carrying a homemade water pipe resembling something out of a chemistry lab. A small metal bowl of water sat on a long stem attached to a glass reservoir. She unwrapped a tiny square of foil and removed what looked like a small piece of chocolate, which she placed in the bowl.

Putting the pipe's mouthpiece between her lips, she lit a match. Carefully she held its flame directly under the little square as she puffed. With each breath the square glowed hot shades of orange. The water in the bowl gurgled to life as smoke circulated inside the glass tubes and filtered through the water. Michael found the sound hypnotic, like a waterfall.

Once the pipe was well lit, she handed the mouthpiece to Michael.

"What is it?" he said.

"Just try it."

Michael hesitated.

"Quick," she said, "before it goes out."

He inserted the mouthpiece.

"Now draw in slowly," she said. "Hold it in your lungs for as long as possible. Then exhale."

Michael inhaled the smoke. He held it for as long as he could, then slowly released it. Unlike cigarette tobacco, which tasted harsh and abrasive, this was soothing and mild. He surmised that the water acted as a distiller, filtering out the acrid fumes.

After a moment he felt light headed. Michael became giggly, laughing constantly for no apparent reason. He lost all concept of time as he and Amanda talked and laughed for hours. When Amanda announced that she had to go to work, Michael was astonished.

It was night when he left her flat. He walked directly to the academy to clean the studios. The euphoria lasted long into the evening. He coasted through his cleaning duties without a care in the world. He even looked at Suzanne's prize-winning watercolor and felt nothing. When Michael returned to his flat, he tore down the black cloth that had covered his windows for weeks.

DAYS AWAY from entering the novitiate—the intensive preparation for becoming a monk—Steven felt he was ready to devote himself to God. Although he wondered from time to time how Michael was doing, and prayed for him daily, his love for his old friend had mellowed.

He did like to test himself, however. One beautiful afternoon, Steven stopped his gardening and let his feet march him down to the stream. After some searching in the high overgrowth, he found the cord, still tied around the tree trunk. The other end disappeared into the water. When he pulled it up, there was another surprise. Although the body of the bottle had broken off long ago, the dark green neck was still intact.

Another time, late at night, he removed a large cardboard envelope from under his bed. He opened it over his bed, and Michael's drawings and watercolors spilled out. Steven looked at each one. It had been a long time since he had seen them. But the moment he felt a lump in his throat, he quickly gathered them up, funneled them back into the envelope, and returned them under his bed.

Both times, Steven regained his composure by taking a deep breath and waiting for the torrent of feelings to pass. Both times, it did.

11

THE DAYLIGHT COMING THROUGH the window was overpowering. Stretching from sleep, Michael put his hand up against the brightness. It didn't help much. Eyes half closed, he slid into his dressing gown and went downstairs to the kitchen to make himself a cup of coffee and some toast. Then he dressed and walked to his new friend's flat.

This time there was no hesitation on Amanda's part when she opened the door and saw Michael standing there. She let him in without a word. Locking the apartment door behind them, she said, "When you come to visit, use the side entrance."

"Why?"

"Because I've got busybody neighbors. It's none of their bloody business who my guests are."

They sat on the carpet in the sitting room and partook of the strange pipe.

"I've added opium to the hash," Amanda said. "It should be nice."

Although Michael had heard those names before, they meant nothing to him. As he drew in more and more of the fumes, the mild, tranquil high they produced became a sedative, shielding him from all worries and ills. It magically transported him to a land free of heartache. He closed his eyes and felt like he was floating in a warm tub of water. Instead of laughter, he entered a deep meditative state, akin to the awe and wonder of a profound religious experience.

Michael opened his eyes and looked at Amanda. She was older than he was, Michael guessed, by about four years. She was his height, with long, straight jet-black hair and sapphire-blue eyes. Her high cheekbones framed two perfect rows of the whitest teeth he had ever seen. Her body was athletic. He found her attractive.

She caught him looking at her. "You don't have any money, do you?" she said.

"Money?"

"Yes."

"For what?"

"Normally I don't do this," Amanda said.

"Do what?"

"I'll be right back."

A few moments later she stood before him naked. Taking him by the hand, she led him into her bedroom. She lowered him onto the bed and without a word slowly undressed him. Michael did not resist. She leaned over and kissed him, then guided her tongue in an S shape down his chest. She licked his nipples in tiny circles as her soft hair brushed his chest. Moving down, she flicked her tongue along his inner thighs. Suddenly, wordlessly, she lowered her lips onto him. She ran the tip of her tongue around him until he became rock hard, his member wet and glistening.

Using her saliva, she moistened a suppository and inserted it into Michael as she continued to hold him in her mouth. Then she released her hold and straddled him. He slid into her effort-lessly. She rode him wildly, the violent motion rocking the bed from side to side. Within a few minutes Michael felt her tightening around him. He stiffened. Unable to hold himself back, his body jerked and writhed suddenly of its own accord.

She collapsed on top of him in a heap of joyful exhaustion, sheets drenched in perspiration and sexual juices. They drifted off to sleep.

Later, Amanda awoke with a start. Jolted from her cocoon of sleep, she looked toward the window. It was dark outside. The clock by her bed read 7:00 p.m.

Carefully she pried herself from Michael, slithered out of the sheets, and went into the bathroom, where she bathed and meticulously applied her makeup. Then she threw on some clothes.

She wrote a note and left it on the nightstand for Michael, who was curled up in the bed. She smiled. For the first time in a long while, she felt happy.

MICHAEL EVENTUALLY roused himself from sleep and saw the note Amanda had written saying she had gone to work. He struggled to get into his shirt and underwear, then shuffled into the kitchen, where he made himself a cup of coffee with teaspoonfuls of sugar and a dash of cream he found in the fridge. He sat down at the wooden kitchen table and lit a cigarette. He did not bother to put on the light. Although it was night, the orange-yellow wash of the alley lights below reflected off the white walls and ceiling of the kitchen.

As he stared out the window sipping his coffee, his stomach suddenly tightened. He rushed to the bathroom and doubled over the toilet. He vomited over and over again, feeling as though his insides would come out. As soon as one spasm passed, another would arrive. He vomited until there was nothing left. Even then, the dry heaves continued.

Sweat instantly broke out all over his body. Hot liquid mucus streamed from his nostrils. His head felt like it was on fire. The hot, feverish sweat beaded up icy cold on his forehead. His skin turned clammy. He began shivering uncontrollably, and his breathing became shallow and irregular. His body lost all its strength.

Clutching his stomach, he curled up on the floor next to the toilet. Finally, when the pain became too much, he passed out.

AMANDA FOUND Michael on the bathroom floor, his face as white as a sheet. Immediately she knew what had happened. Instead of violently shaking him back to consciousness, she retrieved a blanket and a pillow from the bed. She wrapped the blanket around him and positioned the pillow under his head.

For several hours she sat by his huddled body as it rained sweat and shivered with cold. She dampened a towel with cool water and dabbed his burning forehead and face. Dark yellow circles were etched under his eyes. She knew the signs only too well. She had been there herself.

When he regained consciousness, Amanda helped him to the bed. He flopped down on the mattress and she pulled the covers over him. Still shivering, he curled up in the fetal position and quickly fell asleep.

The following morning when he opened his eyes, Amanda was sitting next to the bed, watching over him. "How are you feeling?" she said.

"My head feels like a train rolled over it."

"I've just the thing." She left and returned moments later with a glass of water and two aspirins. "This will fix you up," she said.

She sat him up. Michael downed the pills and drained the glass of water. "What happened?" he asked in a low, hoarse whisper.

"You got sick."

"Sick?"

"Yes."

"From what?"

"From the drug."

A puzzled expression swept across Michael's face. "What drug?"

"Don't you remember?"

"No."

"I put something in you. You don't recall?"

"No."

"What do you recall?"

Michael smiled. "Having sex."

"How was it?"

"Wonderful," he whispered.

"That was the drug."

"It was?"

Michael closed his eyes and fell back to sleep.

AMANDA'S KITCHEN came alive with the sounds of cooking. The clanging of pots and pans mingled with the strains of classical music floating softly from a small wireless in another room.

No sooner had Michael opened his eyes than Amanda appeared, carrying a tray that she placed in front of him. He looked down at the breakfast of eggs, toast, sausages, orange juice, and freshly ground coffee. Closing his eyes, he brought his face close to the food, letting its aroma wash over him. Some of the smells reminded him of the monastery. Then, as if he had finished a silent prayer, Michael opened his eyes and devoured everything on the tray, as though he had not eaten in days.

Amanda pulled up a chair near the bed and watched in silent satisfaction. When he finished, she transported the tray back to the kitchen and sat down beside him on the bed. Michael took a cigarette from a cigarette holder on the nightstand. He lit it and sucked in the smoke.

Amanda realized he had forgotten their earlier conversation. "You had a minor overdose," she said.

"From what?"

She paused. "Milk of Paradise."

"I've never heard of that before," he said.

"Don't you recall yesterday? I put something up you?"

Michael shook his head.

"Well, anyway, it's slang. An expression. Its real name is heroin."

He stared at her in shock. "You mean the drug?"

"Yes, that's right. Your reaction was a bit extreme, but it's always difficult the first time. It's all part of your body rejecting the drug before accepting it. In severe cases such as yours, you experience violent illness, mostly in the form of nausea and vomiting. Diarrhea too. But after you're over that hump, it's all smooth sailing."

Michael sat in stunned silence. He was appalled. Never before had he felt so violated. He threw himself out of bed and jumped to his feet. "Why did you do that?" he growled.

Amanda skittered back across the bed, afraid. "Because I wanted you to feel the same way I do. And you did. You admitted it. Getting sick the first few times is all part of it."

He looked at her with cold eyes. "You cunt! Never do that to me again, do you understand?"

Hurriedly he dressed and stormed out, slamming the door behind him.

DESPITE THE sting of Amanda's betrayal of his trust, Michael found he could not stay away. Visiting her became a ritual. He would come to her flat in the late morning, and they would make love. Amanda was fluent in the Kama Sutra and other Eastern practices of lovemaking. Every morning she would show Michael a different sexual position.

Before he left for work in the early evening, she would make him a hashish cigarette to take with him. Michael watched as she took a razor blade and, with the skill of a surgeon, cut open a cigarette. She then carefully transferred the tobacco into a cigarette roller. She broke off a piece of hashish from a larger square of the drug and sprinkled the crumbs over the tobacco. After inserting a fresh cigarette paper into the roller, she licked it and, with the rolling machine, rolled up the cigarette. Then she wrapped it in tissue and gave it to Michael.

"Remember," she said. "The key is to inhale deeply and hold it. If you smoke it like a normal cigarette, you'll waste it."

Michael smoked it as he cleaned the academy. With it, the hours floated by. As an added bonus, the drug created a childlike magic. If he saved some of it to smoke in the morning, he would walk dazedly through the city, wandering in and out of museums. One benefit of working at night was that he could visit museums during the day. He was still an art lover but no longer felt the desire to paint. The drug turned the mundane into the sublime. He would also be seized by laughing convulsions that sometimes lasted minutes. On one occasion in a museum, he fell into such a fit of uncontrollable laughter that a guard asked him to leave. The drug also made him hungry. After wandering the streets for hours, he would inevitably become ravenous. He would sit down at a café and eagerly devour twice the amount he normally ate when he was sober. In the past, as a result of his grief, his thinking had been muddled and confused. The drug restored a clarity to his mind, which Michael knew was a good thing.

Amanda introduced him to a circus of drugs. One day they smoked pure opium from Thailand; the next she made a delicious chocolate cake decorated with peyote buttons.

"Peyote is a powerful, hallucinogenic Mexican mushroom," she said.

"What does that mean?"

"You see things, that's all."

First they smoked hashish. Soon Michael became hungry. She cut him a slice of cake and one for herself. They shared a glass of milk.

Afterward Michael lay down on the carpet and stared at the ceiling. Within a few minutes he heard beautiful, exotic music, a miraculous choir coming from everywhere and nowhere. The toxic melodies carried him off into another world.

By NOON the powerful rays of the midday sun slanted through the stained-glass windows on the abbey's east side, casting their illustrations onto the stone floor. Steven lay at the foot of the altar, his forehead resting on the floor, arms extended out to his sides, body formed in the shape of a crucifix. On either side of him stood a row of nine monks, with the abbot standing at Steven's head. Steven wore the white robe of the novitiate and prostrated himself in front of his abbot.

Thomas affectionately placed his arm around Dominic's waist, smiling as he fondly remembered the day his friend had transported the infant Steven, in his wicker basket, into their lives. Dominic removed a handkerchief from the pocket of his habit and dabbed his eyes.

For more than an hour Steven was not allowed to move as the monks recited plainchant over him. He was uncomfortable and wanted to adjust his position but was not allowed to. He became increasingly aware of the incense filling the room. When the chanting stopped, Steven rose to his feet in front of his abbot. Slowly he removed the white robe and let it drop to the floor, revealing his naked body. He then knelt to receive the folded, coffee-colored habit of his order from his abbot. Steven rose again and methodically put it on. As was part of the ceremony, Steven turned around to face the others.

"You are now Brother Steven St. Francis," said the abbot. "We welcome you as one of our own."

One by one, each of the monks came up and embraced Steven. Only Dominic and Thomas each held the boy in his arms as a father would and kissed him on the cheek.

After the ceremony everyone filed into the refectory. The long table was dressed with a freshly laundered white linen table-cloth and filled with a feast reserved only for Christmas. Thomas, Ignatius, and Matthew had begun their kitchen preparations at three o'clock that morning. A dozen loaves of fresh bread had been baked. Pheasant and wild duck had been cooked. Even Steven's favorite split pea soup and mashed potatoes were on the menu. The three monks wanted to make sure that this would be a day everyone would remember.

MICHAEL SAID good-bye to Amanda.

The summer afternoon was hot, and Michael decided to walk home by a different route. Threading his way through the tiny backstreets and alleys where Amanda lived, he finally emerged onto Piccadilly Circus. At five thirty, rush-hour traffic choked the city. Streets swelled with impatient commuters. He wove through the great press of anxious people hurrying home and crossed into Green Park to avoid the crowds.

It had been a while since he had walked through the park. He couldn't help but look for the tree he had inscribed when he was with Suzanne. Finding it, he ran his hand over the inscription. It was still rough and sappy, as though it had been carved a few days ago instead of half a year. In an instant he began regretting his action.

Michael hurried home as though pursued by an invisible as-sailant. He visualized the tin containing the hashish cigarettes he had stored behind a row of books on his shelf. When he got home and opened it, however, it was empty. He could not recall having smoked them all, yet the empty container did not lie.

He knew he would be late for work, but he couldn't help himself. He took the bus back to Amanda's flat. He jabbed the doorbell again and again, but there was no answer. Michael guessed she had already left for work. Locating the spare key under the planter outside her front door, he let himself in.

He rushed into her bedroom, trying to figure out where she kept her drugs. A good place to start was the chest of drawers, he decided. He yanked them out and rifled through each one, running his hands back and forth through the sea of garments, flipping over shirts, squeezing sweaters, feeling every corner of silk hose. In the fourth drawer he felt something square and hard. When he pushed aside the underwear, he found a wooden box.

Without bothering to close the drawers, he took the box into the living room and set it on the floor. He opened it and found a small square of foil in one of its compartments. Michael unwrapped the foil, broke off a piece of the dark brown hash inside, and placed it in the water pipe. He lit it and inhaled deeply. The drug filtered smoothly through the bubbling water and down into his lungs.

He waited. Entire minutes passed. Nothing happened. His anxiety was still present.

Michael was growing desperate. In the same box he found a syringe, a frayed silk stocking, a spoon, matches, and a brown paper bag. He opened up the paper bag and looked inside. There were three suppositories and some kind of mold. He remembered how much of a rush he got from the suppository Amanda had put up him. But he also recalled how sick he became afterward. At that moment, though, he did not care.

He took the brown paper bag into the bathroom and set it on the counter. He undid his pants and let them drop to the floor. Removing a suppository from the bag, he tried forcing it up himself, but it was too difficult. Frantically he pulled up his pants and hurried into the kitchen, where he opened several cupboards until he found a bottle of olive oil. He greased the suppository with the oil and put the bottle back in the cupboard. Returning to the bathroom, he dropped his pants, bent over the sink, and inserted the suppository. He was surprised at how easily it slipped in. Uncertain that one was enough to do the job, he went back into the kitchen, oiled a second one, and inserted it as well. Then he pulled up his pants, went into the bedroom, and flopped down on the bed.

Within a few minutes a calm invaded every part of his body as though he was immersed in a warm bath. He closed his eyes. In his mind he ran carefree through the field behind the monastery. He heard music, a chorus of plainchant. He wanted to sing along but could not muster the energy, so instead he just listened.

Michael felt happy.

WHEN AMANDA came home at 3:00 a.m., she saw her bathroom light was on—odd, because normally she left only the kitchen light on. She stepped cautiously into the sitting room and found her works box open on the floor.

Amanda bolted into the bedroom. Throwing on the light, she discovered Michael fully clothed on the bed. She rushed into the bathroom and spotted the open paper bag with only one suppository in it. She tried shaking Michael awake, then slapping him, but in vain.

"Hang on," she said, putting her lips to his ear. "You'll be alright."

Sobbing, Amanda sat at Michael's feet in the back of the ambulance as she watched a paramedic hold an oxygen mask over his face. When they reached the hospital, Michael disappeared on a gurney that sped through swinging doors into the emergency room.

A portly nurse in a starched, white uniform approached Amanda. "Sorry, luv," she said. "You have to stay outside." She held a clipboard in front of Amanda. "You'll need to fill these out."

Amanda took the clipboard to the waiting room and sat down. She glanced at it. It was an admittance form asking for Michael's medical history. When she had finished guessing, she handed the clipboard back. The nurse escorted her to a small office. "Wait here," she said, closing the door behind her.

Amanda sat down in a chair in front of the desk and glanced around the room. There were several bulletin boards, each with bits of paper pinned to them.

A few minutes later a tall uniformed police officer entered, carrying a file under his arm. Without a word he sat down behind the desk. He took his cap off, placed it on the desk, and opened the file.

"Miss Lerner, is it?" the officer said.

"Yes."

"What is your relationship to the patient?"

"He's a friend."

The officer jotted something down in the file. Then he asked for Michael's place of birth, his parents' names, where his family lived, and his current address. The only answers she provided were his name and her phone number.

"What's all this for?" Amanda said.

Without looking up from what he was writing, the officer said, "Drug overdoses are automatically reported to the police. He then becomes a registered addict, and we have a record of it."

This was the first she had heard about the police being called in to interview overdose cases. "But he's not an addict," she said.

He looked up. "If he wasn't, Miss, he wouldn't be here now, would he? Do you know where he acquired the drug?"

Amanda became wary. "I've no idea," she said. "I've never known him to do drugs before."

"Do you use drugs, Miss Lerner?"

"No."

"Have you ever tried drugs before?"

"Never."

There was a moment of silence as he wrote. When he finished, he looked at Amanda and said, "We may need to speak with you again in a few days' time. Thank you for your cooperation."

Amanda sat in the waiting room fidgeting. A white-smocked physician approached her. He wore a stethoscope around his neck and his hair was graying around the temples.

"Miss Lerner?" he said, sitting down next to her.

"Yes," said Amanda hesitantly.

"Mr. Warren will be fine. We'll need to keep him under observation for a few days, then he can go home."

"When can I see him?" Amanda said.

"Tomorrow," said the doctor. He smiled and patted Amanda on the hand, then got up and walked away.

Amanda walked home along quiet streets, relieved. She put her hands in her pockets. The brisk night air brushed against her cheeks.

Who was this mysterious stranger she had adopted so easily? A con man? An escaped criminal? A fugitive on the run?

It was 5:00 a.m. when she arrived at her flat. Tired, she climbed the stairs and did not bother cleaning up the mess Michael had made.

12

STEVEN WAS IN THE garden on his hands and knees, weeding with a trowel. It was fall, and though shaded by a tree he still mopped the sweat from his forehead with a handkerchief and brushed the flies from his face.

Brother Andrew came rushing up. "Come quickly," he said.

"Why?" said Steven. "What's the matter?"

"It's Dominic. There's something the matter with Dominic."

Steven dropped his trowel and hurried behind the monk until they reached the laboratory. Thomas stood anxiously at the door. Inside, Dominic lay facedown on the stone floor, motionless. Steven turned him over and felt his father's wrist for any sign of a pulse. Pressing an ear against Dominic's chest, he strained to hear a heartbeat, but it was as soundless as an owl's flight.

Frantically he began pushing violently on Dominic's chest with both hands.

"Father! Father!" Steven yelled. "Please, Father! Don't die!"

Thomas and Andrew pulled him off, but Steven broke free and clung to Dominic's body. He buried his face in his father's chest, weeping uncontrollably.

STEVEN COULD not bring himself to attend the funeral or burial. Instead, he showered Dominic's empty bed in a blanket of white rose petals he had collected from the garden in the same wicker basket his father had carried him in as an infant. Then he locked himself in Dominic's room and placed the key on the mantel. He remained there for two days while the bells sounded for prayers, offices, and meals, studying the cell that had belonged to the simple apothecary monk. He gazed at the portrait of St. Francis that hung on the wall and at the wooden kneeler at the foot of the bed, cushioned and covered in exquisite purple linen with a simple white cross embroidered in the middle, that Brother Gregory had made for him as a birthday gift. It was hardly worn. Dominic had spent more time praying on the stone floor than on his comfortable kneeler.

Steven painfully recalled the night of his father's secret confession. A few days before his ninth birthday, curious as to why he had a father but no mother, he had asked Dominic who his mother was. Years earlier, all the monks had agreed that the truth was to remain a secret until Steven was old enough to be told. They also had agreed it would be Dominic who would tell him.

That evening Dominic came to Steven's room just before midnight and gently caressed his son until he awoke. "Get dressed," he said. "I've something to tell you."

They walked outside the abbey to where the fields began. Not a cloud obstructed the dark sky. The bright disc of a full moon floated above them, obscuring the stars and covering everything in a mantle of light that made the fields shimmer like a glassy lake. Steven could pick out all the details of his surroundings.

"When you were little," Dominic said, "I held you up to this same sky and prayed you would find happiness with us. But I didn't bring you out here now to speak of that. I brought you here to tell you something else."

Steven felt Dominic's hand slide into his.

"I am not your real father," Dominic said. "I found you in this field when you were an infant. You have a father and a mother somewhere, but we never found them."

Steven was struck silent. Minutes passed. Then he said, "Does that mean you don't love me?"

Dominic bent down and looked steadily into Steven's searching eyes. "Don't ever think that I don't love you. Ever. Your parents abandoned you. I never will. Until the last breath has expired from these lungs, I will always love you."

He took Steven in his arms and held him wordlessly for a very long time. Then father and son turned around and walked back into the monastery.

The day before Dominic's death, they were sitting in the garden, under the shade of their favorite tree.

"Are you still angry with me for burning Michael's drawings?" Dominic said.

Steven was surprised by the suddenness of Dominic's question. He was slow to answer. "No."

"Do you think what I did was wrong?"

From the tone of Dominic's voice, Steven could tell that his father had wrestled with his conscience over this matter.

"I do not fully agree with what you did," Steven said. "What I do realize now is that you were only trying to protect him."

Dominic turned to Steven and put a hand on his cheek. Steven saw his old, tired eyes grow moist.

"You have grown up," Dominic said. "Oftentimes we do not see clearly what our path is. There was much about Michael that opened every one of us up to questions. I know that in some ways you are still struggling with your faith. You can decide these things for yourself. And you will. All in all, you must listen to your heart. I want you to know that you have been the source of my life's greatest happiness."

Steven lit a fire in Dominic's fireplace. He took the Bible that sat on the table by the bed, opened it, and page by page fed it to the flames. When that was done, he removed the wooden crucifix from the wall above the bed and did the same. Now he knew what anger at God was.

Steven went to his own cell. He removed the habit from his body and put on the overalls he used for gardening. Then he went in search of the abbot and handed him the brown robe. "I cannot stay here any longer," he said. "I'm not fit for this. I can't be expected to believe in anything any longer. Forgive me."

"You need a break," said the abbot. "I think I know just the thing. I'll phone Dr. Cotter in the village and ask if he could use an assistant."

THE ONLY monk Steven said good-bye to was Thomas, whom he found in the kitchen.

"I'm leaving," Steven said.

Thomas wiped his hands on his apron. "What do you mean?"

"I'm leaving the monastery."

"For good?"

Steven was silent.

"Where will you go?"

"The abbot has secured me a position with Dr. Cotter in the village. I'm to be his assistant."

"Is this permanent, then?"

Steven nodded, and Thomas gave him a warm embrace. "If you need anything at all, let me know."

DR. COTTER was a tall, affable man who was liked by everyone in the village. He set upon Steven the tasks of cataloging and ordering medicine, organizing the medical supplies, and keeping his records up to date. Steven learned a great deal from this tireless man who listened carefully to his patients' complaints.

Steven lived in the home of the doctor and his wife, Margaret, who was every bit as approachable as her husband. He found Mrs. Cotter endearing in the same way he found Brother Thomas. She always made sure Steven had everything he needed and prepared wonderful meals that often made him homesick. From Brother Thomas, Steven received weekly letters filling him in on all the news at the cloister. Steven looked forward to receiving the familiar envelopes written in the monk's bold handwriting.

AFTER TWO days in the hospital, Michael was glad when Amanda came to collect him. He was worried that he had embarrassed and humiliated her so much that she never wanted anything to do with him again.

On the bus ride to her flat they said nothing. It was only after Michael eagerly devoured the steak and chips Amanda cooked for him when they got home that Amanda broke the silence. "The police know."

"I know," said Michael, regret registering in his voice. "I was hoping you wouldn't find out. They interviewed me in the hospital."

"You haven't been truthful with me," Amanda said. "I deserve to know everything, from the beginning. Something upset you to make you do this."

Nothing was lost in his story. Michael painted for Amanda a vivid picture of a boy orphaned at an early age, his life at the monastery, his burning passion for art, his admission to the academy, and the promise of a bright future. He told her of Suzanne and his subsequent derailment from life. He told her of finding the tree with the inscription, and the avalanche of memories it triggered.

Aside from Steven, he had never told anyone about his past. Now that it was revealed, he felt naked and vulnerable, no longer protected.

"My intention was to annihilate the pain, not myself," he said.

Amanda locked her arms around him and was grateful he was alive.

STEVEN HAD been gone from the monastery nearly two months when he received a surprise visit from Brother Thomas. The two relaxed on the sofa in front of the fireplace in the Cotters' tiny living room. The doctor and his wife were out.

"You need to see something," Thomas said.

"Where?"

"Back at the cloister."

"Is something wrong?"

"No. But I think you should see this."

Steven knew Thomas would not have come if it was not important. The two took a taxi back to the cloister. Thomas led Steven by the hand to Dominic's laboratory. When they got to the door, Steven hesitated.

"I'm not ready to go in," he said.

Since Dominic's death, his laboratory and his greenhouse were the two places Steven wanted to avoid.

"I know," Thomas said in his thick Welsh accent. "But you need to see this. I'm here. Don't worry. It's alright."

Thomas opened the door and walked through first. Steven followed and was immediately struck by the reminders of Dominic's devotion to his work, the books and notes on the table left just as they were at the time of his death. Steven had instructed that nothing be touched except the medicines. Sick friars still needed medication.

Steven could picture Dominic standing in the middle of his laboratory. "I have so many wonderful medicines here," he used to say. Yet in the end, neither they nor his knowledge could prevent his untimely death.

It was winter, and snow blanketed the ground outside. But inside Dominic's laboratory, every flower and plant bloomed as if it were spring. The room was filled with the most wondrous scents and smells, giving off a symphony of intoxicating, seductive perfumes and fragrances that overpowered Steven.

"This is unusual," Steven said. "Have you been watering them?"

"I have," said Thomas. "But I've never—"

"It's the same in the greenhouse?"

"Yes." The monk placed a hand on Steven's shoulder. "I think it's Dominic. He's trying to tell you that he's alright."

Steven was stunned. Then he said suddenly, "I need some bread."

They went into the kitchen, where Thomas gave him half a loaf. Steven tore it into pieces and stuffed it into his pockets. He dashed out the back of the monastery and into the snow. Making his way to the water's edge, he removed the bread from his pockets. He shredded it into crumbs and held it out in his palms. As if summoned by some magic bell, the birds came, first in pairs, then in flocks.

From that moment on Steven knew he belonged at the monastery.

WHILE STEVEN was working in the village, Brother Lawrence stripped Dominic's cell, leaving the laboratory untouched according to Steven's wishes. Lifting the mattress, Lawrence found three leather-bound volumes wrapped in a protective cloth lying neatly side by side on the bedsprings. The dull brown leather books, whose pages numbered exactly one hundred each, were filled with handwritten text. Of his discovery Lawrence told no one, and upon Steven's return he gave the books to him.

That evening Steven examined them. After reading a portion of the text, Steven paused in a moment of conflict. It was evident that these were not notes on medicine or medical practice, but the private notes and inner soul searchings of a monk. The practice of diary writing, of recording one's thoughts and emotions, translated into material possession, which constituted a breach of the rule's order of poverty. Every monk had taken that vow. The material world no longer belonged to them; neither did their own lives, their thoughts, or their feelings. All were deemed the monastery's exclusive property, and no individual had the right to own or record them in any fashion.

Although forbidden, diaries were not uncommon. For centuries, in the quiet hours past midnight, monks scribbled their secrets in their cells by candlelight and kept them hidden under mattresses or in secret recesses. Decades earlier a journal, penned by a long-departed monk at the turn of the century, had been found wrapped in cloth and stuffed into a crevice in the brick wall of a cell. It had been concealed by a loose brick. But neither the abbot's wrath nor the breaking of the abbey's code was enough to deter the determined few. Dominic was astute enough to know that one day his journals would be discovered.

Steven was reminded of how Dominic had treated Michael's artwork. He could, without further delay, obediently bring the diaries to the abbot's attention without reviewing them himself. That would mean the risk of never knowing what was in those volumes, for there was every chance that the abbot would destroy them, as Dominic destroyed Michael's works to protect him from harm.

In the end, Steven decided against handing them over to the abbot. After all, they were the words of his father, and he had every right to know what was inside the mind of the man who had found him and raised him.

Alone in his cell, Steven opened the first volume and saw Dominic's distinctive handwriting in faded blue ink. His hands trembled as he held the journal that the monk had secretly kept from prying eyes. The entries began shortly after Dominic's arrival at the monastery. They spoke of a lonely man struggling to find himself within the rigid structure of this new social order. It was then Steven realized he was not the only one to have doubts about his calling.

STEVEN WENT to work in the laboratory every day. When something gnawed at him, he would sit down in Dominic's chair. The shifting daylight slanted through the large bay windows, flooding the room and pooling across the polished stone floor. He faced the table, built centuries earlier by a friar of their order. The size of an English baron's dining table, it was a vast expanse of cherry wood. When he was alive, Dominic would spread out before him reams of papers, notes, and books that Steven had now stacked neatly at the corners. A lamp illuminated only a small portion of the table. Dominic preferred to work during the day when there was plenty of light, but on occasion he needed to work at night. Steven recollected how much Dominic loved to work at the table. Sometimes, when it was raining and Steven was working, he thought he heard Dominic's voice and familiar footsteps. But when he looked around, no one was there.

Although his father didn't mind the cold when he worked, Steven hated it. He filled the grate of the laboratory's fireplace with logs and relished listening to the crackling fire. Intermittently he would get up to warm himself, standing with his back to the flames as he read.

Since Dominic's death, Steven had been unable to pray. He only went through the motions in chapel during the offices. But now he found new meaning in the ancient words. At night in his cell, he welcomed the ritual by his bed. He prayed in his underwear, his habit resting on a hanger on the closet door.

In Michael's pay packet from work was a handwritten note from the academy principal summoning him to his office. For the first time in weeks, Michael appeared at the school during class hours. He sat in the chair opposite the principal's desk.

The principal was taken aback by Michael's appearance and smell. The young student had neglected himself. It was apparent he had not bathed or shaved in weeks.

"Are you alright?" the principal said.

Michael nodded. The principal put on his glasses and studied a piece of paper in his hands. "Am I to understand that you are no longer attending classes?"

"Yes, sir. That's correct."

"And why is that?"

"I've lost interest, sir."

"We expected you to enter the annual academy competition, but you did not submit anything."

"I've lost my inspiration, sir."

The principal scratched his head. "That's hard to believe, given the dedication you brought to your studies until most recently."

"I'm sorry, sir," Michael said.

The principal sighed. "I see." He scribbled something on the piece of paper, then folded his hands on top of it. "Well, I'm sorry to hear that, but this sort of thing happens. If you change your mind, come and see me. Take until the new term begins to think this through. You can keep your job, provided you show up every night. But you know the college rules regarding scholarships. Should you choose to leave the school, after this term we can no longer finance your living accommodations."

The principal waited several moments for an answer.

"Thank you," Michael said finally before walking out of the room.

"Move in with me," Amanda said.

Michael returned to his flat to collect what few things would be of use to him. His paints, canvases, drawings, books, sketchbooks, and artist's tools he left behind. He scribbled an apologetic letter to his landlord. Before sealing the envelope and slipping it through the mail slot in the door, he dropped in the key.

AMANDA'S OCCUPATION was something of a mystery to Michael. Whenever he asked her what she did, all she said was, "I work nights."

Michael never pursued it any further. Initially he thought she was a waitress, but he later ruled that out. She always came home long after all the restaurants had closed. Perhaps she was a cocktail hostess at one of the casinos in Mayfair?

He began observing her routine more closely. She rose at noon from a comalike sleep. Tugging a dressing gown around her, she sauntered into the tiny kitchen and made herself a cup of tea and some toast. After bathing, she spent the rest of the day doing housework. Except to shop, she seldom left the flat.

At five thirty in the afternoon, a remarkable transformation took place. After bathing again, she applied heavy eye makeup and thick red lipstick, and worked on her hair for more than forty-five minutes. When she stepped out of the bathroom, the strong scent of perfume followed her. Michael noticed that her style of dress did not match her makeup; it was more casual, while there was an air of formality about her makeup. By eight thirty she was out the door, and returned usually around three o'clock in the morning, accompanied by the smell of tobacco.

"What do you do?" Michael said one morning over breakfast.

Amanda lit a cigarette and blew out the smoke. "I'm a working girl," she said.

"Working girl?"

She casually munched on a slice of toast with jam. "On the game. Or to be more polite, a lady of the night."

Michael stopped eating. "A . . . prostitute?" He could not believe what he had heard. "How long have you been doing this, then?"

"Since I was sixteen."

Although Michael was shocked, it all made sense. Her drug taking and her virtuoso lovemaking fit in with her nocturnal occupation. "Why do you do it?"

"The money's good and I enjoy sex. But once I got hooked, I needed to support my habit. In the beginning I thought I could just make some good money, then get out."

"So you're a streetwalker?"

"No," she said. "I don't do that."

"Do you ever bring men home?"

"Used to. I have an office now."

"An office," Michael repeated.

"I linked up with some friends who work the Houses. Since then, it's been steady work, and good pay."

"Houses?"

"Parliament."

"So your clients are . . . ?"

"Mostly civil servants, MPs, peers. I have a few solicitors and businessmen, too, from the financial district. But in the past my clientele were not always so upscale. Streetwalking was rough back then. On occasion I'd come home with cuts and bruises. It all came with the territory." She sighed, taking a sip of tea. "There are always a few rotten apples in the bunch."

Michael had noticed the scars but had said nothing. One was a single knife wound on her upper back, no larger than a shilling. Another ran along her right inner thigh for three inches. With its stitches and serpentine shape, it resembled an insect with many legs.

"How did you get that one on your leg?" said Michael.

"A black man slashed me with a cutthroat razor."

"Why?"

"He wanted sex for free. I refused and so he cut me. Since then I avoid black men."

"I'd like to see where you work," Michael said.

Amanda was reluctant at first, but after a month or so of Michael's badgering, she took him with her to Soho. Next to a Chinese restaurant was an inconspicuous door she unlocked. They climbed a flight of stairs. When they got to the top, she unlocked another door.

"This is my office," she said, swinging it open.

It wasn't what he had expected. Michael saw a cramped bed-sit with an adjoining bathroom and no kitchen. Two windows overlooked the street below. The beige carpet was old and worn, and a battered wooden dresser supported a small pile of fresh white towels. The bed, newly sheeted and impeccably made, was turned down, ready for use. He could smell the freshness of the linens. A single bedside lamp provided the only light. There was no phone.

Michael had expected something elegant or grand, like the paintings and photos he had seen of Parisian bordellos at the turn of the century. Instead, Amanda's office was spartan and clean. In the corner was a wardrobe that had no doors. It was stuffed with bright red bras, lace knickers, garter belts, and hose. Michael realized why Amanda always left the flat in casual clothes; she had the luxury of changing into her working clothes here.

He gulped. *Just what was he getting himself into?*

As BROTHER Thomas reached for his mug of tea, the sleeve of his habit brushed the chessboard, knocking two pieces off. He reached down and picked them up from the ground. With his habit, he wiped the dirt from them and replaced them on the board.

It was four in the afternoon. Thomas and Steven had been sitting on one of the corner benches in the garden since two o'clock, playing chess. Despite the intense sun, it was still a chilly spring day. Thomas had a shawl wrapped around his shoulders. The chessboard lay between them, flanked by two steaming mugs of tea.

"Your move," said Thomas.

After Steven moved one of his knights, he brought his mug of tea to his lips. "Do you ever think about God?" he said.

Thomas intently studied the board. "In what sense?"

"Well, what do you picture God as, an old man on a throne with a long white beard?"

Thomas scratched his head. "Never saw God as anything like that. Mind you, many do."

"Then what?"

"To me, it's not a matter of who God is, but where you find Him. Many find Him in church, for instance. I never do, though."

"Where do you find Him, then?"

Thomas took another sip of tea. "In cooking."

Steven was baffled by the answer. Thomas moved a piece on the chessboard.

"Cooking?" Steven said.

"Dominic, as you know, found God in nature."

Steven remembered visiting his father in his laboratory one morning long ago, when he was just a boy of seven. He found Dominic as he usually did, hunched over his work table, intent on his manuals and medicines. The physician stopped what he was doing when he saw Steven. "What is it, my son?"

"Father, what is God?"

Without hesitation, Dominic rose from the table. He took Steven by the hand and walked him to the open doorway that led to the garden. They stood in the doorway for a moment. Outside, the garden exploded with color from a variety of flowers. Everything was bathed in sunlight. Birds sang, butterflies fluttered from one flower to the next, trees rustled in the breeze. At the far end of the garden Brother Samson sang happily to himself.

"This is God," said Dominic.

Thomas moved another piece on the chessboard, bringing Steven back to the present. "We all find God in our own way," Thomas said. "You must find him in yours."

"Yes, but where?"

"That's for you to discover. Nobody can do that for you. Be patient."

13

Spring made way for summer, although there were few signs in the city except for the heat and the changes in women's fashions. Michael and Amanda had developed a routine, a quiet existence of spending their late afternoons and dinners together before each went off to work in the evening. Michael felt content.

When Amanda didn't return to the living room, Michael went searching. He found her in the bathroom, standing naked in front of the mirror, her middle finger up her anus and her wooden works box on the counter.

"Why do you do that?" he said, sitting down on the toilet lid.

"Because it makes me feel good."

"Can't you enjoy yourself without it?"

"It just makes things nicer, that's all."

She looked at him sympathetically. It was clear he didn't understand. He would never understand unless he experienced it for himself.

"I want to do it," Michael told her. "But I don't want a repeat of what happened before."

Amanda was shocked by his request. "Neither do I."

Curious about Amanda's works set, Michael picked up the velvet-lined mahogany box. "Where did you get it?" he asked.

"I found it on the Portobello Road," she said. "It was originally a case for an old microscope."

Amanda pointed out the different compartments and explained what went where. "You need to know where everything is," she said. "If you're stoned and mistake one thing for another, it'll be your last mistake."

From the box she removed something wrapped in a handkerchief. Next she pulled out a spoon, a white candle, a box of matches, and a small wax-paper packet. She unwrapped the handkerchief, and inside lay the elements of a hypodermic syringe.

"You can learn more by watching," she said, "so watch me carefully."

Methodically she assembled the syringe in front of him. "This," she said, holding it up, "must always be clean. A dirty syringe can do you in just as easily as getting hit by a bus. Boil everything after you use it. Do it first thing in the morning. Boiling water for tea comes after. No exceptions. And never, ever share a needle with someone else."

To Michael, the whole thing sounded like a complicated science experiment.

Amanda cushioned the syringe on a towel. Delicately she opened the wax-paper packet and measured some of the white powder into the spoon. She struck a match and lit the candle, then blew out the match and picked up the spoon. Wrapping the end of the towel around the metal handle, she held the spoon steadily over the flame of the candle.

When the heat had dissolved the powder in the spoon into a clear liquid, she blew out the candle and carefully set the spoon down on the counter. Then she gently blew onto the clear liquid. When it had cooled sufficiently, Amanda lowered the needle into the liquid and carefully pulled the plunger back. It drank up the serum like a large, hideous mosquito.

Amanda leaned close to Michael, showing him a line on the syringe. "Only fill it to this mark," she said.

Pointing the needle straight up, she carefully scrutinized its clear barrel. She flicked the barrel with her middle finger, as though flicking a tiny pebble out to sea. Then she gently pushed the plunger until a bit of liquid squirted out from the needle.

"Why are you doing that?" Michael said.

"Air bubbles," she said. "After dirty works, air bubbles are the next hazard. Get one of those little buggers in your bloodstream and it's all over."

She placed the syringe back down on the towel and removed a frayed silk stocking from the box.

"Take off your shirt," she said.

Michael unbuttoned his shirt and took it off.

"Do everything you can to make it easier," she said. "Whenever possible, shoot up indoors. Shooting up outside, especially in bad weather, is miserable."

She tied the stocking around his upper left arm with a special knot that could be quickly undone with a firm tug. "It has to be tight," she said.

After waiting fifteen seconds, she began violently slapping his inner arm near the elbow. Michael's skin became red. Little rivers of thin blue spaghetti began appearing along his arm. Two large veins dominated.

"There, see?" she said, pointing to the larger vein. "Always go for the biggest one. They're the easiest."

She chose one. Michael's repulsion was matched only by his curiosity. He had believed that needles were the exclusive province of doctors. Now he was learning differently.

Perspiration beaded on Amanda's forehead as she tried to slide the needle into Michael's vein. Twice she tried, and missed. "What's the matter?" Michael said.

"I can't hit the vein. It won't go in." In exasperation she said, "Rollers. Big veins roll away. That's why they're called rollers. Each time you try to put the needle into them, they try to escape. You just have to keep trying."

Nature's defense mechanisms are clever, Michael thought. The vein was trying to tell him something. Like a snail retreating into the safety of its shell, a part of his body was telling him that it didn't want to be poked and injected with dangerous substances.

Then he winced as he felt the sharp needle hit its target. The needle slid into the vein until the metal all but disappeared. Loosening the tourniquet, Amanda slowly pushed on the plunger, emptying the contents of the syringe into his arm. There was no gushing sensation, like a river emptying into his vein, as he thought there would be.

When the liquid had vanished from the clear cylinder, Amanda retracted the needle from his arm and placed it again on the towel. A droplet of blood rose to the surface of Michael's skin. With a tissue she applied pressure at the place where the needle had entered and exited. Then she bent his arm onto the tissue.

"See?" she said. "Easy."

Michael just looked at her, waiting for something to happen. Within moments his entire body began tingling. He felt as though he were floating on a carpet of air a few feet above the ground. He watched as Amanda lit a cigarette and blew long blue-gray columns of smoke toward the ceiling.

He nodded at the empty syringe. "Why don't you do it this way?" he said.

"I used to, but my arms looked a wreck. It just isn't very sexy to have black-and-blue marks. Clients don't want to see that. It's not attractive. So I started shooting up in other places."

"Like where?"

She looked down at her bare feet. "The feet," she said.

"Right on the foot?"

"No, on the soft part of the ankle, under the nails, between the toes. I also did the groin and the inner part of the thigh. When those were exhausted, I shot up under the tongue. Basically, any part of the body that can't be seen. Then I discovered suppositories. But the best way to do Paradise is to shoot it. That way you use very little of the drug to get high. The only drawback is that your arms look terrible."

"Where can I buy these drugs?" said Michael.

"In time," she said. "In time I'll tell you."

In her box was the same brown paper bag Michael had seen before. She opened it and showed him four suppositories ready for use. There was also some sort of a mold. She took it out to show him.

"It's a fountain-pen cap," she said. "I sliced it in half with a cutthroat razor after heating the razor over the stove. The two pieces are held together by rubber bands. I make a paste out of the drug with water and baking flour. When there's no baking flour, I use powdered milk. I put it into the mold and let it dry. Then I remove the rubber bands and pry open the mold. I either store the suppository or use it right away. I have only one mold, so I can make only one at a time. That's why I stockpile."

"How do you put the suppository up you?" Michael said.

"With face cream," she said.

Michael looked at the spoon. A tiny portion of serum remained.

"After you shoot up," she said, "there'll always be a little left over in the spoon. Never waste it." She opened the medicine chest and produced a glass pill bottle stuffed with cotton. She opened the lid and removed one of the cotton balls. After swabbing the spoon with it, she pushed the cotton back into the bottle. "Always save your cottons," she said, screwing on the cap. "For emergencies."

"But how do you get the drug out again?" Michael said.

"The drug stays in the cotton," Amanda said. "It's released when it's boiled."

AMANDA SCHOOLED Michael in the use of heroin, morphine, opium, peyote, and cannabis. She showed him all the various colors, tastes, and smells, and explained how each drug was used, but she never told him where she bought them. That she still kept a secret.

One morning she put two wax-paper packets, neatly folded, on the kitchen table in front of Michael. She opened up one. "This type of heroin is called Baptisma."

Michael inspected the muddy-colored drug.

"It comes from Bolivia," she said. "It's a medium-grade heroin, good and reliable."

She opened up the next wax-paper square. "This is the diamond of heroin," she said. "It's superior because it's the purest. Purity is everything. Paradise—or *Paradiso*, as the Colombians call it—is the best. It's uncut and the most expensive. It's what I use."

"What do you mean by uncut?" Michael touched the fine white powder with his index finger.

"Most dealers," she said, "will dilute the drug with something so they can make more money. Most heroin is cut with either milk sugar or baby's laxative. When it's cooked up in the spoon, the impurities usually dissolve and are burned out. But there are also deadly synthetic versions of heroin, to be avoided at all costs. One is China White. The Chinese export it without conscience in order to make a quick profit. Everyone who uses it dies."

"How can you tell it apart from real heroin?"

Amanda folded up the packets and stowed them away. "You can't," she said. "You have to find a trustworthy dealer."

NOT UNLIKE Dominic, Amanda was an apothecary. But while Dominic's medicine provided healing, hers gave pleasure. Michael realized that both had fatal side effects if ill-used.

The more drugs he did, the more withdrawn he became from the world. He spent his summer days sitting by the window, gazing catatonically down at the street below. The warm pinprick of addiction had taken over his life without him knowing it.

There were nights when he forgot to go to his job at the academy. It needed to be cleaned every night, and missing even one night would be noticeable. Garbage would start piling up and, in some cases, overflow the bins. One day, when Michael opened his latest pay packet, he found a formally typed termination notice requesting he leave his academy key in his pigeonhole.

AN UNCOMFORTABLE distance had developed between Michael and Amanda. Their only activity now was the drugs they shared. Michael became lethargic. The drugs had taken away his sex drive. The only time they went out was to collect Chinese takeaway. They did not socialize because they had no friends.

There were fleeting moments when they found each other, but these reunions often occurred in the haze of drugs and were short-lived. When the high washed away, life returned to what it was. Although Amanda still cared about Michael, her home, which was once her sanctuary, had become a prison. She began working longer hours to keep her mind off the problems at home and had increased her own drug intake substantially. She was now supporting two people and two drug habits. Life had just become more expensive.

IT WAS 5:30 p.m. Amanda was still asleep. Unusual, because normally she was up by noon. When she did not rise by seven, Michael figured she must be feeling ill. He made some hot tea and toast and placed it at her bedside.

Amanda lay unmoving underneath the snowstorm of the bedclothing. Michael tried to wake her by gently rubbing her shoulder. That having failed, he peeled back the blankets and the sheets. Amanda appeared to be in peaceful slumber but looked very pale. Michael touched her cheek with the back of his hand. She was cold. Frightened, he shook her violently.

"Amanda, wake up! Wake up!"

She did not respond. He knew where the phone was, but in his panic he couldn't find it. After searching frantically, he found it buried under the cushions of the sofa. Michael guessed she had placed it there so as not to be disturbed by its ringing. He wasted no time phoning for an ambulance. One of the men who arrived had a stethoscope draped around his neck. He plugged it into his ears, bent down, and placed the flat circular end on Amanda's chest. After ten seconds, he looked up at his colleague and shook his head.

Michael stood at the foot of the bed, numb.

They transported Amanda to the hospital. The amount of time Michael had to wait to hear from a doctor seemed like forever. Finally, a man with dark wavy hair and a white lab coat approached him in the waiting area.

"Mr. Warren, is it?"

"Yes," Michael said.

The man extended his hand. "I'm Dr. Thompson. I know this is difficult for you."

"What did she die of?"

"We'll be running some tests. We should have the results by tomorrow. Come back then."

When Michael stepped outside, the night was clear and the air was warm. He decided to walk back to Amanda's flat, just over a mile and a half away. As he made his way along the streets, his hands buried deep in his pockets, symptoms of withdrawal began to claw at him. Michael promised himself that until he found out the test results on Amanda, he wouldn't touch any of the powders in her box.

Back at the flat, he sat on the floor of the sitting room, the water pipe between his legs. Sucking on the mouthpiece, he lit a small piece of opium. At least he knew that was safe. After the first inhale, he sat in the darkness, with only the streetlights illuminating the room.

He became sleepy and shuffled into the bedroom. He was about to lie down when he looked at the unmade bed.

Someone has died in it, he thought.

Michael removed the blanket and a pillow and dragged it into the sitting room. The couch was too small for him, but he didn't care. He curled up on it and lay his head on the pillow.

THE RINGING of the telephone awoke Michael. Dr. Thompson was asking to see him.

As if in a fog, Michael got ready and was at the hospital in less than an hour. Once inside the building, Dr. Thompson led him down the busy corridor. They entered an office lined with medical books. The doctor closed the door and sat behind the desk, motioning Michael to a chair. He put on his glasses and looked at some papers in front of him. "We ran lab tests on Amanda," he said. "Heroin was present in her blood sample, but not a sufficient quantity to cause death. However, large traces of strychnine were found."

"Strychnine?" said Michael.

"Yes. Do you have any reason to suspect that she wanted to take her own life?"

"Not in the slightest," Michael said.

"Was she a regular heroin user?"

Michael was hesitant for a moment. "Yes," he said.

"Then she must have purchased tainted heroin. These street dealers mix it with anything. I'm afraid this could be such a case."

He made a note on his papers.

Michael searched his mind. *Could it be that in order to economize, she had bought low-grade heroin?*

Thompson finished writing. "What is your association with Amanda?" he said. "Are you a relative?"

"No, just a friend."

"My condolences."

In a choked whisper Michael said, "May I see her?"

"If you wish." Thompson closed the file. He folded his glasses and put them into his breast pocket. "Come with me."

He led Michael through a labyrinth of corridors and finally down a group of stairs into what looked like a large basement. It was distinctly cold. An odd, unpleasant chemical odor hung in the air. The large room was dimly lit, and there were six metal tables with green sheets draped over what Michael assumed to be corpses. Thompson approached the first table. Lifting aside the sheet slightly, he examined the name tag tied to a big toe. Then he moved to the second table and did the same. "This is she," he said. "I'll leave you alone."

He turned and left. The room seemed to grow colder as Michael pondered the sheet. He was frightened to pull it back because only yesterday he had seen Amanda alive.

Mustering the courage, he gingerly folded the green sheet back. Amanda's face was pasty white, and there were dark blue circles around her eyes. Michael bit his lip. Tears slipped from his eyes. He desperately wanted to shake Amanda awake and tell her everything was alright, that he was sorry. With his index finger he touched her pale white face and cold blue lips. He had never touched a dead person before. All the softness had gone out of her. He gently pulled the sheet back into place.

MICHAEL FOUND the paper bag in Amanda's works box. Two suppositories were left. Most likely they were tainted as well. He dumped them in the toilet bowl and pulled the chain, but as he did so he was reminded of his own discomfort. Withdrawal began eating at him. He tried to think of other things, but the pangs grew more intense by the hour.

In one of the small compartments of the works box, there was some powdered Paradise. He reasoned that if he cooked what was left, he could boil the poison out. It was risky, but his aching body urged him to take the chance. He cooked the drug and let it stand to cool. Then he cooked it once more, hoping to purge any remaining impurities from it.

Michael injected a small amount into his right arm. Fifteen minutes passed. He slumped onto the bed and lay motionless for hours as the drug flooded his body with relief and washed over him like a warm, ebbing tide. Nothing adverse happened.

THE FOLLOWING morning Michael groggily got up and took stock of how much of the drug he had left. By the size of the packet, he gauged that he had enough for a week to ten days, taking into consideration he would have to cook it thoroughly and use it sparingly.

Michael began sifting through Amanda's things. In a closet, buried deep behind a stack of shoeboxes, he found a large brown envelope. From it he extracted several worn black-and-white photos. In one, a man with a bushy mustache hugged a little girl in a frilly white lace dress. Another showed a young boy and girl reluctantly clasping hands in a cardboard pose as they looked at the camera. *A brother?* In a third picture, the same girl hugged a shaggy dog in a small garden in front of a tidy house.

Is this Amanda as a little girl? Michael wondered. *If so, why hadn't she shown him these before?*

He remembered asking Amanda about her family and where she came from. She had answered that she was from Hertford-shire, that she was an only child, and that her parents had died several years before.

As he walked across the room to put the aging envelope on top of the bureau, Michael's foot caught on the corner of the area rug under the bed. He stumbled but recovered. When he looked down, he noticed he had flipped up the corner of the rug. He was about to press it back down when he noticed a small square panel in the floor. He pushed the rug back until the panel was fully exposed. Digging his nails under the edge, Michael tried to lift it out, but it refused to budge.

After thinking a moment, he pressed one side of the panel, and the other side popped up easily. He lifted it off. In the cavity he found a candy tin. He carefully edged it out. The lid was stuck tight. He took the can into the kitchen and with a knife pried open the lid. A roll of paper was tightly wedged inside the can, and even when he turned the can upside down and slapped the bottom he could not dislodge it. Finally, one by one, he began peeling off the contents of the roll. The first leaf he pulled out was a ten-pound banknote. Then another, and another. Finally, when enough of the notes had been removed, he turned the can upside down again and gave the bottom a good thump. The rest of the roll spilled out. Banknotes flew everywhere, littering the counter and floor like autumn leaves.

Michael gathered up all the notes and sat down at the kitchen table. He separated the money into piles by denomination. When he finished counting, more than three thousand pounds lay on the table.

What was the money for? Had Amanda planned to make a fresh start, free from drugs and prostitution? What other reason would she be saving for?

Michael went through the remainder of her things but found nothing—no letters, no passport, no driver's license or any form of identification. Michael guessed they existed but had been carefully hidden, like the money, and the chances of finding them were slim.

In the sitting room was a small desk that Amanda used to pay bills. It had a single drawer in the center. When he opened it, he found a stash of envelopes rubber-banded together. He looked at every one. They were bills—phone bills, electricity bills—but not a single bank book or bank statement, or any other record for that matter. Amanda had paid everything in cash. Michael realized then that everything in her world, from drugs to her services, was transacted in cash. The rent, for instance, had always been paid in cash directly to the landlord downstairs. But with the bills it was different. He surmised that she must have paid the electricity, heating, and phone bills with postal orders.

In the same drawer he found an address book. He scanned it page by page, hoping to find a name that could be a relative or friend. But they all looked like the names of her clients. He threw the book away. Keeping it could land him in hot water if the flat was ever searched.

He went to her office in Soho and asked the two girls who shared the apartment with Amanda if they knew anything about her family. The girls seemed to know even less than he did. One was so high she was practically incoherent. Amanda's clothes, hanging in the wardrobe, were the only evidence that she had ever existed.

Michael made a trip to the Hertfordshire public records office but found nothing under her name. It didn't surprise him. Amanda could have changed her name years ago.

He informed the hospital that there was no next of kin. No funeral was held, and Michael paid for and attended the cremation. On a Sunday morning he scattered Amanda's ashes among the bushes in Hyde Park.

14

ALTHOUGH AMANDA HAD ALWAYS stopped short of revealing the name of her drug supplier to Michael, on one occasion she had let a name slip. Price.

Is he a dealer in Piccadilly? Michael thought.

By now he knew that most drug connections were made in Soho. That Sunday evening after scattering Amanda's ashes, he headed there. Soho's small, cramped streets were brightened by flashing, multicolored neon signs advertising Eastern and Oriental cuisines. Their bittersweet odors drifted into the hot night air, mixing with the humidity that made Michael's shirt stick to his skin. Barkers stood in doorways cajoling passersby to enter topless revues. Cabaret music spilled from basement cafés. Pedestrians meandered in aimless, intoxicated ballets.

Michael wandered the back alleys where toothless whores leaned from broken windows. Just as he was questioning the wisdom of being there, a short, skinny black man stepped out of the shadows into the yellow wash of the streetlights.

"Fancy some shine, mate?"

The man's thick Jamaican accent threw Michael off.

"Paradise," Michael said.

"What bag are you looking for?"

"Bag?" said Michael, puzzled.

"Bag. Amount, mate."

"What have you got?" said Michael.

"A fifty-quid bag, or a fiver, good for one fixer."

"I'll take the fifty-quid bag, if it's clean."

"Pure as mountain snow, mate. Meet me back here in half an hour."

After walking the streets for thirty minutes, Michael returned to the same spot. The small man stepped out of the shadows and handed him a brown paper bag. Michael opened it and peered inside. In the dim light he saw several wax-paper packets.

"It's all there," said the man, annoyed.

Michael closed the bag and fished a wad of money from his pocket. Peeling off five ten-pound notes, he placed them in the man's open hand.

"Do you know Price?" Michael said.

The dealer stepped back. "Now, what do you want with him?"

"Where can I find him?"

The dealer shook his head discouragingly. "Shouldn't be messing with him, mate."

"And why not?"

"He's bad magic, man."

"What do you mean?"

"Price? Why, he's the biggest dealer in Piccadilly. He's got juice."

"Juice?"

"Got a whole network of people working for him, you know. Enforcers. People who kill for him if he don't get payment." The dealer pushed the money into his pocket. "Also been said he don't sell to ladies."

"You mean they get powders for free?" said Michael.

The dealer shook his head. "If they want shit, they have to fuck him for it. That's the deal. Anyway, rumor has it he's been selling bad shit recently. People have died."

Michael felt his anger rise inside him. He stared into the little man's dark, shiny eyes. "What does he look like?"

"White guy," said the dealer. "About your height."

"Where can I find him?"

"Piccadilly Underground. Between ten and eleven thirty."

"Every night?"

"Most nights, mate. But you're looking for trouble."

PICCADILLY CIRCUS blazed with scores of glittering neon lights and signs. While dozens of people strolled by taking in the sights, Michael sat at a café, an uneaten steak pie on the plate in front of him. He drained the last of his coffee, grasping the cup carefully so as not to let it slip from his sweaty hands. At eleven-twenty he walked down into the Piccadilly Underground. There was a steady stream of people heading to and from the trains. Small groups of teenagers clustered in corners. Michael spotted an out-of-order chocolate machine and leaned against it, waiting.

Soon a man in a white open-collared shirt hurried down the steps and quickly dodged into the men's lavatories. Michael followed. He saw the man urinating and stood at the urinal next to him, pretending to pee.

"Price," said Michael. "I'm looking for some Paradise."

The man stared down into the urinal bowl. "How much?"

Michael struggled to keep his voice calm and impassive. "Two hundred quid," he said.

The man casually shook himself dry and buttoned his fly. "Come back tomorrow."

THE LARGE stainless-steel blade gleamed in Michael's hand. "I'll take it," he said.

Michael placed three pounds on the counter. The clerk in the sporting goods store wrapped the hunting knife and sheath in brown paper and placed it in a bag. Michael thanked the clerk and left.

Back in his bed-sit, he used his belt to strap the knife around his waist. He put on his lightest jacket. Looking in the mirror, he saw the sheath sticking out from the bottom of the jacket. He raised the belt to the level of his chest and positioned the knife just under his left armpit so that he could draw it easily. But the line of the belt ran across his shirt like a large black ribbon. He would have to keep his jacket zipped until he needed to use the knife.

Michael stood in front of the mirror and practiced opening his jacket and drawing out the knife. He rehearsed it over and over again, drawing and jabbing, drawing and jabbing, until the movement was fluid. He contemplated the knife's long, shiny blade and bone handle. From his anatomy classes at the academy, Michael knew that getting a blade past the chest and rib cage was difficult. The abdomen, too, was risky, as it meant one had to face one's adversary. Only the back offered an unobstructed route to the heart and other organs.

He remembered something else he learned from Brother Thomas. Whenever something was too stubborn to cut, like a loaf of bread, Thomas would run the blade under the tap in the kitchen sink. Once wet, the blade easily sliced through whatever he was trying to cut. Michael lubricated the blade with olive oil and returned the knife to its sheath.

One question remained: What would he do with his blood-soaked clothes? Michael decided to take with him a small duffel bag that he could sling over his shoulder. In it would be a change of clothes. Dealers knew most of their clients were near-transients anyhow and always on the move. He would not arouse suspicion.

MICHAEL SAT in the same café as the previous night, across the street from the Piccadilly Underground. It was another hot, humid night, and at the last minute he had decided not to wear a shirt under his jacket. Despite that, he was still sweltering.

At precisely eleven twenty Michael descended into the tube station. Price appeared at eleven thirty and entered the men's lavatory. Four youths who had been standing outside the lavatory followed him in. Michael waited for the youths to leave, then walked into the lavatory. Price was washing his hands.

Michael went to the basin next to him and began washing. Price had black hair, a round face, and the pug nose of a boxer. He had a day's growth of beard, and his hairline was receding.

"We spoke yesterday about the Paradise," Michael began.

"Got the cash?" Price said, drying his hands.

"Yes," said Michael.

"Follow me, but stay well back."

Michael noticed his slight gait and trailed behind at a moderate distance. Price never looked back, walking as though Michael did not exist. Michael was led through Soho's grimmest backstreets to a dilapidated building with storefronts and restaurants on the street level. He struggled to calm the butterflies in his stomach. Although his nerves were drawn wire tight, it made his mind sharp and lucid.

Price entered an alley and disappeared through the back door of an Indian restaurant. Michael followed him up some dimly lit stairs. The carpet smelled of mildew. They climbed to a second-floor landing, where the narrow hallway was illuminated by bright, naked lightbulbs, some of which had gone out. Price walked halfway down the hall, took out a set of keys, opened a door, and drifted inside. Michael squeezed in behind him.

The room was dark. Michael felt for the knife. Suddenly Price flipped a switch, and a single blue bulb, dangling at the end of a bare wire, lit the room. The light distracted Michael, and he quickly moved his hand away from the knife.

Struggling to adjust to the strange light, Michael saw they were in a sitting room. Hundreds of phonograph records lined the floor along the walls. The only piece of furniture was a reading chair and ottoman. On the floor next to the chair was a phonograph. The smell of garbage hung in the air. Michael could see a half-opened door leading to a darkened hallway.

"The money?" Price said.

Michael handed him a roll of banknotes wrapped in a rubber band. Price removed the rubber band, turned toward the blue light, and began counting the notes. His back was to Michael.

"Do you know Amanda Lerner?" Michael said.

"Yes," said Price absently as he counted the money.

Could there be a remote chance that I have the wrong man? Michael thought to himself.

Mentally he tallied up everything in his mind. Amanda had mentioned someone by the name of Price. The Jamaican drug dealer had said that Price was doing business with women, accepting sex as payment for dope. Now Price himself admitted to knowing Amanda.

No, Michael concluded. *I have the right man.*

Before Price could turn around, Michael unzipped his jacket, drew out the oiled knife, and with all of his strength buried the blade deep in the drug dealer's back.

Michael withdrew the knife. A dark area immediately appeared on the surface of Price's shirt. Horror-stricken, Price spun around, the banknotes slipping from his hand. He lunged at Michael but met only his knife. With a gasp, Price doubled over. Michael sank the blade into the dealer's abdomen again until the dealer collapsed in a heap on the floor.

Bending over Price's still form, Michael checked for vital signs. At that moment he heard wheezing noises. Michael did not realize it was the last of Price's air escaping through his stab wounds. Fearing he was about to rise up and attack him, Michael thrust the blade wildly into the dealer's back again and again until Price's shirt was shredded.

Down the hall, jazz music played on a gramophone. There was a clatter of footsteps on the landing below. In the blue light Price lay motionless.

The archbishop of bad dope is dead.

Fear engulfed Michael. His racing heart pounded in his ears. Rivers of sweat ran down his body as he struggled to catch his breath. Michael's throat was dry. Finding his way to the kitchen, he used a washcloth on the kitchen counter to turn on the tap. Sticking his face underneath, he guzzled the water. Then he washed his blood-soaked hands and the blade of the knife and dried them with the same washcloth. He replaced the knife in its sheath.

There was a knock at the door. Michael froze.

"Eh, Pricey? You in there, mate?" said a booming voice. "Freddy here. Jeff's with me. We're feeling peckish. Fancy a bite?"

The man began talking to someone else. Michael caught the phrase "he's probably out." Then he heard footsteps going down the hall, away from the door.

When Michael returned to the sitting room, he saw a dark, shapeless mass creeping outward from Price's body. In the colored light he could not tell if his own clothes were bloodstained, but still he decided to proceed with his plan. He quickly unzipped the duffel bag, changed his clothes, and stuffed the clothes and jacket he had been wearing into the bag. He then collected his money, which had been scattered about the floor. Some of it was bloodstained. He rolled up the notes and stuffed them into the bag as well.

Using the same washcloth he had dried his hands on, Michael opened the door and let himself out. He tossed the cloth into a rubbish bin behind the Indian restaurant and walked out into the street, where he lost himself in the crowded Soho night.

The monks had taught him that revenge was a cardinal sin. But Price's bad drugs had robbed a young woman of her promise.

MICHAEL CLOSED the bathroom door and locked it. He plugged the bathtub and turned on the cold-water tap. When the tub was half filled, he removed the clothes from his duffel bag. Surprisingly they were no bloodier than he had feared: just a few areas on his jacket and pants. He dunked the clothes in the water and scrubbed them with a bar of soap until the water turned a pale crimson. Letting the clothes soak, he stretched out on the floor to rest and calm his nerves. He would have liked nothing better than to take a bath himself, but washing out all the blood was his first priority.

After a while he massaged and squeezed the clothes, wringing whatever blood remained from them, and then unplugged the bathtub. He turned on the cold water and rinsed the clothes a final time, then wrung out the excess water. He hung them over the side of the bathtub to dry. Returning to the bedroom, Michael took off his sweaty clothes and collapsed on top of the unmade bed. He fell into a corpselike slumber.

The next morning he buried the knife under some bushes in Hyde Park.

THE JAMAICAN dealer Michael had met on that fateful night became his connection. Aside from his name—Russell—Michael knew little about the man. For Michael, however, this relationship was a love affair. Whenever he saw Russell, he shook and perspired with sexual pleasure. At times he even got an erection. Although Russell was always late, Michael never grew tired of waiting for him. Oftentimes, as he waited for Russell in the night, he watched the other junkies roaming the streets in search of their connections. They were always easy to spot. They drifted up and down the pavements of Soho like wind-blown leaves.

They stood in the corners of the Piccadilly Underground, studying their feet, shifting their weight from one foot to the next, waiting. They were soldiers of a broken army, seldom speaking to one another.

As Russell grew to trust Michael, he agreed to meet him in a crowded café near the Piccadilly Underground, away from the shadows of Soho. Michael would arrive early and park himself at a table beside a window. Sipping his coffee, he scanned the city's faces, imagining his dealer among the hurrying crowds. Late as usual, Russell would saunter in, sit down, and order a coffee. After a few pleasantries, Michael would slip him the money. Russell would expertly count the banknotes under the table, fold them up, and push them into his pocket, then hand Michael a small envelope. The entire transaction took place smoothly and surreptitiously under the table. Michael took the envelope and slipped it into the breast pocket of his jacket. Back at his flat, Michael opened the envelope and found two wax-paper packets. Unwrapping them carefully, he inspected his purchase with the zeal of an antiques dealer examining a rare find.

Eventually Russell began inviting Michael back to his own flat for a fix after a purchase. One night, as Russell lit a few candles and some Indian incense, he stared into the flame of one candle and said, "Be careful in dealing with the police, mate. They're bastards." He tugged a cigarette out of a pack and lit it. "Sometimes they detain addicts for a long time. Don't mess with them."

"What should I tell them if they stop me?" said Michael.

"Tell them any old rubbish. Just keep talking. It's what they expect from junkies. If you clam up, they'll detain you."

Although Michael hated the idea of injecting the drugs, for the sake of economy he took up the needle. It wasn't long before his arms were black and blue, the veins dilapidated canals. Fortunately no police officer ever stopped Michael and asked him to roll up his sleeves, only to discover a motorway of track marks running up and down his arms. Even in the heat of summer, Michael always wore long-sleeved shirts.

One afternoon Michael returned to his flat with a bad case of the shakes. When he went to fix, he found there were no drugs left in the works box. He had used them all. In desperation he began ransacking the flat, jerking open drawers and emptying them out onto the floor. In the kitchen, he opened and dumped out coffee cans, biscuit tins, and sugar and salt containers into the sink to see if Amanda had secretly hidden anything. He rushed from one room to the next, wildly throwing things out of his way. In the bedroom, he careened into the end table, sending the lamp crashing to the floor and shattering the lightbulb. He slumped in a corner of the bedroom, sobbing in frustration.

Once he had calmed down, he remembered the cotton in the medicine chest. In his mania he had forgotten to search there. When he opened the chest, concealed within the ranks of other medicine bottles was the smoke-brown glass pill bottle stuffed with cotton balls that had absorbed the surplus drug. He searched the rest of the cabinet and found an added bonus. Buried in the back of the cabinet was a small unopened vial. The label read MORPHINE. He guessed Amanda had kept it for emergencies.

Michael broke open the glass top and emptied the vial into a teacup from the kitchen. Anxiously he lowered the syringe into the liquid and filled it to the mark, as Amanda had instructed. After he fixed, he delicately poured what remained in the teacup into an empty pill bottle and stored it in the refrigerator.

The drug relaxed him, first in his back, then his legs, and then his neck. Warmth spread all over his body, and he floated away on a golden tide.

MICHAEL REALIZED he was being extravagant with Amanda's money. *How many times did she have to fuck to earn three thousand quid?*

He decided to ration it. At fifteen pounds a week, the flat was pricey. It wasn't difficult finding a new place. He found a small, boxy, furnished bed-sit in Ladbrook Grove at eight pounds a week.

Amanda didn't have many possessions. Besides her clothes, there were a few framed posters on the walls, a row of worn paperback books that stood on the mantel of the fireplace, and a small collection of jewelry. Inside the books he could find no inscriptions, no underlined passages, nothing that made them personal or indicated ownership. He left the books on the mantel and most of the posters on the walls. Within two days he had packed up everything he wanted to keep, including Amanda's jewelry and her works box, which he carefully wrapped in a towel. But the rest—her clothing, her vanity chest, even her family photos—he boxed up and gave to Oxfam.

THE NEW flat had several drawbacks. It was on the fifth floor, which meant walking up several flights of stairs daily. He shared the bath and toilet with other tenants on his floor. Like the first flat he lived in when he was at the academy, he had to get up in the middle of the night and feed the shilling gas meter to avoid freezing.

He decorated the walls with the few posters he had brought with him from Amanda's flat. One he used to cover a stain on the wall. He put the money in a glass jar, concealing it behind rows of canned foods and other jars. Frequently Michael took it out of the jar and counted it, fanning the notes out on the kitchen table. After counting them, he would roll them back up and force them back into the jar. For the time being, he did not have to worry about money. He could not believe his good fortune.

Michael kept to himself, living like a hermit. His days were spent alone, wandering through museums and taking long walks. He missed Amanda. There were moments he craved a sympathetic ear, someone to talk to, a warm body to hold.

Occasionally he had flashes of inspiration and would get a sudden urge to draw. But every time he picked up a pencil and began sketching on a brown grocery bag or sheet of newspaper, it reminded him of Suzanne, and he abruptly stopped.

The drugs brought him euphoria, but they also chipped away at his confidence and trust. He developed a paranoia about the world. He became suspicious of people and did not talk to anyone for very long.

It wasn't long before Michael began to neglect his bed-sit. As the weeks passed, dust built up everywhere in his room. Unwashed dishes lay in his sink, encrusted with a covering of green mold. The white sink itself had turned a grayish black from lack of scrubbing. Lining the wall next to his door was a row of empty milk bottles, also unwashed and mold-ridden. He slept in the same white sheets until they turned cardboard hard and a brown color. He wore the same clothes for weeks. The tips of his fingers turned a sticky yellow brown from smoking cigarettes. All around the flat, piled high on plates and crunched in used coffee cans, were cigarette butts. Sometimes Michael would sit at the edge of his bed for hours, smoking one cigarette after another, then stubbing them out into the coffee cans. His body shook from all the coffee he drank, and he ate only one meal a day: sweet-and-sour chicken from the Chinese restaurant down the street.

Michael's entire life now revolved around one thing—the drug.

15

STEVEN MADE THE SIGN of the cross over his chest. His legs ached from the hour spent in prayer at the altar railing in the chapel. Unsteadily he rose to his feet, rubbing both knees.

He contemplated whether he had said his prayers correctly, and often wondered if they were ever heard. He remembered what Michael had said about prayer. *Prayers are for those who can't take responsibility for their lives. They are for those who can't make their own decisions.* More than a year later, Michael's words still burned through Steven.

Was becoming a monk the right path? Sometimes Steven thought his prayers were performed simply by rote. He could not help reflecting on how many times he had repeated the same words hour after hour with little result, and he was tortured by the fact that his friend might have been right. Maybe God did not hear him after all. He found that thought frightening.

His laundry lay neatly folded on the bed when he returned to his cell. Something about the smell of freshly laundered sheets reminded Steven of his childhood. But that memory did little to comfort him. He placed the clean sheets and bedclothing on the first shelf of his chest. Three undershirts and three pairs of underwear were stored on a shelf in the next compartment. He rolled up three pairs of socks and placed them in a drawer.

Dominic had taught him how to pray. He had taught him the correct posture and the proper way to fold his hands.

"You must give yourself up to the words completely," his father had said. "You must surrender yourself to their meaning and let them fill you, just as you let music fill you when you sing. The sacred words cannot be uttered. They cannot be said as one normally speaks but must be enunciated clearly and spoken in a manner that they enter the heart directly. Whenever you catch your thoughts drifting, you must begin again. You cannot teach anyone to pray unless the heart believes."

Steven had been taught that fervor in private prayer was the greatest proof of religious sincerity. Only through active prayer could one prove the belief one professed. Yet for some time Steven had been aware that his heart was no longer present in his prayers. Each day he became more and more racked and tormented by Michael's argument that prayers were for people who didn't have lives.

After putting away his laundry, Steven sat down in the chair by his bed. For a long time he stayed there, questioning his decision to serve God. Finally he concluded, *I must not think about whether God hears my prayers or not. I should concern myself only with whether I said them well.*

MICHAEL WAS just starting to warm up from the freezing rains as he finished the arduous climb to his flat. A note from the landlord was pinned to the door. The rent was late. Realizing he had not taken inventory of his cash in a while, Michael promptly sat down and counted his banknotes. To his dismay, he found he had only twenty pounds left. All that Amanda had saved was gone, in five months.

His expenditures on Paradise had cost him. Twenty pounds would last only a few days. He cursed himself for his extravagance and even regretted giving Amanda's things to Oxfam. He could have sold them instead. At the back of his mind, Michael had always known the money would run out, but he had not anticipated it would be so soon.

Hoping to scrape together some cash, Michael took Amanda's jewelry to a local pawnshop, but that yielded little money. Instead of being able to purchase enough of the drug for two weeks at a time, he could now afford to buy it only on a fix-by-fix basis.

As Russell prepared a syringe, Michael said, "I'm running out of cash."

"You want my advice, mate?" said Russell. "Is that what you're looking for?"

Michael rolled up his shirt sleeve past the elbow. He yanked the decaying leather belt from around his waist and passed the strap through the buckle. Then he slipped his hand through the loop and wrapped it tightly around his upper arm near his shoulder, holding the end with his free hand.

"I could find a job," said Michael. "That would pay for my rent and food, but it wouldn't begin to pay for my fixes."

When the drug had finished cooking in the spoon, Russell blew on it to cool it down. He then dipped the needle into the spoon and watched it drink up the serum.

"You could always hook, mate," he said, peering into the glass cylinder. "You're good-looking enough." He pointed the syringe toward the ceiling and flicked the barrel with his index finger a few times. A minuscule bubble scampered up to the top of the needle.

Michael was incredulous. "You mean a gigolo? Pick up women?"

"No, man," said Russell. "Blokes. A male prostitute. Pay's good."

Russell pushed gently on the plunger. Liquid spurted out of the needle's tip. Michael's breath became short with excitement at the sight of the full syringe. His hands shook. "Blokes?"

Nodding, Russell slapped Michael's forearm, then slid the cold needle into his flesh. "You'd make it, mate." He eased the plunger in as Michael loosened the belt. "My friend does it down on the King's Road. Makes good money."

Russell withdrew the needle. Michael closed his eyes and pressed the spot on his arm where the needle had entered. A warm wave of pleasant relaxation rolled through his entire body. As a smile of contentment spread across his lips, he let the belt drop to the floor.

"Thank you . . ." he whispered breathlessly. "Thank you."

ON THE King's Road Michael had been followed almost immediately. The stranger kept a safe distance behind as Michael entered a crowded café. In short order the man sat down next to Michael. After a moment Michael felt a hand drop onto his thigh under the table. A nervous coffee and cigarette later, Michael followed the stranger to a cheap hotel and watched as the stranger slid a ten-bob note across the reception counter without a word.

In the room Michael took off his clothes and neatly folded them on a chair, then slipped into the bed beside the strange man. The stranger lubricated himself from a tube of gel. In less than fifteen minutes it was over. They shared a cigarette in bed before getting dressed. Outside, the man reached into his pocket and paid Michael. They nodded and went their separate ways.

Although Michael realized that Russell had been right about the King's Road, he came to discover that he could pick up more clients in the public toilets in Kensington and not have to find a hotel. The tricks would follow him into a toilet stall, and the door would be locked. They would drop their pants. Some customers wanted to be played with until they sprayed the toilet wall. Often they preferred to be bent over the toilet and entered. Then, likewise, they entered him. Michael found it excruciating. His clients would use their own saliva to lubricate themselves, but it was not enough. Michael began carrying his own tube of gel.

The majority of his clients were businessmen in suits. Most of the time Michael did not see their faces. Obscured by the dim light of the public toilets, they were merely shapes with genitalia. There was never any chat; they simply wanted to get on with it. Usually the act itself lasted no more than ten minutes and ended in a grunt of ejaculation. Michael set a time limit of twenty minutes, unless the client paid extra. Some came sooner, which pleased Michael all the more.

Most paid promptly, but a few took some persuading. The first time a client refused to pay, Michael's fists became his debt collector. He knocked the man to the toilet floor and took his wallet. Michael's hands ached for a week. On another occasion he wrestled one trick's head into an unflushed toilet bowl filled with dark yellow urine and floating feces.

Russell had shown Michael the cosh he carried for protection. It was a lead pipe, six inches in length, wrapped in cloth that was taped to the pipe to muffle the blow. Michael made his own cosh and carried it with him. Just tugging it out was enough to convince a reluctant customer.

One trick turned around after he was done and punched Michael in the face. As he fumbled with Michael's pockets, Michael retaliated, brandishing the cosh. He beat the man, grabbed his wallet, and ran away. After that incident, he thought of exhuming the knife he had buried in Hyde Park but knew the blade would be rusted by now.

In the Victoria Station public toilets one evening, an Italian offered to pay only half of Michael's fee. When the man turned around to button his pants, Michael brought the cosh down hard on the Italian's skull. The man collapsed in a heap. Michael reached inside the trick's pockets and turned them inside out, grabbing the man's wallet and all his jewelry. Only after several incidents such as this did he learn the wisdom of making clients pay upfront.

Michael began avoiding the toilets at Victoria Station. He figured the police would be looking for him. He also worried that if he did not stop turning tricks, it would be only a matter of time before he killed someone.

Despite his efforts, Michael was not making the money he needed. He barely managed to feed his addiction on a daily basis. As the weeks passed, he looked more disheveled. His filthy appearance made it difficult to attract well-paying clients. It didn't matter. He had had enough of dealing with tricks anyway. Briefly he thought of returning to the academy and asking for his old janitorial job back. But the pay was barely enough to keep him fed, much less support his habit. There was also the possibility of bumping into Suzanne.

So Michael became a good thief and an even better con artist. At night he stole from sleeping drunks on platform benches in train stations and at bus stops. He would snake a hand into their pockets, extracting anything he could—cash, wallets, rings, jewelry, watches. If a drunk happened to wake up, Michael would simply touch the man suggestively on the thigh, pretending to be looking for quick, anonymous sex while stealthily robbing the drunk of his possessions.

He would sleep until noon, then rise and wander to the East End, where he would cash in his booty. Generally he made enough to pay for rent and two fixes a day. On a bad night when he was hungry and his pockets empty, he would steal food from the crowded open-air markets on Berwick Street. Pretending to be a shopper, Michael would stuff the pockets of his coat with bread and fruit as he meandered past the displays.

MICHAEL ARRIVED at Russell's one night, soaking wet from the rains. "I've been turfed out," he said.

Russell handed Michael a towel, and Michael began drying his hair. "From your bed-sit?" said Russell.

"For not paying rent."

"Listen, mate. It's about time you squatted."

"What's that?"

"Sharing a condemned building with other vagrants. Tomorrow I'll take you to a place I know nearby that's not too crowded."

The next day Michael eyed warily the second-floor room in the old, dilapidated building that Russell had led him to. It seemed to have functioned at one time as a sitting room. Four large, grime-covered windows, two of which were broken, lined one wall. The walls had darkened to a dull beige from cigarette smoke and lack of cleaning, and the room had no furniture. The entire house reeked of spirits, vomit, and urine. There was no electricity, no heat, no running water, and no working toilet.

Russell patted Michael on the back. "You'll be OK here, mate," he said. "At least you'll be out of the rains."

Michael slept in the middle of the floor on a worn mattress with a threadbare blanket Russell had found for him. He had no sheets or pillows. All night long he heard footsteps throughout the building. The cracked paint was peeling off the walls. He was often smacked out of a sound sleep by chunks of plaster falling from the ceiling. He found a decrepit Bible in one of the hallways and began rolling cigarettes out of Deuteronomy.

In the mornings he would try to dry shave, but the blade of his razor coarsely scraped across the rugged, stubbly landscape of his face. Deciding it was too uncomfortable, he gave up shaving altogether.

The winter cold and dampness invaded every part of the old building and seeped into Michael's bones. He was cold when he went to sleep and stiff when he woke up. He could see the clouds of his breath in the room. Because of the cold and the lack of running water, he seldom bathed. If he had to pee, he did so against the brick wall of the alleyway outside, teeth chattering. Sometimes a freezing wind danced through the room, and he would stuff the holes and cracks in the windows with newspaper. Nothing helped. The cold was inescapable and paralyzing. Its misery provoked vague memories of his mother and of hot monastery meals, especially the fresh-baked bread that Michael could smell in his mind. He imagined sleeping in one of the soft beds with clean linens and sinking into a warm bath as the steam rose from the surface of the water.

Michael slept by day and went out by night. The cold stung his cheeks when he ventured outside. Long strands of mucus ran from his nostrils. He blew his nose so much it began bleeding. Wrapping his coat tightly around him, he turned up the collar against the raw wind and buried his hands deep inside his pockets. Often he entered the warmth of pubs just to get out of the rain and cold. But when he did not buy a drink, the publican told him to leave.

Soon Michael began wrapping newspapers around his torso, legs, and feet to insulate himself from the bitter cold. An old vagrant in the park had shown him that trick. "Newspaper," said the old man, "is the best insulation against the cold. The feet are the body's thermostat. Keep them warm and the rest of the body will be warm. Remember, as long as your feet are warm, you can wander around in a blizzard and never be cold."

Michael kept the newspaper wrapped around his body for days until it disintegrated.

When he came back to his room at night, he would lie on his back, counting the lines and cracks in the ceiling and watching the shadows made by passing cars creep across the walls.

If it rained hard, his ceiling leaked. A series of cans on the floor collected the drops. Each can made a different sound as the water steadily dripped into it hour after hour.

Then Amanda's works box went missing. Michael had hidden it as best he could under his mattress, but one evening he returned to his room to find it gone. Beside himself, he searched everywhere. Michael did not have roommates, only a steady stream of vagrants with different faces. Save for that box, he had no other possessions. It was the last remaining vestige of Amanda. And now it too was gone. For days he wept.

THE SQUATTERS were finally evicted from the derelict building, and once again Michael found himself without a place to stay.

During the freezing winter days he slept on park benches until he was told to move along by the police. He slept under the bridges along the Thames with other vagrants. There, at least, under their resounding vaults, he could sleep undisturbed. At one bridge a soup truck pulled up every night. Everyone who lined up was handed a bowl of soup and a roll. The smell of the soup reminded Michael of the monastery.

Michael also did the rounds of the local doss houses. Few of them had proper beds. Most were just rooms with mattresses strewn on the floor, six to a room, with hardly a gap between them. Michael shared one room with five bearded men reeking of alcohol, urine, and body odor. During the night some wet themselves in their sleep, and by the morning the stench of dried urine was stifling. One regular was a drunken Irishman in a tattered coat who sang calmly to himself and always introduced himself as the Savior's spokesman. There was also a blind man who tapped his stick along the hall, entered the room, and without a word lay down quietly on an empty mattress.

For Michael, the doss houses were the only place he knew to keep warm. By night, wrapping his long coat around him, he lay down on a sheetless mattress that sunk in the middle and smelled of dried urine. By day, the anteroom was full of elderly people who sat unmoving, like old bookends.

The house Michael frequented the most had a balding, bespectacled caretaker. He had an unlit pipe in his mouth and always wore a threadbare button cardigan that was missing two buttons. Even though he knew Michael was one of his regulars, he still repeated the same thing to him whenever he swung the door open to the room: "Two bob. In advance."

Sometimes when he was hungry and didn't have any money, Michael rummaged through rubbish bins behind restaurants in search of food in the early hours of the morning. Even the stench of rotting vegetables and decaying meat was not enough to deter him. He would stuff himself until he was full.

One late afternoon as vendors were packing up for the day, Michael was caught thieving two oranges and a banana from an open-air market. Pursued by two men, Michael sprinted through the streets with all the strength he could muster. Turning into a blind alley, he found himself cornered. Michael surprised one of the men by rushing him. He pulled out his cosh and swiftly brought it down on the man's head. The man fell to the ground. He turned to the second pursuer, who stood motionless and wide-eyed before running off into the fading afternoon light.

Michael's terror left his mouth and eyes dry. He bent over his unconscious victim and ran his hands through his pockets. After removing the man's wallet and wristwatch, Michael quickly left the alley.

LIKE ALL monks who got seasonal colds, it began with the sniffles. After bouts of continuous sneezing, however, there was the risk of spreading his cold to others, and so Brother Thomas was forbidden to work in the kitchen. A day later he took to his bed. Steven and the other friars thought nothing of it. Everyone had bad colds from time to time.

Steven brought Thomas herbal teas and restricted his diet. But with the passing days, Thomas's condition worsened. With the help of Ignatius and Matthew, he was moved to the infirmary. But despite Steven's watchful eye, Thomas's fever and coughing turned into bronchitis. When Thomas fell into pneumonia, the abbot called Steven into his study.

"There are many here," said Daniel, "who feel that Thomas would be better served if he was in hospital. They are imploring me to call for an outside doctor or an ambulance."

"I do not agree with that," Steven said.

"All the same, Steven, Thomas's condition has deteriorated, and it's time you acknowledge that."

"I assure you I can help him."

"This is not the time to be testing yourself, Steven. Even Dominic knew his limitations. I don't wish to bring up a sore point, but Dominic knew when it was time to call an ambulance when your own condition had moved beyond the boundaries of his skills."

"I know I can help Thomas," Steven repeated, "but I need a few more days."

"A few more days may be all he has."

Thomas continued coughing so violently it scared Steven. Whenever he wasn't by Thomas's side, he was studying and preparing medicine in his laboratory.

"They want me to call an ambulance," Steven said as he applied hot compresses to Thomas's forehead and had him sip calendula. "They say you should be in hospital."

"You can do this," Thomas whispered hoarsely.

"The truth is, I don't know if I can," Steven confessed. "I've consulted Dominic's manuals and his notes. Nothing makes sense."

Thomas opened his eyes. "Ask Dominic for help."

That night, when Thomas appeared to be sleeping, Steven sat next to the bed and in silence asked his father for help.

The next day something wonderful happened.

Steven awoke with a peculiar insight that he decided to follow. With the help of Brothers Gregory and Christopher, Steven constructed a tent out of two sheets over Thomas's bed. Christopher created the frame by lashing four metal rods to the legs of the bed. Sheets were draped over the rods. A table was placed at the foot of the bed, which was covered by the same sheet that tented the bed. Every hour a cauldron of hot water was brought in and set on the table. It too was draped by the same sheet. Steam filled the tent. Next, Steven poured eucalyptus oil into the cauldron and rubbed linseed oil over Thomas's bare chest. When the muscles in his hands and arms grew sore from massaging, he soaked towels in the hot cauldron and wrung them out. He sprayed them with eucalyptus oil before placing them on Thomas's chest. In addition, he placed a small cloth, also soaked with hot water and eucalyptus oil, over Thomas's face.

As Steven slowly and methodically rubbed the monk's chest, he felt something, like a shiver, move through his entire body, from his head to his toes. Suddenly he felt a pair of hands on his, but when he glanced around there was no one else in the room.

For two days Thomas lay in the tent, sweating so profusely that the sheets from under him had to be changed every few hours. But at the end of the second day, when Steven took Thomas's temperature, he was utterly astounded: Thomas's fever had vanished. Within a short time the cook was talking and joking again, drinking mugs of hot tea and even getting up and going to the bathroom unaided.

When the abbot came to see for himself, Thomas was still in his tent. "Quite like this tent," he joked. "I may erect one in my room."

All the brothers crowded into the room, happy and grateful for Thomas's recovery. After the well-wishers had left, Steven and Thomas were alone in the infirmary. Thomas asked Steven to sit down beside him. He reached out and held Steven's hand.

"I told you, didn't I?" he said. His red hair was still soaked in perspiration. "You had a divine intervention. It came from Dominic. I told you that you would find God in your own way. You've done so through the practice of medicine, with Dominic's help."

No one ever questioned Steven's abilities again. From that moment on, everyone took the monastery physician seriously.

FOR TWO cold months Michael slept on the streets, surviving only to feed his addiction. He decided to rob one last time, a haul big enough to pay for his cure and start over. But the only place where he could find that kind of money was a bank, and robbing a bank was out of the question.

While he was walking through the rains one afternoon, he passed a church, and an idea came to him.

Churches.

Churches housed collection boxes brimming with donations. Their altars were adorned with gold chalices and silver candle-holders encrusted with precious and semiprecious stones. Even the chalice and the candleholders at the monastery were opulent, he remembered. He also knew that the doors of churches were always open to the faithful and the penitent. This also left them vulnerable and undefended. He could have the place to himself. Best of all, he knew that if he was caught, no priest would ever bring charges against a Catholic orphan boy.

Michael remembered a small church in Bayswater, on the corner where he once lived. The church was a 170-year-old brown stone building, with a high vault and stained-glass windows. He had visited the church once out of curiosity and knew that the altar was always set for service, even if no one was in the church.

On a rainy afternoon he entered the church through its thick oak doors. As he predicted, the building was empty. Without hesitation Michael walked straight up to the altar, his footsteps echoing under the stone vault. He stepped over the wooden railing running the width of the room and stood in front of the altar, neatly laid out with a white cloth.

From under his coat he produced a canvas gunnysack. On the altar was a pair of ornate silver candlesticks encrusted with semiprecious stones. But as he reached to grab the first one, a mysterious force suddenly compelled him to fall on his knees and abandon all thoughts of robbery.

Michael closed his eyes and found himself surrounded by echoes of the abbey of St. Martin's. In his mind he smelled the mowed lawns after the rains. He felt the warm waters of the bath against his skin and smelled the lavender soap as he rubbed the bar on his skin. In the distance he saw the sandstone and granite buildings in the pale pink dawn. He felt a soft breeze on his face that came off the fields and heard the rustling of the trees as the breeze caught them. He also heard the familiar chattering of the stream and, far off in the distance, the ringing of St. Martin's bell.

He opened his eyes. His cheeks were soaked with tears. Michael looked up at the large, polished wooden crucifix suspended on the wall above the altar. He stared intently at it for several minutes, then slowly rose and left the building.

16

A CROWD HAD GATHERED around one stall in the Underground public toilet. Michael finished relieving himself and stood behind the others, trying to see what all the commotion was about, but he could not see over the heads of all the onlookers.

An ambulance arrived, and the medics shouted at everyone to get back. As the crowd parted, Michael could see a skeletal excuse for a man lying sprawled on the toilet floor on his back, his eyes staring blankly into space. A syringe lay close to his hand. The medics picked up the body, placed it on a stretcher, and left with the victim. The crowd dispersed.

Michael remained, staring at the empty, stained floor. He saw himself lying there, and that terrified him.

He looked at himself in the cracked lavatory mirror. What he saw reflected was a stranger's face—cadaverous, devoured by drugs, hollowed out by hard living on the streets. His orbits were dark, sunken wells in a pale, pasty landscape, so deeply recessed they were mere outlines of dark shadows. His eyes danced nervously.

Michael turned his head from side to side, scrutinizing himself more closely. Reaching out to touch the image in the mirror, he then brought his hand back to his face. Meticulously he felt every inch of his flesh, every stubble, every pimple, as if he were blind.

"I WANT to quit," Michael said.

"Easier said than done, mate," Russell said. "But well worth considering. This really isn't your style. Never was. You should go back to your monks, to your three hot meals a day and a warm bed."

"How did you kick?" Michael said.

Russell lit a cigarette. He took a long drag and blew the gray-blue smoke up into the air. "Doctor's help."

Michael looked around Russell's tiny flat. Russell slept on a camping mattress on the hardwood floor with only a thin blanket to cover him. A battered wooden box held a radio, a few white candles and some books. On his walls hung a few posters and postcards. A corner of one poster was curling up and needed to be tacked back onto the wall. There were no other furnishings.

"How many years were you using?" Michael said.

"Eleven."

"How much did the treatment cost?"

"One fifty."

Michael rubbed his forehead. "Was it easy?"

"Piece of cake. The doc put me on methadone. I slept a lot."

"How long did it take?"

"Three weeks for the treatment, two weeks sleeping it off."

"I just don't have the money," Michael said.

"You can try it yourself."

"How?"

Russell shrugged his shoulders. "Drink plenty of orange juice."

"What made you quit?"

"After a while, nothing mattered except junk," Russell said. "Life isn't worth living for a drug." As an afterthought he said,

"Nobody gives a damn about a junkie. No one's gonna light candles at your funeral, mate."

"Why do you sell it, then?"

"Good money," Russell said. "My last straight job was washing corpses. That paid well too. Hundred quid a week. But it really got me down." He rubbed his eyes with his knuckles and yawned. "These days, all I do is sell. Never touch the stuff myself."

Michael considered his predicament. *Two weeks*, he thought. That was too long. Two weeks without the drug was an eternity. Deep down he knew he could never last that long. Stealing money for his cure was also out of the question. The day he had walked out of that church, he made a commitment not to steal or rob anymore. Going cold turkey was his only option. Russell was kind enough to offer his floor and spare mattress. At least Michael would have a roof over his head.

The first day without the drug was easy. But midway through the second day, despite the orange juice, Michael began experiencing excruciating aches and pains in his muscles and joints. His entire body began shaking and shivering uncontrollably. A screeching sound rang in his ears, as if the room were full of confused, storm-tossed seagulls. The symptoms gnawed at his body and tore at his bones. Like a frenzied monkey they clawed at him, never letting go. Violent vomiting and diarrhea were followed by uncontrollable fits of sneezing that left him gasping for breath. Then he experienced a debilitating weakness as if his blood were too thick to circulate. He felt as if all the cells in his body were dying, all at once.

By this time he was too weak to get off the mattress, but he couldn't lie still. His nerves were on edge. The drug sickness had taken over his body. He wanted desperately to sleep, yet his chattering thoughts banished all hope of rest.

For three days straight Michael lay on the mattress, shivering, soaked in cold sweat. It coursed down his face and body, drenching his clothes. He began to feel like a bag of bones. Soon he was unable to move. When he couldn't get up and go down the hall to the toilet, he urinated into an empty milk bottle Russell had given him.

Paralysis crept through him, closing down every part of his body. First his lips became numb, as if he had been punched in the mouth. Then his face went cold. He lost all feeling in his knees and legs. It was as though his limbs were no longer attached to his body. Warm saliva filled his mouth, and his eyes became so dry he had to keep them closed. Leaving them open hurt too much. His heart palpitated wildly, racing out of control, and his breathing became short. Anxiety gripped his body. He felt his hands and face swelling but was unable to get up to look in the mirror.

Michael tried calming himself. "It will be alright," he said repeatedly to himself out loud.

He endured the nightmare for five days. When he felt he could no longer take it, he conceded the battle. Now only one thought obsessed him: the searing pain could be banished with a single fix. He summoned Russell, who did not hesitate to act. Michael recited a shaky Hail Mary as Russell edged the needle into his arm. Within minutes relief flooded every part of Michael's body.

As he lay on Russell's floor, Michael felt as if he was awakening from a bad dream. He remembered that Steven had once warned him that his talents would turn against him if he turned his back on them. More than once, Steven had mentioned that Michael had it in him to be a great painter. Those words haunted Michael now. For a brief moment, the belief he once held—that he could do anything and rise to the pinnacle of success—came flooding back. But at the same time, he became guilt ridden as he realized how far he had sunk.

All his life Michael had done everything alone. He had taught himself to paint. Whenever there was a problem, on his own he had found a solution; an ailment, the cure; a question, the answer. For the first time in his life he was facing something he could not do alone. He felt like a spark flying off into space, helpless.

Then, as if from nowhere, it came to him. Brother Dominic was a doctor. *Yes*, Michael thought. *He can help me.*

Michael was comforted by the thought of Dominic's medical talents. A sudden urge to see both Dominic and Brother Thomas again filled him. But just as quickly he was reminded of all the reasons why he had left the abbey in the first place. He did not want to return as a junkie. At the very least, he wanted to come back as he had left.

But that was only a fantasy now.

"I'm taking your advice," Michael said to Russell. "I'm going back to the monastery. There's a monk there who's a doctor. I know he can help me."

At daybreak Michael bundled himself up. He shook Russell's hand and thanked him for everything. He stumbled out into the cold February morning where the streets were shiny with rain. Michael turned up his collar and began walking against the cold that burned his cheeks and nostrils.

STEVEN WAS mixing medicines in the laboratory, concentrating on measuring the precise amounts called for by the prescription. A novice barged in.

"What is it?" Steven said without looking up.

"There's a man looking for Brother Dominic," said the novice.

Distracted, Steven sighed and stopped what he was doing. Slowly he walked to the front entrance. A rain-soaked figure sat hunched over on the bench in the foyer. There was a puddle of water on the stone floor at his feet. The man's smell was so overpowering Steven had difficulty approaching him.

"Yes," said Steven. "May I help you?"

The man raised his head. He looked ill. Sagging dark circles hung under his eyes. Pale and gaunt, his face was mere skin stretched over bones. His long hair and shapeless beard were matted from neglect. His entire appearance was disheveled and windswept. His hands were dirty, and there was black grime under his fingernails. Clothes tattered and threadbare, he looked like he had not bathed in weeks.

For a moment there was no recognition on Steven's part. Then he stared into the man's vacant, ice-blue eyes.

Steven lost his breath momentarily. "Michael," he uttered.

Michael looked at Steven's habit with bleary eyes. "This is a joke, correct?"

"What do you mean?" said Steven.

"Where's Dominic?"

"He's dead."

"Very well," Michael said. "If you insist on playing games, I'll find him myself."

Michael struggled to his feet and was about to march off in the direction of the laboratory when Steven caught his arm. "That won't be necessary," he said.

Under the protection of an umbrella, Steven led Michael through the pouring rain to the cemetery. They stopped at Dominic's headstone. Michael stared at the grave marker bearing the monk's name as the rain beat down on the umbrella.

"When?" Michael shouted over the din of the rain.

"Fall, more than a year ago," Steven shouted back.

"How?"

"Heart failure. It was sudden."

Steven helped Michael back to the monastery and led him to the infirmary. He handed Michael a towel. Catatonically Michael undressed and dried himself off. He pulled back the sheets on one of the beds, crawled underneath, and within moments was fast asleep.

Michael's arm hung over the side of the bed. Steven gently lifted it and was about to place it under the covers when he noticed how black and blue the inner arm was. Looking closely, he saw tiny puncture marks that ran up and down, like the footprints of a drunken insect. He covered Michael with another blanket.

Turning his attention to Michael's clothes, Steven bundled everything up and left them on the floor. Before bundling Michael's coat, which was tattered and threadbare in places, Steven went through it thoroughly. Emptying out all the pockets, he found a spoon, a box of matches, a packet of cigarettes, a makeshift cosh, and seven pounds. He also found two wax-paper packets. When Steven opened one, he saw that it contained a white powder.

His fingers felt something long and cylindrical, thin, like a fountain pen, trapped in the coat's lining. He fumbled through the cloth until he found an opening. Carefully he guided the object out. It was a syringe.

Steven was puzzled. He didn't remember Michael having any health problems. He took everything he found and locked it away in a cabinet drawer in the infirmary.

MICHAEL AWOKE in the middle of the night, his body crying out in pain. He didn't know where he was. Groping in the dark, he felt a night table and a long, slender candleholder. His probing fingers encountered a box of matches. Striking one, he lit the candle. Looking around in the darkness, he remembered he was in the monastery infirmary but could not recall how he got there.

Using the light of the candle, he found all his clothes on the floor tied in a bundle. His coat hung from a hanger. He ran his hands through the pockets and found nothing.

Michael became desperate. Guiding the candle around the room, he came across Steven sleeping. His bed blocked the door. Michael went back to his bed and sat down.

Russell had donated three fiver bags, a syringe, and ten pounds in cash to keep Michael going until he reached the monastery. The trip, mostly on foot, had taken four days. Michael used one bag sparingly. At nights he slept under trees and in barns. During the day he tramped along the roadside in the winter cold. He ate little. His only plan was to make it to the monastery to be cured.

Perhaps Steven knows enough to help me, he had told himself. *Dominic most likely has trained him.* But Michael had dismissed the idea. No one could replace Dominic. Now, with his death Michael's hopes vanished. He needed the drug's warm oblivion, and what little he had brought with him was missing.

Michael knew he would need money to buy more drugs. He also knew the monastery possessed a chalice from the Middle Ages rumored to have belonged to a Frankish emperor. Cast in pure gold, it was studded with precious stones. It was kept on permanent display, locked behind a thin pane of glass in a wooden cabinet in a corner of the chapel. It had been there for as long as he could remember. He could make his way to the chapel via the sacristy. In his mind he could hear the metal lock squealing as he forced it open, and he could almost feel the cold metal chalice in his sweaty palms. He could slip it under his shirt or into his coat pocket and escape back to London with his prize.

It would be easy, he thought. There was just one problem: how would he get past Steven? Although he was sleeping peacefully, moving Steven was out of the question. Michael could climb out a window, but he knew the infirmary windows all opened onto an enclosed garden with twelve-foot-high walls.

The pain of withdrawal sharpened.

Michael's only option was to render Steven unconscious. He knew there was a possibility of killing him, but his only thoughts were acquiring the chalice. Without further contemplation he searched in the dark for a weapon. He lamented not having his cosh. It could have done the job quickly and silently. Fumbling under his bed, he came across a loose metal strut that supported the mattress. Working quietly, he unscrewed it free. He wrapped the strut in his pillowcase so as to inflict the minimum amount of damage.

He held the candle in front of him and tiptoed over to Steven's bed. It was late at night, and not a sound would be heard. Silently Michael raised the iron bar above his head. In that instant, the candlelight caught Steven's angelic face, wrapped softly in blissful sleep. Michael's grip weakened and his arm sank to his side.

Dear God. What has become of me?

Michael stood there for a moment, the bar in his hand. After laying it on the floor, he shook Steven awake. "I need my medicine," he said. "Where have you put my medicine?"

Groggily Steven got up. Using Michael's candle, he found his keys, wandered over to the cabinet, and unlocked the drawer.

"Are you diabetic?" said Steven, slipping the cosh under his nightshirt when Michael wasn't looking.

Michael shivered. "Something like that."

Steven gave the candle to Michael. He walked back to his bed, climbed in, and went to sleep.

Michael sat down on his bed. By the light of the candle, he poured some of the white powder into the spoon and struck a match under it. He held the spoon with the end of the towel he had used to dry himself off. He wrapped his leather belt around his arm, filled the syringe, and darted the needle into his arm. Within moments his trembling body dissolved into a tranquil calm. He lit a cigarette and inhaled deeply. Smoking was forbidden in the monastery, but he didn't care. He finished his cigarette and stubbed it out on the stone floor, then blew out the candle and went back to bed.

STEVEN AWOKE early and found Michael still asleep. He went into the lavatory and studied the contents of the toilet bowl Michael had neglected to flush. The dark, cloudy yellow urine was an indication of toxicity.

Picking up the empty syringe and spoon from Michael's bedside, Steven brought them to the laboratory. A few drops remained inside the glass cylinder. He carefully removed the plunger from the syringe and transferred the liquid to a glass slide, which he inserted under the microscope. He studied the slide. In a worn notebook that sat beside the microscope, he listed in pencil all of Michael's symptoms, then what he observed on the slide. He consulted the rows of medical books on the bookshelves, searching the pages on toxicity. Within an hour he had matched Michael's symptoms.

The substance Michael was injecting was not a drug to treat diabetes. It was heroin.

Steven asked Brother Thomas to prepare a tray of food. When Steven brought the tray in, he found Michael sitting up, staring off into space.

"Thought you'd be hungry," Steven said, setting the tray of bread, bacon, eggs, and a cup of tea on his lap.

Michael did not say anything. He began to eat the food slowly. Steven picked up the bundle of Michael's clothes and took his tattered jacket off the hanger. "I'm going to take your things to be laundered and mended," he said. "I'll be back in a few minutes."

When he returned, he found Michael had devoured everything on the tray. "Well," Steven said, "looks like you were hungry." He picked up the tray. "I'll trot off to the kitchen to drop this off. Be back in a moment. Anything else I can get you?"

Michael continued to stare straight ahead, saying nothing.

Nobody but Thomas knew that the patient was Michael. In the kitchen Thomas looked at the empty plates and said, "Well, he hasn't lost his appetite, has he?" He put the dishes into the sink and began running the water. "I'm glad he's back. And how's he doing?"

Steven didn't want to lie to Thomas. "He's a drug addict."

Thomas turned off the water and quickly dried his hands. He turned and faced Steven. "Repeat that for me. I don't think I heard you clearly."

"He's a drug addict. Heroin."

"That's what I thought you said." Thomas sighed and shook his head. "Now who's going to tell the abbot?"

"I'm going to. But I'm going to tell him that he's got a severe cold. I'm counting on you to say nothing, Thomas. Please."

Thomas approached Steven and put a hand on his shoulder. "I give you my word. I know how fond of him you were. There's the possibility that you won't be able to help him. And nothing is worse than knowing you can't help someone you love."

Steven said softly, "But I did help you."

Thomas smiled.

17

LATER THAT DAY WHILE Michael slept, Steven, Thomas, and Andrew stripped the linens from his bed and fastened his arms and legs to the four posts with cloth strips. Steven had read in his medical texts that addicts could become dangerous to themselves and others when their supply was unavailable. One volume, published in 1902, even compared the drug withdrawal process to a demonic exorcism. All the books stressed the importance of vigilance throughout the entire ordeal.

Looks could be deceiving. Although Michael was skinny, Steven knew that even addicts who were emaciated and appeared weak could possess considerable physical strength.

Michael awoke just as his legs were being fastened. "What's all this?" he shouted.

"It's for your own good," Steven said.

On the empty bed next to Michael's, Steven laid out fresh cloths and towels. An assortment of metal bowls of different sizes were placed on the floor. An ancient metal trolley was wheeled into the room. Dominic had used this portable tabletop to transport medications when administering bedside treatments to infirm brothers.

"So when did you sink to this level?" said Michael.

"What do you mean?"

"What the hell do you think you're doing? You don't have a clue, do you?"

Steven casually unfolded and laid out towels. Another monk came in and began filling some of the metal bowls with boiling water.

"So you're a monk now, is that it?" Michael sneered.

"Yes."

"Self-denial, is it? A lifetime of conformity, confinement, commitment to an intangibility?"

"You'll never understand."

"You're absolutely correct. I don't. I credited you with more intelligence."

Steven dunked some of the towels in the hot water. "It doesn't matter what you think. It's what I believe that matters."

"Prayer impoverishes the soul," Michael said. "How many times did I tell you that? And now look at you!"

Steven said nothing.

"Your God will disappoint you. He'll let you down. And your fucking religion will not save you!"

After the knots were secured and checked, Steven nodded to Thomas and Andrew. They retreated from the bed.

"And what the hell do you think you're doing, taking Dominic's place?"

"He trained me to do this."

"Did he, now. Well, I've news. The only thing you've ever been trained to do is to wipe your own ass. And it's questionable whether you can even do that!"

Years earlier, Michael's verbal jabs would have been a knife to Steven's heart. Now he knew it was only the addiction talking.

"I am a sinner," said Steven, "just like any other. I have my faults, my weaknesses. I am content to serve God."

"I'm not getting through that thick skull of yours," Michael hissed. *"A monk's life is a wasted life!"*

Steven shook his head. "I am not like you," he said. "Unlike you, this is not my prison. I am not enslaved by my beliefs, as you may think."

Squirming to escape his bonds, Michael yelled, "A monk's life is a wasted life!"

Ignoring Michael's tirade, Steven began preparing the medications. Even though Steven had never treated narcotic addiction before, he knew he could rely on Dominic's manuals. From his reading, Steven was able to predict the course of his patient's withdrawal. The process would be uncomfortable, lasting anywhere from four days to a week.

Andrew stepped forward to hold Michael still. Steven began inserting acupuncture needles along the meridians and points of Michael's body that would help relieve the withdrawal symptoms. He placed a cluster of needles on his chest and on his feet. It was going to be a difficult night.

STEVEN KEPT Michael isolated in the infirmary, away from the others. Many wondered why Steven was nursing this vagrant, this disheveled London tramp. Aside from Thomas and Andrew, Steven told those who asked that Michael had a bad case of influenza and was simply passing a fever. That ended the questioning.

Michael showed no outward reaction to the treatment on the first day. He just slept.

That night the abbot paid a visit to the infirmary. Seeing Michael raised his suspicions. "Steven, why does a patient with influenza need to be bound hand and foot?"

Steven knew the time would come when he would have to be truthful to his abbot, and that time was now. "Abbot, you remember Michael Warren. He does not have influenza. He's addicted to heroin."

By the flickering candlelight, Daniel looked closer and recalled Michael. "It is not your place," he said, "to treat or care for
those outside our walls."

"Abbot," said Steven, "I was raised here, and so was Michael.
I believe there's an unwritten rule that any orphan who leaves us
can always return if he is in need. Apart from that, I am the physician here. And all matters of health are my jurisdiction."

"He may stay until he is well," said the abbot. "Then he must
go." He gave Steven a piercing look and added, "I knew he would
turn out badly."

THE SECOND day Michael began perspiring. His sheets and bedclothing were so drenched in sweat that they had to be changed
every few hours. Hot towels were wrung out and pressed against
his burning flesh. Cold towels were applied to his face and forehead.

Thomas allowed Andrew to assist Steven in handing him towels and ointments. For hours Steven massaged Michael's muscles
and joints in an effort to bring the toxins to the surface more
quickly and speed up the withdrawal process. The smell was awful.

Michael was tormented by a terrible thirst, and his mouth was
always dry. Steven knew liquids were the key to his patient's recovery. Every four hours he would lift Michael's head, raise a
glass to his lips, and administer a chamomile solution mixed with
water to cleanse Michael's body of the toxins.

By the second day Michael's thirst was compounded by a fever
that Steven knew had to run its course. Michael's sweating continued. As his fever escalated, Michael began having severe hot
and cold flashes throughout his entire body.

On the third day Michael was at times wide awake and alert,
and at other times delirious, hardly recognizing Steven or his surroundings. In his delirium Michael talked of a tingly sensation,

like an electrical current running the length of his arms and legs, akin to ants crawling over and under his skin. He also mumbled about sharp pains that stabbed at his bones and muscles.

Steven was plagued by self-doubt and worry. Despite the fact that he had followed Dominic's manuals to the letter, he still agonized over whether he had left something out. When he leaned over the bed and looked into Michael's expressionless, sleeping face, he wondered if he had checked his manuals thoroughly against the copious notes he had made.

An incessant prayer, Dominic had never hesitated to get down on his knees on the cold stone floor of his cell to ask for guidance or an answer. As Michael slept, Steven knelt by the side of his patient's bed and prayed to God for help. He removed the cross that hung from his neck and placed it on the wooden table beside Michael's bed.

Soon after, things took a turn for the worse.

Heavy rains beat down all night. Lightning flashed, and loud claps of thunder echoed throughout the monastery. The wind hammered severely against the windows of the infirmary, shaking them with such intensity that it seemed the glass would shatter in its casements.

But the cacophonous weather helped to mask Michael's tortured screams. Steven watched in horror as Michael's body convulsed and shook uncontrollably, as though possessed. His limbs jerked and twisted against their restraints. Then his entire body began bucking and writhing. Michael's red, sweaty face twitched and contorted. Mucus ran from his nostrils, and his blue eyes turned bloodshot. Four monks had to hold Michael down on the bed so that Steven could open his mouth and give him the chamomile-and-water solution.

"Do you want anything?" Steven said to Michael.

"You know fucking well what I want, you idiot! Where the hell's Dominic? He's the doctor around here."

Steven knew that hallucinations and delusions were part of the withdrawal process. "He'll be here soon," he said.

Hovering at Michael's side that night, Steven monitored his patient's progress. The minutes felt like hours as he watched sweat gush from every pore of Michael's body and endured his unceasing, nightmarish screaming.

Finally, at three thirty in the morning, Michael's tense body, drained from its struggle, surrendered to exhaustion. Like a stone sinking to the bottom of the ocean, he collapsed into a deep, fathomless sleep. At the same time, the thunderstorm passed, and a ghostlike stillness settled over the infirmary.

FEELING THAT Michael was no longer a physical threat, Steven untied him. Michael complained of body aches for days after the withdrawal. Fatigued and racked, he slept as though he had melted into the sheets. Whenever he was awake, he would stare aimlessly into space, dark yellow circles etched around his glazed eyes. Many times Steven had to repeat himself in order to be understood.

Using a pestle and mortar, Steven ground a compound into powder on the portable table. He poured the powder into a wooden cup and added water. The powder turned the water green. Steven helped Michael sit up. He gave him a straw.

Michael took one sniff. "Smells like sewer water," he said, handing the cup back to Steven, who pushed the cup back toward him.

"To the very last drop," he said, "if you want to get well."

Michael took a sip. "It tastes like soap."

"Drink it," said Steven.

Michael put the straw back into his mouth.

"Look at it this way," said Steven. "In the eighteenth century they would have bled you. Be grateful."

Michael's lips twitched slightly into a smile.

"Can you remember anything?" said Steven.

A collage of fragmented images whirled through Michael's mind: Suzanne kissing a strange man in a doorway, a ticking clock, the sharp smell of whiskey, something about the rain.

"I only remember bits of things," he said.

Within twenty minutes of drinking the liquid, all Michael's previous symptoms returned with a vengeance. His body flashed hot and cold. Every joint and muscle ached. When Steven saw Michael was about to vomit, he swiftly brought up a metal bowl he had placed on the floor at the side of the bed. Michael retched, then collapsed back onto the bed in a heap and passed out. Steven maneuvered the rest of his patient's body onto the middle of the bed and drew the covers over him.

In his dreams Michael kept hearing singing. He was convinced he had died and was being serenaded by a heavenly chorus of angels. But when he opened his eyes, he saw only Steven sitting next him, reading a book.

Groggily Michael said, "Where am I?"

Steven looked up. "You don't know?"

Michael silently surveyed the room. "The cloister?"

Steven nodded.

"But how did I get here?"

Steven knew the treatment would cause temporary amnesia. He wiped Michael's forehead with a warm, damp cloth. "How are you feeling?"

Michael had forgotten how comforting it was to have someone looking over him. "Tired," he said. He took a deep breath and recognized the sweet smell of freshly laundered sheets. In the distance the singing continued. "What's that?"

"Choir practice," Steven said.

Michael listened for a moment. "It's beautiful," he whispered.

"Yes," said Steven. "Yes, it is. I arranged for choir practice to be held in the hallway outside the infirmary." Steven smiled. "Doctor's orders." After a pause he said, "Would you like me to open the door?"

His face wooden, Michael nodded. Steven opened the door and, like a refreshing breeze, the lilting strains of plainchant wafted into the infirmary. Closing his eyes, Michael reveled in the uplifting melodies, which seemed to dance in the air and fill him with warmth and comfort. After a short time he felt his eyelids grow heavy.

Steven had inherited Dominic's love of music. Long ago he also recognized its healing properties. In his gut he knew that music was medicine to a tortured soul and that the stirring melodies of plainchant would reach the deepest parts of his friend's being.

Years earlier, the same music had meant nothing to Michael. He had been unable to appreciate the simple beauty of the canon, the long-drawn-out melismatic strands of plainchant hanging magically in the air, as if suspended by an invisible thread. Chills did not shoot down his spine when he heard the long note of the Ave. But now, its haunting quality intoxicated him.

When the choir had finished its practice, Steven brought a tray of food into the room. With his friend's help, Michael sat up in bed. He lifted the bowl of hot soup to his face. As the steam rose, his eyes closed in rapture. Having not eaten any solid food in five days, Michael raised the spoon to his lips and ate slowly. He resisted the temptation to gulp everything down, and savored it all.

After the meal, Steven ran a hot bath. He helped Michael out of bed and wrapped a towel around his thin waist. With much effort, Michael tried to stand. The illness of withdrawal had weakened him. Steven offered his arm, but Michael refused it. Legs shaking like a newborn colt's, he managed to take a few steps, then collapsed.

"*Shit!*" Michael shouted.

Michael felt Steven take him by the arm and guide him toward the bath. He couldn't remember the last time he had bathed. He eased himself into the tub until only his head was above water. The warm water soothed his aching bones.

Too weak to wash himself, Michael lay still. Steven sat on a stool behind the tub and washed his hair. There was a mirror by the side of the tub. Michael picked it up and looked at himself. His face had been devoured by the drug. His cheeks were so sunken that his cheekbones protruded. Welts and pimples covered his face. Unable to look at himself any longer, he put the mirror back.

"Dominic taught you well," Michael said while Steven scrubbed his scalp.

"Now that's a compliment," Steven said.

"Are you happy here?"

Steven didn't answer. Michael dunked his head under the water and washed all the soap out of his hair. Steven began shaving Michael's beard with a cutthroat razor. When he was done, he handed Michael a towel and Michael dried himself off. "It doesn't bother you, being locked up here?" said Michael.

"No," said Steven. He pointed to a chair. "Sit down. I'll cut your hair."

MICHAEL'S RECUPERATION, now peaceful, was monitored closely by Steven. During the night Michael often would awaken with a start to find Steven sitting there, watching over him. Steven continued to administer the green powder medication over Michael's objections.

"It tastes like shit," said Michael.

"It's for your own good," Steven said. "It'll flush the toxins out."

Gradually the color came back into Michael's face, and he began to gain back the weight he had lost. For the first time in months, his bowels moved easily. At night he always woke up thirsty and guzzled water from a large pitcher by his bed. No matter how much he drank, he still felt thirsty. And all night long he sweated.

When awake, Michael lay listlessly in bed, catatonically staring at the ceiling. Disabled from fatigue, he often gazed at Steven with half-absent eyes. His muscles ached from the long periods of spasms that he could not remember. He frequently snapped at Steven, but Steven remained unperturbed, wise enough to know that his patient was far from fully recovered.

Each night Michael fell asleep to the smell of freshly laundered sheets. When he slept, he lay on his back, arms folded across his chest, an expression of exhaustion carved on his strained face. Steven would tuck in his sleeping friend before retiring himself. One evening he stood there in a moment of reflection, gazing at Michael. Secretly he had hoped his friend would one day return. *How glad I am that you are back, my friend,* he thought. For two years he had waited, and hoped.

IT HAD rained all night, and it was still raining the following morning.

Steven gently nudged Michael awake. "Get up and get dressed. I've something to show you."

Michael grunted. "Go back to sleep, you imbecile."

"It's important."

Rubbing the sleep from his eyes, Michael sat up. "This better be good."

Michael groggily threaded his arms through his shirt and a jumper, and was about to step into his shoes when Steven said, "Don't worry about those. Come with me."

Curious, Michael followed Steven to the kitchen, where he watched Steven open a small bin on the counter and remove some bread. He handed Michael a large chunk. It was stale and hard.

"I know your spartan discipline calls for a bland diet," Michael said, "but stale bread? Isn't this carrying mortification a bit too far? I could break a window with this. Is that all there is for breakfast?"

Steven laughed. "Just put it in your pocket and follow me."

A row of rubber Wellington boots lined the stone floor at the monastery's back entrance. Jackets and coats hung from a rack. Umbrellas and walking sticks rested in an oak bin. Steven pulled on a pair of boots and slipped into a raincoat. "Go on," he said, "pull on a pair and put on a coat."

Michael stuffed the chunk of bread into his pocket and followed Steven's example. He trod behind Steven in the light rain until they arrived at the stream. A mist enshrouded the area, limiting visibility. At the water's edge Steven looked around, his horn-rimmed spectacles splattered with raindrops.

Steven removed the bread from his habit. "Take your bread," he said, "and shred it into crumbs. Then hold it out like this." Steven held his arms outstretched.

Bewildered, Michael reached into his pocket. He removed the chunk of bread, broke off a piece, and crumbled it. He held up his bread-filled palms, but his arms sagged unconfidently.

"No! No!" Steven said. "Higher, higher. Hold them up higher, so that your arms are level with your shoulders!"

Michael felt this was all a crude prank, retaliation for all the wrongs and hurts he had brought upon his friend. Just at that moment, a single bird flew out of the blanket of mist and alighted on Michael's left arm. It looked around nervously, confused. For a moment the tiny creature did not move. Then, cautiously, it hopped toward his open hand and pecked at the bread.

Michael did not find this too unusual. Sometimes, by complete mistake, wild birds had been known to land on humans. But within moments his entire body was surrounded by a flock of flapping birds summoned as if magically by some silent bell. They clung to his coat and crowded his outstretched arms and hands. Some even landed on his hair, perhaps mistaking it for a nest. Their uncanny boldness, the lack of fear they exhibited toward their greatest predator, amazed Michael. For the first time something was touching him that he had previously admired only from a distance. The birds appeared to accept him unconditionally as one of their own. He breathed as one with them. They became part of his skin, and he part of their feathers.

He crumbled more and more of the bread. As soon as he did, the birds devoured every morsel. Steven looked over at Michael. He saw elation fill his friend's face. Feeling a sense of joy he had never experienced before, Michael laughed with abandon. Relief flooded his entire body. His chest heaved and expanded with happiness. In an instant the weight of the sadness that had plagued him for so long was lifted.

If Michael's arms grew tired, he didn't notice. For a long while he stood there, touched by the same joy he had felt when he painted and when Suzanne showered him with soft kisses. He wanted to shout out his happiness.

After the final morsel had been eaten and the last bird flew off into the mist, Michael stood, strangely quiet. He stared out into the pale grayness, empty hands still raised toward the sky. The smile had disappeared from his face. He looked disappointed.

In an instant his mind drowned in a sea of a million memories that rushed through him. Without warning his legs buckled, and he sank to his knees in the mud, his body quivering. Out of his mouth came a wail wrung from his soul.

Steven knelt down and gathered his friend into his arms. He helped Michael to his feet again and walked him back to the monastery.

"HERE," SAID Steven. "Put this on. It should fit."

Michael looked at what Steven had handed him. It was a monk's habit, but made of soft cotton, not the coarse wool he was used to seeing.

"What's going on?" said Michael.

"Look, just do what I say. And bring your old clothes."

Michael pulled the habit over his naked body.

"Follow me," Steven said.

Dutifully Michael followed Steven to the very back of the garden, where there was a small patch of dirt.

"Alright," Steven said. "Put the clothes down."

Michael dumped them on the ground. Steven walked over to the bushes and fetched a can of kerosene. He removed the cap and doused the clothes with the liquid.

"What are you doing?" Michael said, horrified.

"This is what we do here when one of us becomes ordained. The old clothing is burned. It symbolizes releasing the old life and entering the new. Releasing the old is important so that you can move on. It's a ritual."

"No offense to your bloody rituals, mate," said Michael, "but maybe you can tell me what I'm supposed to wear. The ashes?"

"What you're wearing now, until we make you some new clothes," said Steven. "Now we must say a little prayer." He bowed his head and closed his eyes. "With the burning of these garments, O Lord, comes the releasing of Michael Warren's former life forever. With the ashes comes the freeing from the bondages of his past."

Steven lit a match and threw it on the damp clothing. There was a sound like a gust of wind, and the clothing burst into flame.

Wordlessly Michael watched as the flames consumed the remnants of his former life.

BACK IN his cell, Steven was folding his laundry and putting it away in his cupboard when the abbot paid him a visit.

"I thought I made it very clear to you that he must leave upon his recuperation," Daniel said. "Did we not have an agreement about this? He should have been gone by now. Why is he still here? Is he not cured? And why is he dressed in a habit? Where are his clothes?"

Before Steven could respond, the abbot became distracted by a series of pen-and-ink drawings hanging on the wall beside Steven's bed. He put on his glasses. "Oh my," he said. "What's this?"

"Michael Warren drew them years ago," Steven said. "He does have an extraordinary talent, don't you think?" Daniel did not answer but continued admiring the drawings. "Part of his therapy is to paint again," Steven continued. "When he has done that, then he is ready to leave, he is rehabilitated. Let me show you something."

From under his bed Steven tugged out the cardboard envelope of Michael's drawings. He turned it upside down and out cascaded dozens of drawings. One by one the abbot reviewed them all.

"Once upon a time, Brother Dominic had refused to show the abbot Michael's work. I am showing it to you now. This man has great talent, great promise. It's only through that that he can be healed."

Daniel was visibly stunned. "I never knew about any of this," he said. "Why didn't you bring this to my attention before?"

"Because, Abbot, I wanted to make sure you saw how he has flourished and not just a few drawings he did years ago, when it would have been difficult to judge his potential. Michael Warren has always been talented. It's just that when he was here, nobody wanted to see it. Finding himself through his art—allowing him to reconnect with it—is vital to his survival. Would you send him away now, at this crucial juncture?"

"What are you suggesting?" said the abbot.

"I would like to set him up in the storage shed, where his art therapy can begin. I'll buy the paints and canvas. He won't bother anyone."

Sighing, Daniel picked up one of the drawings. "Alright, I'll go along with it for now. But we'll review this again soon."

MICHAEL WAS given a small, spare room with a single window, a bed, and a bookshelf. A chair and tiny desk were next to the bed, a candle on the desk. In his new surroundings Michael withdrew into a shell of silence. A few times Steven lingered outside Michael's door, contemplating his friend's sobbing.

A brooding Michael tramped around the newly blossoming flowers in the gardens and paced up and down the colonnaded galleries. Many days he roamed the countryside, returning to the monastery only for meals. No one bothered him.

Each night before retiring, Steven checked on Michael in his room. Unaccustomed to a soft bed, Michael had grown used to a harsher world. He had removed the mattress from the bed and placed it on the floor. In the mornings Steven would find Michael on the floor, curled into a ball.

ONE AFTERNOON Steven was on his hands and knees pulling out weeds from one of the flowerbeds. The ground was warming up with the coming of spring, and everything—wanted and unwanted—was growing. Seeing Michael approach, he smiled.

"It's time to talk," said Michael.

Steven put down his trowel and brushed the dirt off his habit. They walked over to the bench at the far corner of the garden and sat down.

"You ask the questions first," said Michael.

"Alright," said Steven. "What did you do with your evenings in London?"

"I painted," said Michael. "I listened to music or a play on the wireless while I painted. I read a lot."

"Did you go out much?"

"Not really. After being at the college all day, I enjoyed being at home."

Steven paused for a moment. "Have you ever been with a woman?"

"Yes."

To Steven, the idea of exchanging intimacies with a woman was foreign. It simply never occurred to him. All his life he had lived surrounded by men. He had never known any women, save those he encountered in the village. He did have trouble, however, believing the biblical lessons that had taught him that women were the enemy. After all, his father, Dominic, had been in love with a woman whom he had held in great esteem.

"So how did you make the journey here from London?"

"Mostly on foot," Michael said. "It was cold. It took me four days. Strangers gave me food along the way. I'd stop just before nightfall to find shelter, sleeping under trees or in abandoned barns."

For the next three hours Michael told his story from beginning to end, from the day he left the monastery on that snowy morning until his return. No detail was left out. He talked of his dreams of becoming a famous painter, and how those dreams died the night he saw Suzanne's watercolor hanging on the academy's wall. As he described how he had sealed his windows for months, daylight began to fade.

"Why did you come back?" Steven said.

"I knew that question was coming. I wanted to be cured, and I knew I couldn't do it alone. I thought Dominic could help me."

"But how did your addiction begin?" Steven said.

"When Suzanne broke it off with me," Michael said, "I began looking for anything to numb the pain. I took long walks and tried finding answers in books. When those failed me, I became desperate. I found the answers in the bottle and the needle. My only happiness was injected. The drug was my whole world. Relief came only when I fixed."

Michael talked about Amanda, the woman who had introduced him to the drug. "When I found all the money she had stashed, I believed she had every intention of starting a new life." He grew quiet. "I killed the man who killed her."

Steven was shocked. "Killed?"

"He poisoned her with bad drugs."

Michael told Steven about the mysterious force he encountered when he tried to rob the church in Bayswater, and how it had irrevocably changed him and made him want to change his ways.

"When I learned from you that Dominic was dead," Michael said, "I wanted to kill you."

"Why?" Steven said.

"You were blocking the door. I had to kill you in order to get past you to steal the chalice from the chapel. That was my plan."

"Money for drugs?" said Steven.

Michael hung his head.

"You didn't have to kill me," Steven said. "I would have given it to you gladly and taken the blame."

"I had just enough junk to make it here," Michael said. "I believed you couldn't cure me."

Michael's voice was devoured by emotion, every sentence filled with anguish. In the dim light of the setting sun Steven could just make out the tears that filled his friend's eyes.

"Now it's my turn," Michael said. "What happened to the monastery orphanage?"

"Closed down," Steven said.

"Why?"

Steven pulled out a handkerchief from his pocket and gave it to Michael to dry his eyes. "Times changed. Orphanages are state run these days. The boys were all transferred elsewhere. To tell you the truth, it was a relief. Teaching by day and endeavoring to carry out our duties by night proved too much of a strain." Steven chuckled. "Frankly, many of the brothers were grateful to get their old lives back."

"When did it close down?"

"About a year ago."

"And Brother Richard and Brother Basil?"

"Gone."

"What happened?"

"Transferred. They couldn't stand what became of the monastery. They said they didn't sign on to take care of young boys."

"How did you take Dominic's death?" Michael said, changing the subject.

"After his death, I lost the will to go on. I lost everything, even my faith in my religion. I didn't care about life. Of course, I hid that from the others."

"He was a wonderful man," Michael said. "He was certainly to me. It's obvious why you miss him."

A part of Steven had never recovered from his father's death. But having Michael back was like a new beginning. The crucifix now was back on the wall above his bed. Steven was singing in the choir again, for the first time since Dominic's death.

18

FAR FROM THE NEON lights and seedy corners of Soho, Michael thrived. The rhythms of nature and the stability of life at the abbey had been his best medicine.

Each night the tree outside his window lulled him into a deep, childlike slumber as its leaves rustled and its branches gently tapped the glass. Every morning Michael was awakened by songbirds. Once dressed, he went to Brother Thomas's kitchen, where pots and pans hung on hooks from the ceiling and the intoxicating aroma of fresh coffee and baking bread permeated the room.

Thomas was getting old. Rheumatism filled his bones. His hands were so arthritic they resembled an eagle's talons. Groaning, he stopped to massage them. "Growing old is one of nature's brutal punishments," he said to Michael.

Despite this, Thomas refused to give up his kitchen duties. Although he could not physically carry out most of the tasks, he would sit in a chair in the corner and direct the others. And no matter how painful it was, he still insisted on making the bread himself every day.

As Michael watched, Thomas was his usual jovial self, humming and singing while he worked, white apron wrapped around his torso, hands buried in a large bowl of dough. He looked at Michael and sighed. "Every day it's the same. Ten loaves a day."

"That's ten loaves of the best bread in England," Michael told him.

He meant it. Thomas walked over to the sink to wash his hands, which were caked with white flour, then dried them on his apron. Michael sat down at the small table and ate a plate of eggs, bacon, and hot toast spread with freshly made jam, washing it all down with a cup of hot coffee. Truly grateful for the food, Michael never let even a single crumb fall.

ALTHOUGH STEVEN'S herbal medications helped reduce Michael's craving for the drug, Michael still struggled with his addiction. Every day he fed the birds by the stream. He took long walks in the countryside, trudging through the occasional summer downpour without an umbrella. The rains beat on his forehead, then down the back of his neck when he tilted his head forward. After a while he could no longer feel the weight of the wet clothes hanging from his body or the dampness seeping through to his bones. The rains turned the roads into a muddy broth, and at times he lost his footing and slipped. He walked and walked until fatigue replaced his hunger for the drug and his legs felt so heavy from his excursion that it was all he could do to peel off his clothes and plop into bed upon returning to the abbey.

But on most days the weather was sunny, and he would lie in the tall grasses by the stream and let the fresh country air fill his lungs as he watched the rolling, tumbling succession of clouds whip across the open blue sky. In the distance a cow lowed in friendly greeting.

As summer turned into autumn, vivid red and golden brown leaves fluttered down from the belt of towering trees that ran along the monastery drive, peppering the dark green manicured lawns. As Michael strolled along the drive, the leaves tumbled and danced all around him in the afternoon breeze. At the top of the drive, two monks solemnly raked the leaves into mounds and incinerated them. Ribbons of gray black smoke coiled into the air. Aware of the strident smell of freshly cut grass, Michael stopped in front of the old apple tree in the vegetable garden that still held its far-reaching branches in the same way it always had. Sometimes he wandered into the mist-enshrouded forests near the cloister.

One afternoon Steven found Michael down by the stream, sitting against the trunk of the same elm tree they had known as students. He was feeding a family of ducks swimming in the water. Steven sat down beside him as a breeze blew through the trees.

"There are days," Michael said, "when I can't stop hungering for the drug. Addicts call it the thirst. There are days when my thirst is unquenchable, and I wonder whether I'll ever get my confidence back."

Steven said, "Describe to me what addiction is like."

"Addiction," said Michael, "is like a hanged man swinging from the gallows in the empty air, his hands tied behind him and his eyes blindfolded. Yet he is still alive, helpless and hopeless. You know I don't believe in the devil in the religious sense. But I do believe evil resides in drugs. Craving for the drug is a living example of that evil."

"I can only imagine how difficult it must be," Steven said. "But the yearnings will go away. You'll see. There will come a time when they will leave completely, I promise you. Doing drugs did not remove your pain. It only numbed it. That's what drugs do. The pain is still there. Now you are working through that pain. You must be patient."

The ducks had moved on. Steven tossed a pebble into the water. "I read in my books how drugs unfortunately rob you of your spirit and your life. They also rob you of your will to create."

Michael felt the pressure of Steven's hand in his and looked down at his friend's hand. "But you know what to do now," Steven said.

"Yes," said Michael, "the birds. Feeding the birds and going for long walks. Sometimes standing in the pouring rain helps."

"But there is something even more important than the birds. You must draw. When was the last time you drew?"

Michael was somber. "Ages ago."

"Nothing else is going to work for you. Until you start drawing again, the cravings will persist. Only through your art will you truly be healed."

"I can't anymore."

"You must try."

A breeze flowed across the fields and blew against their faces.

"I'm going to say this to you only once, so listen carefully. You must put every need you ever had into your work, all the love you have ever known and lost, every joy, every sorrow. Don't talk to anyone about your suffering. They'll see it and feel it through your work."

Michael shook his head and stared off into the distance. "I can't," he said. "I just can't anymore."

Steven put a hand on Michael's shoulder. "My friend, if you expect your every desire to be met by someone else, you will always know disappointment. But your art will never betray you. Use your tears to irrigate your genius, and they will not have been in vain. If you are not willing to do that, you will never achieve greatness, and the world will be a poorer place for it.

"There's something else: the challenge. With your art, you must build where nothing stood before, climb mountains that no one has climbed, sing more beautifully through your paints than anyone has ever sung, and create works that move people to the core. Your gift to the world is your soul, and it can be conveyed only through your art. You have an obligation to use that gift.

You have known heaven and hell, joy and suffering, on a scale most have not. Now you must tell us what that is like. You must create something that will last longer than we do. That is your mission. You've fallen off your horse. Now it's time to get back on."

Michael grew annoyed. "Can't you hear what I'm saying? My talent—it's gone."

Steven had anticipated this moment. "I've something to show you," he said. "Follow me."

He led Michael through the garden gate and to the small storage shed. When they entered the hut, Michael saw jars of paintbrushes lining the windowsill and a table with sketch paper laid out on it. In the middle of the room, an easel held a blank canvas. Pinned to the walls were his old drawings.

Michael was flabbergasted. "What's all this, then?"

"I wanted to show you this," Steven said. "It's a space for you to work. It was once a storage shed. Brother Benedict helped me clear it out and sweep it. Brother Christopher made a makeshift easel in his carpentry shop. From an art supply catalog I ordered canvas, wooden bracings, paints, thinner, paper, pencils, and brushes."

"I remember these," Michael said, looking at the drawings on the walls.

"All the ones you threw away, I saved," Steven said. "Believing he was protecting you, Dominic began burning them. When I found out, I started rescuing the ones I wanted before passing the rest on to him. For years I never forgave him. It was through these works that I first came to know you. I just want you to know that all is not lost. Once you start, it will all come back. You'll see. All those wonderful feelings you once knew will return. Remember back then? Nothing else in the world mattered when you drew. It was your refuge, your sanctuary, your entire life. The key to regaining your happiness is to return there. And this is your place, ready for you when you are."

Steven patted his friend's shoulder. "From great hell comes paradise."

Michael reached out and touched the coarse brown fabric of his friend's sleeve.

"What are you doing?" said Steven.

"I was just remembering when you wore the same shirt and pants as I did."

When he took his vows, Steven's pants and shirt had been traded for a brown haircloth habit. He was now a servant of his religion, a soldier of God. Yet, although Michael envied Steven's monastic discipline, he struggled to understand the things his friend held sacred. He could not understand what Steven saw in the cross above his bed or heard in the whispered words of his prayers. Michael wondered how Steven could get on his knees every day and pray to a dead, naked, emaciated man on a cross. What did Steven see when he looked up at that crucifix? What did those green eyes see in those two pieces of wood nailed together? Was it love? Redemption? Sacrifice? Comfort? Fear? This perplexed Michael, because to him Steven might as well be worshipping houseflies. He knew Steven to be intelligent and thoughtful, yet he openly genuflected in front of these empty symbols.

It was then that Michael finally became aware of the central divide between them. While Michael found the singing of psalms beautiful, when the bells rang for evening prayer he preferred instead to go for a stroll in the garden. During the Mass, Michael did not believe that bread turned into Christ's body or wine into Christ's blood. To him it was ignorant metaphysics, nothing more. Stripped to its bone, Steven's religion was vulgar. It espoused poverty, chastity, silence, and obedience—all hideous rules to Michael. But it did serve to remind Michael of the life his friend had chosen to live. Steven would never see the excitement of a city or hear the nonstop bustle of a metropolis. He would never visit a museum and marvel at a Rembrandt. He would never leave the countryside where he was born. The only art he would know would be the self-denying portrait of poverty, and the only traveling he would do would be to a monk's simple grave.

"You pray to statues and paintings and find comfort," Michael said. "You look at a cross and see forgiveness. I see only a dead man nailed to it. What is God, anyway?"

Steven took Michael's hand and led him back to the garden gate. They stood looking into the garden. "This is God," Steven said.

To Michael, who had never seen the outdoors from this perspective, the scene was at once arresting and beautiful. But while he admired his friend's stamina for the monastic life, he found Steven's lifestyle intolerable. Michael could not put up with a life regulated by duties and prayer bells. He was not destined to inhabit the confines of a cloister or to live out the rest of his days in prayer, fasting, and silence. Never could he be a part of any collective community that thought, ate, and breathed in unity. No haircloth habit would ever torment his skin. For all these reasons and more, he knew he did not belong at the abbey.

Michael did note, however, that the only time Steven appeared to be relaxed and happy was when they were together out in the fields collecting medicinal plants. From Steven, who administered his potions to the sick, picked thyme and parsley in the pale pink dawn, and worked alone in his laboratory, Michael had learned what unconditional love was.

"Why did you become a monk?" Michael said as they walked back to their bench in the garden.

"I thought I could make a difference," Steven said. "Dominic taught me everything he knew, and when he died I thought I should carry on after him."

"Dominic taught you well," said Michael. "I'm proud of you. You haven't wasted your life. You've become a great doctor."

They sat down. The rays of the afternoon sun highlighted their faces. Michael held up a hand to shield his eyes. "Thomas said the way to overcome my grief was to carry on after Dominic," Steven said. "For months his suggestion haunted me. Finally, when I made the decision, it was like magic—all my sadness vanished. But I am proud of you too. God has given you a divine gift. You must use it now."

19

MICHAEL STOPPED READING ON the bench under the linden tree and instead watched Steven in the garden. If there was one thing Michael knew about his friend, it was that Steven loved gardening and singing above all other things, for they lifted his spirits and washed away his ills. To Steven, no other place on earth was like the garden. It was a magical world that thrived and teemed with life. When Steven was little, he had been fond of collecting insects in jars that lined the shelves of his room. In later years the garden's tranquility became a balm that soothed him in troubled moments, a welcome escape from the rigors of monastic life. The moment he walked out the door and felt the soil beneath his feet, a serene peace flooded his body.

In the mornings, as the sun warmed the stones of the buildings' facades, Michael often watched the monks rise early and begin their strenuous day. Some toiled laboriously in the flower beds and vegetable gardens.

Michael looked around. The trees and foliage exploded in a magnificent display of colors, particularly yellows, oranges, and reds. Sunny butterflies in ragged flight flitted from one flower to the next, rising and vanishing as capriciously as hummingbirds. Bees hovered intensely over the flower beds as birds sang and the grass basked in the warm sun.

His curiosity piqued, Michael asked Steven what he found so comforting in the dirt, leaves, plants, and bugs. Obviously the garden divinely inspired Steven, lifting him up from his doldrums to, at times, a state of euphoria.

"The moment I slice the blade of my trowel into the soil," Steven told him, "all my problems evaporate. There's something consoling about burying my hands in the dirt. I can't explain it. But the garden can be maddening too. The soil is pitted with muddy streams after the rains. Sometimes it turns hard as clay. In winter I have to abandon the garden altogether, as the cold and the hard soil make it impossible to work with." Steven inhaled deeply. "But the roses! I swear that God made them just to tempt us outdoors. And the vegetables I planted are now ready to be harvested. Come, have a look."

Michael followed him to the vegetable garden. Steven yanked some of the carrots from the soil and brushed the dirt from them before putting them into his basket. "A good crop of carrots is a divinity unto itself. Thomas will make a fabulous soup out of these."

From his time at the monastery Michael remembered that Steven had always assisted Dominic in the garden or out in the fields. So it was no surprise as to how Steven had inherited his love of the outdoors and gardening.

Inspired, Michael began helping his friend, fetching a trowel here, a shovel or rake there. He accompanied Steven on his rounds of the fields and woodlands, collecting herbs for medicines.

Once Steven had taught Michael what to do, Michael worked all day in the garden. Much to the dismay of the monks, he even worked on Sundays. On his knees, Michael scooped up the cool earth with his bare hands and placed the soil in a wheelbarrow. He dug with his trowel and hacked at the weeds until perspiration cascaded down his forehead. In the mornings, after finishing his prayers, Steven would look out his window and see Michael on his hands and knees, laboring in the flowerbed. As if under some hypnotic spell or trance, Michael would forget the time and forsake meals. Steven would bring his friend a bowl of soup and some bread to stop him from working, if only momentarily.

Michael had been searching for something to expel the discomfort of his addiction. He had hoped that working in the garden would bring him the permanent succor he desired. But the long hours spent struggling with the muddy soil in the garden, feeding the birds with handfuls of stale bread, and trudging the countryside through heavy rains brought only temporary relief.

EVERY DAY while Michael was out wandering the countryside, Steven put a fresh piece of paper and a sharpened pencil by his friend's bed in an attempt to encourage him to draw. But Michael always snapped the pencil in two, balled up the paper, and tossed both into the dustbin before crawling into bed at night.

One morning Michael sat up in bed, staring out the window at the late winter rain. He was listening to its arrhythmic tapping when a bird alighted on the large sill seeking shelter. It fluttered its wings, shaking the water from its tawny brown feathers. Taken by this unexpected sight, Michael hurriedly retrieved the broken pencil and balled-up paper from the bin. He smoothed out the paper on his lap and began sketching, racing to capture the image of the bird drying itself. An hour later, long after the bird had flown away, the drawing, although crude and lacking detail, was complete. Not since art school had he drawn anything.

Something else had happened. The weight of his addiction had lifted, replaced by a clarity of thought and elation he had not experienced in a long time.

Still in his underwear, Michael raced out to the lawn, oblivious to the pouring rain, and began dancing and shouting in jubilation.

"I can draw!" he crowed. "I can draw! I can draw!" He got down on his knees and thumped the wet grass with his fists. Two monks gazed out the window to see what all the commotion was about.

"Brother Steven," said one without looking away from the window, "can you come here for a moment?"

Steven approached the window. The monk pointed. "Who is that?"

Steven grinned as he looked at the dancing figure on the lawn. He opened the window. "What are you doing?" he shouted.

Michael twirled in the rain, drunk with ecstasy. Losing his balance, he fell on the grass shouting, "I can draw! I can draw!"

In his friend's cell Steven studied the drawing as Michael sat in the chair, drying his hair with a towel. Steven beamed. The time had arrived.

THE STUDIO was small, but it was all Michael needed. There was plenty of sunlight, and the windows gave him a view of the garden. At five forty-five every morning he awoke to a bowl of hot porridge and a strong cup of coffee served by Thomas. Then he disappeared into his studio, rarely venturing out for the rest of the day.

At first Michael played with the paints on the blank canvas, refamiliarizing himself with the colors. He brushed and stroked the stark white canvas until he came alive. Every color was a different happiness that lifted his spirits and made him forget the past.

All spring and into the summer Michael painted, leaving the studio door open to let in the fresh, sweet country air. On sunny days he took his canvas and easel out into the fields or the garden and painted until the light faded. He painted cauliflower clouds crawling across cobalt skies, wheat fields bending in breezes, verdant landscapes ringing with color. He even painted the buildings of the monastery in the pale pink twilight.

In the late afternoons when the light was too dim to paint, Michael would go for long walks with Steven, or the two friends would play badminton in the garden. Once Michael backed up in order to return a volley and promptly fell backward into the pond. At dinner they would discuss their respective days before retiring early. Michael would run a bath in which he languished until bedtime. He would flop into bed, but not before removing the single freshly cut red rose Steven had placed on his pillow.

There were days, however, when he did not work. Michael was more than happy to help out with odd jobs around the monastery as payment for his room and board. He helped repair buildings and paint walls.

STEVEN DID not disturb Michael while he was in his studio, yet he burned with curiosity to see what his friend was up to. Weeks passed without Michael offering even a glimpse of his efforts.

Late one afternoon Steven grew impatient. Under the pretext of bringing him a pot of tea and a tray of hot scones, he went to the hut. Steven knocked on the door and entered. "Thought you'd be hungry," he said, putting the tray down. "Am I welcome?"

Michael stopped painting and put down his brush. "You never have to ask."

Steven pointed to the canvas Michael was working on. "May I see?"

"You know my rule," said Michael. "I need to finish it first."

Steven wandered over to a white sheet draped over what appeared to be a large rectangle. "How about this one?" he said.

"I was keeping it a secret," Michael said. "It was going to be your birthday present. But go ahead."

Steven gently lifted the sheet. Reflecting the style of the late Italian Renaissance, the work depicted Christ rescuing three fishermen on the Sea of Galilee. The Godhead's long hair and white robes flowed behind him in the wind as he strode above the troubled seas. The Savior's face was transformed by an inner rapture.

Michael dragged the easel closer to the window so that Steven could see it better in the light. Steven stood transfixed. The image was vivid and commanding and made his knees weak. Without taking his eyes off the painting, Steven slowly sank into an empty chair and could not refrain from crossing himself.

"The gift the drug stole from you," he said, "God has given back to you."

"You were right all along," Michael said. He was silent for a moment. "How can I ever repay you? You have given me so much. What could I possibly give you in return?"

A radiant smile spread across Steven's face. "You already have. It has always been my wish to see you develop your talent. Now God has granted me that wish."

STEVEN KNEW Michael would not be in the hut. It was a perfect summer's day, and not a cloud hung in the cobalt sky. He knew Michael was out painting in the fields somewhere.

"Everything you see here is the result of his stay," Steven said to the abbot as he showed him around Michael's studio. "Because of the environment we have provided him, his talents have been allowed to emerge safely. But I have the sense that you feel Michael is not pulling his own weight, is not contributing. We could use some new artwork here, could we not? You yourself said not long ago that even the chapel could use some 'dressing up.' I believe those were your exact words. Some spiritual depictions, perhaps? I'll leave that up to you. I'm asking you to give him a chance. This is the way he can give back."

Daniel intently studied all the artwork in the small studio. He was particularly moved, as Steven had been, by the painting of Christ and the fishermen.

"It's an interesting proposition," the abbot said after a moment. "Let me ponder it. I'll give you my answer tomorrow."

"WHAT THE hell am I going to bloody paint?" said Michael, cleaning some of his brushes in his hut as he learned of the news.

"Well," said Steven, "the abbot suggested you do something for the chapel."

"Yes, but what?"

"I'll leave that up to you. You're the artist in the family. Come up with some drawings and bring them to me. I'll present them to the abbot."

IT WAS while he was painting in the garden that Michael got the idea. That evening he and Steven were having dinner alone in the kitchen. Thomas had made beef stew and had left for the night.

Michael tore off a chunk of bread and dunked it in his stew. "I know what I want to do for the chapel," he said, his mouth full.

"What were you thinking?" Steven said.

"A large mural."

"Where?"

Michael scooped up another mouthful of stew. "It would span the entire length of the chapel wall behind the altar. I've measured it. It would be twelve by twenty feet."

Steven raised his eyebrows. "Hmm. I think the abbot had something smaller in mind. But how would you do it? It's a wood wall."

"I'd paint it on canvas first, then glue the canvas to the wall."

"Ambitious. And what would it be about?"

Michael chewed thoughtfully. "Haven't decided yet. Just wanted to present the idea to you first." He wiped his lips with his napkin. "I have a debt to pay to you and to the others. Let me do this for you."

Over the next month Michael labored away in his studio, making dozens of sketches. Eventually he shared them with Steven, who submitted them to the abbot for review.

"Don't get your hopes up," Steven said. "Changing a room that's been around for over five hundred years might not go down too well. By the way, I have something of yours." He pulled out a small box and a yellowed envelope from his pocket and put them in front of Michael. Opening the box, Michael immediately recognized the gold crucifix Dominic had given him when Michael was leaving the abbey. Michael was glad he had left it and the letter behind. Probably he would have ended up pawning the crucifix and destroying the letter.

A lump formed in Michael's throat. Steven took the crucifix from the box and hung it around Michael's neck.

AFTER THINKING it over for a few days, Michael had an idea. "I left a lot of art behind in London, you know," he said to Steven over dinner. "There's a triptych I did that would be very suitable."

Steven tore off a piece of bread. "Chances are that's all gone now."

"I'd still like to go back and see."

"Are you sure you're ready for that?"

A few days later in London, Michael stood in front of the tall white house in which he had lived. The paint was peeling and the numbers were faded, but it was familiar to him all the same.

He knocked on the door, expecting to see his former landlord, but instead found a tall man with a head of shiny black hair and a beard.

"I'm sorry to bother you," Michael said apologetically, "but I used to live here when I was a student at the academy. I left some paintings behind, large ones."

"Students leave things behind all the time. I put them in the garage until the academy tells me when I can chuck them."

The tall man led Michael out to the garage and pointed to stacks of paintings leaning against the back wall. Michael's paintings were not hard to spot. But only two of the original panels survived. They were now reduced to two large, dusty rectangles, badly damaged, water stained and torn. One brace was broken, causing the canvas to sag. He recalled how he had painstakingly created the wooden stretchers for the canvases. It took him the better part of a week, and in the process he nearly drove a nail through one of his fingers.

The triptych, painted in the style of the old masters, showed a monk discovering a child in the fields in the first panel. In the second a group of monks were playing with the child in a garden.

Michael smiled. In his mind he already had the panels shipped back to the monastery and restored.

STEVEN WAS surprised that, after some deliberation, the abbot gave his consent. Because the painting was so large, Michael had to paint it in sections. Each took up practically his entire work space; there was hardly any room to move around.

The entire mural took eight months to complete. Michael would work all day and often at night by candlelight. As a chilly winter gave way to scented spring days, Steven saw little of his friend. Forbidden from entering the studio, Steven left trays of food by the door. He would knock on the door to alert Michael, then leave. But many times when Steven returned hours later to collect the tray, he found the food untouched and festooned with flies, bees, and other insects.

The mural was painted in eight large sections. When all were completed, the next step was to install it one section at a time on the wall behind the altar. Michael built scaffolding, and each section of scaffolding took a week to put up. During the mural's installation no one was allowed inside the chapel. For two months the monks held their offices in the refectory.

There were few electric lights in the chapel, so Michael woke up early to take advantage of the natural light until it drained away at dusk. Methodically he glued each section of the canvas onto the wall until the panels joined seamlessly. Then he ironed each section into place. The fumes from the glue were overpowering. He had to open all the chapel windows or risk passing out on the scaffolding.

As Michael was completing the mural's final two sections, Steven caught a cold. For days he walked the halls sniffling, but he still performed all his duties. When his stubborn cold would not go away, he put himself to bed, thinking a few days' rest would be the answer.

"It's just a slight fever," he said to Michael. "Nothing more."

But it turned into influenza and worsened to the point where Steven was too weak to get out of bed at night and urinated in his sheets.

"I wouldn't mind it so much," he joked with Michael, "if only the moisture didn't turn so cold."

"Do you want us to call a doctor?" said Michael.

Steven shook his head. "Not necessary. Put me in the infirmary. There is more room to maneuver around, and the toilet is close by. And bring me the medications I ask for. Don't worry, everything will be fine."

Thomas and Michael placed a plastic sheet on Steven's mattress in case he couldn't make the brief journey to the toilet in time.

"Right now he has influenza," Michael told Thomas. "I'm just worried it might escalate into pneumonia."

"Well," said Thomas, "if it gets to that point, we'll call for outside help. But he knows what he's doing. He is a doctor, after all."

Michael knew what Thomas meant. Bad colds were seasonal. As a junkie Michael had known such weakness himself. Back then it took every ounce of his strength to lift himself off his lumpy mattress and go outside to relieve himself.

Twice a day Michael brought his sick friend meals Thomas had prepared. He followed Steven's bedside instructions and brought him all the medications he requested. When his work was done for the day, Michael sat by Steven's bed talking until Steven fell asleep. Michael then crawled into the spare bed next to his friend. During the night he often was awakened by the sound of Steven retching in the darkness. Michael would light a candle and find Steven bent over a bucket by the side of the bed. Without a word Michael would get up and assist his friend.

Steven began sleeping later and later in the mornings. Only when he stirred did Michael bring him a tray of food. It was difficult for Steven to eat. He could only manage plain toast and hot tea with no lemon or honey.

One afternoon when Michael brought in some tea and toast, Steven said, "How's the painting going?"

"Only two more panels to go," Michael said. "How are you feeling?"

"Thirsty," Steven said hoarsely.

Michael sat Steven up and put the mug of tea to his lips. When Steven had had enough, he raised his hand weakly. "Are you pleased with it?" Steven said.

Michael tucked a napkin into Steven's collar. "Yes. I hope everyone else will be too."

"I want to see it," Steven said.

"You'll be the first to see it when it's done, I promise."

"No," Steven said stridently. "I want to see what you've done now."

"But I still need to install the last two panels, and besides, you're not well enough."

"Don't tell me how I feel!" said Steven. "I want to see it now!"

Michael removed the napkin and the tray. He rolled up a wheelchair that was parked in the corner of the room and helped Steven out of bed. Once Steven was in the chair, Michael covered his lower body with a blanket.

When they got to the chapel, Steven's eyes were immediately drawn to the massive painting above the altar. Despite the two missing panels at the end Michael had yet to install, there was enough of the painting to give Steven an idea of what it was going to look like. The early afternoon sunlight streamed through the chapel windows, brilliantly illuminating the painting set in the style of the late Italian Renaissance. It depicted St. Francis of Assisi, dressed in a dark brown habit, standing alone in a garden with a white dove in his cupped hands. The face of St. Francis was Steven's. At the bottom of the painting was an inscription in Latin in large gold lettering on a black border.

From great hell comes paradise.

For a long time Steven stared at the painting, saying nothing. Michael made no attempt to ask him what he thought.

"Alright," Steven said finally. "You can take me back now."

Michael wheeled his friend back into the infirmary and helped him back into bed. He laid the blankets over Steven and placed the tray on his lap. Steven raised a frail hand and put it on Michael's cheek. Michael smiled and took Steven's hand in his.

"You've come a long way," Steven said. "I can't tell you how proud I am of you. Your stay here has brought me much happiness."

He chewed on the toast and sipped on the tea, which by now had turned cold.

"Come lie down beside me for a moment," Steven said.

Michael put the tray back on the table. He removed his shoes and climbed onto the bed, stretching out next to Steven and putting his arm around his friend. He stayed until Steven fell asleep, then eased himself out and tiptoed from the infirmary with the food tray. Dropping it off at the kitchen, he returned to his work in the chapel.

At dinnertime Steven was still asleep. Michael went to the kitchen, where Thomas had Steven's dinner tray ready. "He's still sleeping," Michael said. "I think it's better to let him rest."

"I agree," said Thomas. "But here, sit down. I've made you your dinner."

Thomas smiled as Michael sat down at the kitchen table.

MICHAEL WAS up at five thirty as usual, slipped on his clothes, and went straight to work in the chapel. At eight thirty he went to check on Steven. His friend still appeared to be sleeping peacefully. In the kitchen Thomas had breakfast waiting.

"Sleep well?" said Thomas.

"Yes, thanks." Michael took a bite of scrambled eggs.

"And Steven?"

"Sound asleep. My guess is he'll probably wake up around noon."

Thomas washed dishes in the sink. "How's the mural going?"

Michael wiped his lips with a white cloth napkin. "Two more panels, and then a week for the glue to completely dry."

"I'm looking forward to seeing it," Thomas said.

Finishing his breakfast, Michael folded his napkin neatly next to the empty plate.

"Thanks, Thomas. I'll see you at noon."

At noon Michael came and collected Steven's food tray from Thomas. In the infirmary he put the tray down on the night table and sat down on the bed.

"Come on, my friend," Michael said. "Time to eat."

It appeared Steven was still sleeping, but Michael could see that his chest was not moving. He put an ear close to Steven.

There was no sound of breathing. Michael checked for a pulse but could not find one. Steven's body was still warm.

Michael raced to the kitchen. "Thomas, there's something wrong with Steven. He's not breathing. We need to call an ambulance."

Thomas quickly wiped his hands on his apron. He rushed to the infirmary and examined Steven for himself. "Good God," he muttered.

Without telling Michael where he was going, Thomas rushed to the abbot's study, where the only phone in the monastery was located. The abbot was not there. Thomas lifted the receiver and made the call. Within fifteen minutes an ambulance came racing up the gravel drive. Two attendants emerged and were escorted into the infirmary by Thomas and Michael. By now all the friars were standing outside the infirmary door.

One medic brought out his stethoscope and plugged it into his ears. He checked Steven thoroughly. After a minute or two he removed the stethoscope and shook his head.

"What was he ailing from?" said the medic.

"I personally think it was hepatitis, but it could just as well have been a bad cold," said Thomas.

"Did he have a high fever?"

"Yes."

"Possibly complications from influenza. Pneumonia, perhaps. Why didn't you call a physician?"

Thomas hung his head. "He is a physician."

"Did he have any previous illnesses?"

"He attempted to take his own life with belladonna years ago," said Thomas. "Doctors said it could affect his liver."

"Liver failure," said the attendant. "Then hepatitis makes sense." He put away the stethoscope. "We'll remove him now. Some tests will be run to determine cause of death, which will be noted on the death certificate."

"That won't be necessary, thank you," said Thomas. "We bury our own here."

Thomas covered Steven's body with a white sheet, and the two medics left.

THOMAS SPENT the rest of the afternoon alone in the refectory, his face buried in a dishtowel, weeping. The monastery was unusually quiet.

At suppertime Thomas came into the kitchen and found Michael seated at the table, catatonically staring out the window.

"Did I give him the wrong medication?" Michael said tearfully.

Spontaneously, Thomas took Michael in his arms. "There was nothing you could do," said Thomas. "It was his damaged liver—"

"What are you talking about?" said Michael.

Thomas let Michael go. "Remember his attempt?" Thomas refrained from using the word *suicide*. "His poisoning years ago left his liver severely weakened. Truthfully, he was never well after that. Dominic said he might be susceptible to hepatitis and other illnesses. If he ever got sick—really sick—he could die."

Michael had forgotten about Steven's suicide attempt. "But he didn't have hepatitis. It was something due to his cold."

Thomas looked at Michael. "Are you a doctor, my lad?"

"No."

"I'm convinced that it was hepatitis. He was weak for so long. That was no cold, laddie."

Michael thought for a moment. "But why didn't he say anything? If he knew he had hepatitis, why didn't he get outside medical attention?"

"Because," said Thomas, "he must have thought he could cure it himself. You know how stubborn he was. He was more stubborn than Dominic. I'm sure he tried every remedy from his books. Steven was very proud, you know. Complications brought on by hepatitis. Yes, I'm sure that was it."

Michael said, "But do you think he knew that his poisoning had weakened his liver?"

Thomas could not reply. He buried his face in his hands and sobbed.

IN THE storeroom were two plain wooden coffins Brother Christopher had made. They had been kept ready for the inevitable. Steven's limp body was laid into the pine coffin and taken to the chapel. All night Michael sat by it.

At sunrise a Mass was said for Steven. It was the first time the entire monastery had seen the nearly completed mural. Michael had hoped everyone would see it under different circumstances. A mixture of awe and sadness filled the room. What the monks did not expect to see was Steven's face as the face of St. Francis.

Still in shock, Michael did not pay much attention to the service. In his eulogy the abbot talked of not being able to say good-bye to Steven and that they should do so in their hearts, but Michael was not listening.

Much to Michael's surprise, Steven was buried not in the monastery graveyard but down by the stream. The significance of that location was not lost on Michael.

"An unusual request, really," Thomas mused as he kneaded dough in the kitchen. "Generally we're buried in the cemetery. A few years ago the abbot requested that all of us submit in writing our wishes for our funerals, which he would keep on file. You know, favorite hymns, Bible passages, that sort of thing. I just read Steven's last night. In his detailed instructions he even specified the tree he wished to be buried under."

Michael sat at the kitchen table, his head cradled in his hand. "I vaguely recall Steven mentioning, when we were schoolboys, something about how he wanted to be buried down by the stream," he said.

"Yes, but why that place?" said Thomas.

"That is where Dominic found him. The spot also served as a sort of secret meeting place for us. But like everything else during that period, I didn't take anything anyone said to me seriously."

MICHAEL, BROTHER Christopher, and Brother Samson pushed their shovels into the heavy, moist dark soil under the alcove of trees that leaned over the stream. The grave was being dug under one tree in particular, and it took them more than four hours.

Steven's pine coffin was carried from the monastery by Michael and seven monks. As it was slowly lowered into the ground, the piece of paper in Michael's hand shook as he read. "We were here before, lost under the shade of this tree's branches. But now your love belongs to the ages. It is not for us to know why you were taken from us. We can only say farewell."

Michael read the Twenty-third Psalm, and everyone picked up a handful of dirt and dropped it on the coffin.

"STEVEN'S ROOM has to be dismantled," said Thomas the next day. "It's the rule. I could have someone else do it, but . . ."

Michael knew one of the monks would be assigned to remove the drawings, watercolors, and paintings from the walls of Steven's room. Only a small wooden crucifix would remain hanging above the bed. All Steven's worldly possessions would be boxed up and given to the poor. His bed would be stripped and the blankets folded neatly atop the bare mattress.

"No," said Michael. "I'll do it."

He sat down on the bed in Steven's cell. As he looked around a disquieting silence filled the small room. Everywhere, Michael's drawings and watercolors covered the walls. Sunbeams from the high-walled window carved their way into the room, and the pictures seemed to come alive in the light. Above Steven's bed, the plain wooden crucifix had been replaced by a small painting of *The Last Supper* that Steven had asked Michael to paint for him. He gladly undertook the commission; he had always liked the idea of close friends coming together over a meal.

The tiny room Steven had chosen to live in all his life reminded Michael that his friend's lifestyle was everything Michael's was not: plain, claustrophobic, constricting. Yet, it was in this overbearing claustrophobia, these monastic restrictions, that he saw how Steven had come to know peace and contentment.

As he sat there, struggling to make sense of his friend's death, Michael recalled Steven's eager enthusiasm and his clear, strong words of encouragement whenever Michael had presented his drawings and paintings to his friend. Steven had immediately taped the drawings up on his walls. But it was his words that kept Michael going. Steven was proud of how far Michael had come.

In a sudden whirlwind of desperation, Michael craved the drug he knew would remove him far from the reality of the moment. Quickly he fought back the temptation. Michael knew he had a job to do. One by one he removed the drawings, the watercolors, and the paintings from the walls and laid them neatly on the bed. Thomas had given him a cardboard box for Steven's things.

Michael opened the closet and removed the coffee-colored habits Steven had worn virtually all his life. He held the rough fabric, woven by hand from the coarsest material, against his cheek. For so long it had been the only cloth next to Steven's skin.

He opened the drawers that contained underwear, socks, and shirts. They too went into the box. Michael then turned his attention to the bookshelf. There were two shelves of books on medicine and spiritual life. They would be going to the library.

The only thing Michael kept of Steven's was his worn leather Bible, its cover cracked with age and use. While Michael did not believe in the teachings of the Bible, he knew it was a book his friend held dear to his heart.

Satisfied that he had gone through everything connected to his friend, he sealed up the cardboard box. Next, he removed the sheets from the bed and tied them in a bundle. He plopped the bundle on the floor. Later he would take the sheets to Brother Gregory's laundry. He folded up the blankets in a neat square and placed them on the bare mattress at the foot of the bed, with Steven's pillow on top.

He left the cardboard box on top of the bed in the room that now looked like it had never been occupied. Michael took the drawings, the watercolors, and the paintings with him to his studio, where he placed them in a corner of the room against a wall.

THE MURAL sat unfinished. In the mornings Michael still rose at the same time, but he could not muster the courage to go either to his studio or to the chapel. Instead, he walked outside and watched the sun throw up a pastel blanket in the early dawn. Its tinted hues painted warm oranges and light reds against the sky, reminding him of a Turner painting.

In the midafternoons Michael walked for miles along the country roads or if the weather turned bad, he paced the colonnaded galleries as the rain came down in sheets and leaves tumbled behind him in the wind. For the first time he was unaware of the monastery's familiar damp, mossy smell.

One afternoon Thomas found Michael sitting in the garden. He sat down next to him on the bench.

"You're not working on the mural," he said.

Michael looked at Thomas with faraway eyes. He fought the lump swelling in his throat. The instant Thomas saw the tears welling up in Michael's eyes, he took him in his arms. Michael buried his face in Thomas's habit and could no longer hold back the torrent of tears that made his body convulse and heave with each sob.

Thomas rubbed Michael's back. "Steven would have wanted you to continue," he said. "He would have wanted you to finish."

He took out his handkerchief and gave it to Michael, who dried his eyes. "You were never meant to be part of us," he said. "I, like Dominic, knew that from the very beginning. It wasn't your calling as it was ours. I believe each one of us is fated to do God's work in our own fashion. We glorify Him through our own unique talents. God has blessed you with an extraordinary talent. Every time you pick up your brush and paint, you are preaching His gospel. Honor Him, then, with your work. You must show the world the gift He has given you. If you follow it, it will never let you down. You can go far with it. But do not deceive yourself into thinking it will always be easy. Like prayer, it will require constant effort. It has always been my wish, as it was Steven's, to see you develop your gift. And so, for the rest of your life your task is to paint, as mine is to cook. That's how we serve God diligently, every single hour of the day."

Leading Michael by the hand into the chapel, Thomas made him stand in front of the unfinished mural.

"It's time you finished it," Thomas said. "There's nothing to be afraid of now."

THOMAS WAS out in the garden, walking with two other monks, when Michael approached him. "I've something to show you," he said.

Quickly Thomas excused himself from the others and followed Michael into the chapel. He stood there for a moment, looking at the mural. Michael had spent two weeks installing the final two panels. He had carefully joined them together and ironed them until no creases or separations were visible.

Without looking away from the painting, Thomas said, "You're leaving us now, aren't you?"

"Yes," said Michael.

That night Thomas made Michael a shepherd's pie for dinner. The two sat alone in the kitchen.

"Back to the city, is it?" Thomas said.

Michael did not answer because his mouth was full. He nodded.

"Where will you live? Well, not that it matters. When do you plan on leaving?"

"Maybe in a few weeks' time. But I've no money and no place to stay. And I'll need to find some clothes. Can't be walking around London in a monk's habit now, can I?"

Thomas chuckled. "Who knows, you might start a new style. Stay until spring, when the weather is milder."

"No," said Michael. "I need to get going. I'd like to return to the academy—that is, if they'll take me."

"Don't be daft," said Thomas. "Of course they will."

"Can I leave my paintings and drawings here until I find digs?"

Thomas patted him on the shoulder. "Your studio will be kept as you left it for when you visit, which I hope will be often."

The following day the mural was officially dedicated to the entire abbey. All the monks stood in front of it in silence. Many pressed handkerchiefs to their eyes when they saw once again the face of Steven as St. Francis.

Michael spent the next two weeks cleaning up his studio and packing the things he needed. On the evening before his departure, Thomas prepared a feast for Michael. At the end of the meal, he sat down with Michael at the kitchen table. He reached into the pocket of his habit and pulled out an envelope. "Just a little something," he said, "to help you on your way. Consider it payment for the altarpiece." Thomas put a hand on Michael's and smiled. "This time you won't have to walk back to London."

Michael opened the envelope. Inside was a small sheaf of five-pound notes.

"We took up a little collection," Thomas said. "Everyone loves the mural and donated generously."

"But don't you need this?" said Michael.

"Some of the brothers make arts and crafts and sell them at the annual fair in the village," said Thomas. "We take the money and put it away, saving it for a good cause. There's also something else."

From behind a chair Thomas produced a stack of new clothing and a pair of new shoes. "I hope they fit. Some of us went to the village a few days ago and argued over what to get you. We also bought you two duffel bags for your things."

Michael got up from the table and walked over to the window, struggling to conceal the tears welling up in his eyes.

The old cook's eyes grew moist. "You must write and let us know of your progress," he said. "Wherever you go, part of us will always be with you."

Thomas went to the double doors leading to the refectory. "There are a few others who would like to say good-bye to you as well."

He opened the doors. When Michael turned around, he saw the entire monastery standing there. They all entered. Some, like Thomas, embraced him in farewell. Others thanked him for the mural.

When all had said their thank-yous and good-byes, the group filed into the chapel, where a special Mass was said to bless Michael's journey. The entire chapel was brilliantly lit with hundreds of candles, and it seemed to Michael that the monks chanted more beautifully than ever before.

THE NEXT morning at dawn Michael slipped into some of the new clothes the monks had bought for him. Everything had been packed into the two duffel bags, and Michael parked them at the monastery's front entrance. When he was ready, Thomas would call for a taxi to take him to the train station.

Outside the abbey Michael followed his feet to where the path met the stream. He cut through the tall grasses and arrived at the small row of elms guarding the stream. They swayed gently in the breeze, their leaves faintly stirring.

Michael sat down next to Steven's grave and took a deep breath as he looked around at the verdant countryside and the soft, swelling hills in the distance.

Yes, he thought, *I shall miss it here.*

He stood up and fished some stale bread out of his pocket. The autumn air was brisk. Michael could see the clouds of his breath in the air.

Turning to face the stream, he raised his arms toward the sky and closed his eyes. The familiar fluttering of feathers all around him grew louder and louder . . .

Acknowledgments

The Monk's Son began life on October 3, 1983. Six computers later, it was finally finished on August 15, 2005. On this long road trip, I was fortunate enough to stumble upon a network of people who helped me bring it from my Epson printer to the printing press.

Thank you to my book designer, Beverly Butterfield, and my cover artist, Catherine Lau Hunt, for bringing this story to visual life.

Thank you to my copy editor, Dianne Woo, who took up her needle and thread and carefully stitched up the fabric of this narrative.

Thank you to my secondary editor, Daniel Gilbertson, for making valuable suggestions and additions.

Thank you to my primary editor, Beth Lieberman, whom I asked to make the words of this story rise from the pages. She did not fail me.

Thank you to Nina Wiener at Taschen Books, who started me on this wonderful journey.

Lastly, this book is for my longtime friend Michael Earle. On a cold and overcast autumn morning in 1971, when we were teen-age students living in London, he showed me how to salve my broken heart by feeding the birds in Regent's Park. That incident became the inspiration for this book.